AN ALIEN FOR THE FARM

A NEW HOME
BOOK ONE

A.G. WILDE

PETRONIE
PUBLISHING

This book is dedicated to all those humans who feel invisible.
You aren't.

AN ALIEN FOR THE FARM

Eleanor

I thought starting over on this quiet farm would finally give me a chance to heal. But the moment that towering alien walks through my door, I know real trouble has found me. Zynar is all corded muscle and raw masculinity—nothing like the weak men who've used me. Worse, this alien hunk stirs feelings in me I swore were long dead. Each time his intense yellow gaze locks onto mine, my resolve weakens. I tell myself to keep my distance, that this attraction can only lead to heartbreak. But as Zynar proves himself gentle yet strong, passionate yet restrained, I start to crave the pleasure his touch promises to unlock in me once more.

Zynar

From the moment I lay eyes on the delicate creature named Eleanor, my core-beat quickens in a way I hadn't thought possible. This fragile flower survived abduction and abuse, yet her spirit remains unbroken. I want nothing more than to make her feel safe and cherished. But this female threatens to expose vulnerabilities I've long tried to bury. As a displaced Kari without a homeworld, getting close means risking all that little remains of my past. Yet keeping my distance is torture. Eleanor calls to the very core of my being. Each smile, each caress makes opening my heart seem less impossible. How can I resist a female who awakens feelings I swore were dead?

BEFORE YOU READ!

Hi there!

While this book is intended to be a heartwarming journey, it does contain themes and situations that some readers may find sensitive:

Passionate encounters: This book does not shy away from depicting the fiery and sometimes primal nature of the characters' connection, including an intense mating ritual that involves power dynamics.
Past trauma: The main characters have both experienced significant trauma in their pasts, including abduction, war, the loss of loved ones, and past relationship trauma. These experiences are discussed and explored throughout the story as part of their healing journey.
Possessiveness and dominance: The male protagonist, Zynar, exhibits strong possessive and dominant tendencies, particularly during his mating rut. While these behaviors are ultimately consensual within the context of their bond, they might be triggering for some readers.

Medical scenes: There is a scene involving an injury and medical treatment.
Animal distress: There are brief scenes of animal distress.

My goal is to create a safe and enjoyable reading experience for everyone. If you encounter any content that triggers you or that you believe should be added to this list, please don't hesitate to reach out to me on social media. I'm always open to learning and improving.

Till then,
Happy reading!
🖤 AG

ELEANOR

I grab my bag and step off the shuttle, pulling a chestful of air into my lungs. This is the first day of my new life and...

And it smells like shit.

Maybe I inhaled too hard because the scent of what can only be fresh manure wafts straight into my nostrils and fills my lungs. I almost choke but manage to compose myself as I see the offending pile of animal excrement being carted off down the street.

Strange alien beings look my way. Some with horns, some that look like bulls from back home, others that look like birds... Some with tails, some with more than two legs, some with only one. My eyes widen as they pass, but none stop to look at me. Their gazes fall my way and then shift away a second later.

They...don't see me. It's almost like being transported back to Earth and dropped in the center of a city. I'd be invisible there, too. And that's a good thing right now, isn't it? I just stepped off a shuttle into a brand-new world. The last thing I want to do is stand out like a sore thumb.

Clearing my throat, I fix my glasses on my nose as I look one way down the street and then the other. Behind me, there's a low hiss as the doors to the shuttle close, and the operator, a furry guy who looks like a cross between a goat and a human, gives me a wink before pulling away.

"Hey, I—" But he's already gone. "I...don't know where to go..."

I frown, my words fading into the hustle and bustle of the town around me. Slight panic rises in my gut. I'm on a new world and I'm all alone with no idea where I should go or where to find the person who's supposed to meet me.

Forcing the lump of panic down my throat, I reach into my bag and pull out the flyer. Something squawks near my ears, nearly toppling my glasses off my nose and nearly sending the flyer into the air.

"Get out of the way, female!" A gruff alien that looks like a set of boulders stacked on each other lumbers past with a flock of...ostrich-kiwis? following closely behind him. At least, they look like kiwi birds...if God made them seven feet tall.

His remark has me looking around to realize I am, in fact, standing in the middle of the road. "Oh!" I grab my little bag filled with all the clothes and things I could carry and hurry to the other side of the street. There, I swallow down that ball of panic again and make sure I'm not standing in anyone's way before I lift the flyer again.

"The New Horizons Initiative," I murmur, gaze skipping over the words. "The New Horizons Initiative offers a fresh start on a peaceful farming planet to individuals facing significant life changes—such as widowhood, retirement, divorce, or personal hardship. Each female receives a homestead in the Hudoian planes, creating opportunities for growth and fulfillment."

It's actually written in English. These New Horizons people seemed legit.

I release a breath, turning the flyer to its back. "Someone's supposed to meet me," I murmur, biting my bottom lip as I look at the name I'd scribbled down. "I'm sure of it."

I'd written everything down. I'd double and triple-checked. Living on a refugee ship for the last ten years after being abducted from the only planet I knew, I'd made sure I got every detail right.

Lifting my chin, I use the hand holding the flyer to keep my sunhat on my head as a gust of wind blows down the street. I'd worn the sunhat just in case and it seems like I made the right decision. The sun's shining hot and there's barely a shadow to hide underneath. Hudo III is supposed to be a minor planet with relatively calm weather and low danger. I'd heard someone on the refugee ship laugh and say it was like a huge farming colony and it sounded perfect. A slow life, perfect for rebuilding. I took the flyer and signed up for the New Horizons placement. Only now...now I'm wondering if there's something I missed.

Am I supposed to find my way to the farm on my own?

Just as I square my shoulders and decide to ask someone for possible directions, I hear a voice at my back.

"You must be the human! Eleanor Tabitha Taylor?"

I blink, turning around to face a...male with a perfectly white coat of fur, rabbit ears, and the tiniest nose I have ever seen. His big albino red eyes blink at me. "I am Xarion, your guide."

"Oh!" I release my hat and fumble with the flyer, turning to the back where I'd put down the name of the person I'm supposed to meet. "Xarion Naga...mooshi...favel, right? Nice to meet you!"

He gives me a flourish that makes me blink several times.

"At your service, Eleanor Tabitha." He's dressed in clothes that make him look like a human butler for a very wealthy family. "I do apologize for my tardiness."

"Oh, no! Don't worry, it's fine!" I grab my bag, clenching my teeth slightly at the ache that goes through my thumb. "And it's just Eleanor." I'd packed light to take the strain off my hands, but it seems even that wasn't enough. Ignoring the pain, I smile at Xarion. "So, where to?"

"Well," he stands, his long ears almost brushing against the soft fabric of the flowing brown tunic I'm wearing as a summer dress. Not exactly the type of clothes for a farm, but I assume I'll find a garment shop somewhere and can sew myself some over-alls. They'd advised that I shouldn't carry anything with me, anyway. "I was supposed to take you to have your language implant installed. However, you can understand me, so I assume you're already in possession of a language device."

I smile. "Oh yeah. Just a present from those Isclits that took me from Earth in the dead of night."

Xarion blinks at me. His lids closing over his big eyes in a slow blink filled with the silence makes me want to laugh at my joke. Only a human can joke about their abduction from their planet like it's just another thing that happened. Most other races I met on the refugee ship didn't even speak about that part of their past.

"Well then," Xarion recovers, adjusting his collar with one hand. "We shall set off."

It's my turn to blink at him, wondering if my translator is purposely making him sound like a character from an old-timey novel. Or maybe it's just the way he carries himself, all formal and proper. His ears flick slightly, a sign of mild annoyance or maybe impatience; it's hard to tell.

I nod. "Right behind you."

Luckily for me, I used to live in the city before being ripped from Earth. Walking behind Xarion and dodging the many other aliens coming from the other direction is easy. But this reminder of city life isn't what makes a little ball of energy swirl in my gut. It isn't what makes tingles go across my skin, anticipation filling me with each step. I'm going to a place where I can just be. Where life won't be determined by someone else but me. A fresh start and not like the one from a decade ago.

Soon, Xarion slows down and bows before me again, causing me to blush. I glance behind me at the other aliens, vendors and purchasers alike, but none of them seem to find his behavior out of the ordinary.

"Here is our transportation." He does another flourish and when I look at where he's pointing, I almost drop my bag.

"That—"

"Is an ooga." Xarion pats the hippo-like animal, and the creature lifts its head before going back to the orange grass it's eating. "This one is yours."

"M-mine?" But he's already heading around the rear of the animal. He walks to stand just on the other side, putting the massive creature between us. I look on in dismay as he mounts an ooga on the other side of the one before me, then turns to watch me. I blink at him, because he's waiting on me…to mount the animal before me.

"I've never even ridden a horse before…" I murmur, eyeing the harness on the creature's back.

"I can assure you, an ooga has a much better temperament than a horse from Earth." Xarion states it so matter-of-factly, I don't even have it in me to ask how the hell he knows anything about horses.

There's a basket balancing on the creature's rear and I suppose that's where I'm supposed to place my bag. Reaching up, I ignore the pain in my hand again as I place my bag inside the basket. Now, to climb on to the thing.

"This is just one of the animals that will be on your farm." Xarion speaks with the assured tone of someone who knows what he's saying is true, and I wonder if he always talks like that.

"Say what now?" I partially don't even hear what he's saying next because I'm focusing everything I have on grabbing on to the harness and pulling myself up. It takes two tries and when I see Xarion hopping off his mount to help me, I shake my head.

"No, no, I can do it."

"I apologize. Once again, I've left an unfavorable impression. First with my tardiness and now with this. I was not told that you had no experience with oogas."

I cringe as he rounds the mount, despite my protest. I'm halfway on the thing, balancing on my belly, my ass on display and so will be my britches if I don't get on the damn thing.

"Permission to touch you," Xarion says from behind me. I cringe again. It's the first time in a long while some man is standing face to face with my ass, but in my dreams, I'd imagined myself climbing on all fours on top of a bed or, I don't know, something adventurous like the kitchen counter or something. Not a frickin' ooga.

"It's okay, Xarion!" With a grunt, I haul myself onto the animal, almost losing my balance but managing to set myself straight before I fall. Sitting, I hold the reins and clear my throat. Xarion blinks up at me before dipping his head slightly in another bow and making his way back to his ooga. He climbs on like it's nothing and makes a sound in his throat. A sort of click that the animal responds to. I have no clue how to replicate it but luckily, as his ooga starts to move, so does mine. They lumber down the busy street at a steady pace, allowing me to finally take a look around without feeling out of sorts.

It's pretty here. Pink sky. Warm sun. The aliens in the town don't seem rushed as they go about buying and selling and there are so many variations of species here, it's clear it's an inclusive sort of place. I could get used to this. At least, I think I can. I was looking for a new start to life and this is it, but as soon as we leave the hustle and bustle of the little town behind and the oogas make their way across the plain, another ball of worry swells in my gut.

Xarion is silent and I'm forced to listen to my worry-filled thoughts. Worries like the fact I'll be all alone out on the plains. And that this will be a whole undertaking. That I have no friends here. I'm fifty-five and starting over. Women my age are mostly married and living out their happy lives with their husbands and grown kids. Nice house in the suburbs. White picket fence. Friends to come over and have tea. I have none of that.

Looking down at the ooga, I swallow hard. Can I really do this?

"It will take about three hors to reach your estate," Xarion finally says, breaking the silence and the sound of the soft breeze.

My *estate*. It sounds almost too good to be true.

"Three hors?"

"Yes," he says, looking over his shoulder. "Not to worry, I am escorting you the entire way."

"Right," I murmur, squinting through my glasses as I look ahead. "And you said more of these animals are already there?"

"The New Horizons Initiative has provided you an estate that already has several oogas grazing on the land, as well as a few wild tilgrans."

"Wild?"

"Not to fear. They are not dangerous animals, though the tilgrans can be a bit...hazardous."

"Right." I frown a little, images flitting through my mind. "I thought this was supposed to be a...farm?"

"As it is," Xarion responds over his shoulder. "There are crops also. Whether you wish to maintain it as a farm is up to you, but your crops would provide you with good income if you decide to grow and sell them."

"What type of crops?"

"There's a maize that is eaten by most species living on this part of Hudo III. There are also fruits and grass-feed for animals like the oogas here."

"Right." I close my eyes briefly.

That doesn't sound too bad, does it? I knew this wasn't going to be a walk in the park, but a part of me was still imagining growing flowers and drinking tea on the porch as I watched the sunset.

"Maybe I could grow flowers and sell them?" I don't even disguise the hope in my voice. "I used to garden back at my house on Earth. Well, a little more than gardening. My degree is in, *was* in, horticulture. I used to even teach it. My garden was like a little paradise. But that was before..." I clear my throat. This isn't a part of my life I really talk about, but Xarion already knows everything. He must have seen my file. The one that has all the information about me, my past, and everything that happened since the abduction, too. He knows I'm divorced. It's one reason they accepted me into the program. And still, I can't seem to shut up. "Well, before my ex-husband took everything I had and destroyed everything I thought my life would be. And then..." I sigh. "Then there were the Isclits and the Tasqals. The Restitution helped us and I ended up on a refugee ship when the Tasqals attacked their base. It's all fuzzy now and I haven't had a chance to do any gardening since Earth, but I'm sure I still have my green thumb."

"Hmm," Xarion hums low in his throat. "Green thumbs are a sign of rot in humans, is it not?"

I chuckle. "It's just a phrase."

"Understood." He faces ahead again but says nothing else. Considering my long spiel, I suddenly feel like a fool for telling him my life story. For the next few hours, I keep my mouth shut, because, clearly, I've had no one to talk to in so long that I'm willing to tell all my secrets at the barest sign of friendliness. Back on the refugee ship, it was so hard making friends with anyone that this wasn't a problem. I was forced into loneliness even though I was surrounded by other creatures.

Turning my gaze forward, I take in another breath of fresh air. The air out here is so clean, so clear. It feels like I'm feeding my brain with each inhalation. When a structure appears in the distance, I perk up, sitting straighter as I peer ahead.

"Is that…"

"Your homestead? Yes, it is." Xarion hums a tone underneath his breath and the oogas go into a trot.

I stare at his back, wondering why he didn't do that from the start. We could have probably cut the time in half. But I realize shortly after why we didn't dash across the plains on running oogas. In about two minutes, the ooga in front of mine lifts its short tail and releases a cloud of yellow gas. I cough, covering my nose a moment too late because I still catch a whiff in the wind. This is just as my ooga vibrates beneath me and I hear it fart too.

Okay, so don't make the oogas run. Got it.

As Xarion leads the animals past what looks like a broken-down fence and into an overgrown yard, I get my first glimpse of the place I will call home for the rest of my life.

I wasn't expecting much, and at first glance, the homestead looks run-down and dilapidated. But as I squint through the harsh sunlight, I can make out the solid bones of the place beneath the neglect.

The main house looks like a quaint little cottage built from sturdy stone, the walls still standing firm despite cracked windows and a sagging roof. Outbuildings that were most likely once a barn and stables spread out behind it. The landscape beyond is a wide open prairie, the waving grasses stretching out as far as my eyes can see. And, just like Xarion said, I can spot several oogas and some tall animals that must be tilgrans off in the field. This place has good bones, I think. It just needs some tender loving care to bring it back to life. Just like I do.

My lips stretch in a soft smile. We can do it together, me and this place. Work on myself while I work on it.

A spark of pride flickers inside me at the thought of restoring this place to its former glory with my own two hands, and I sit higher on the ooga, taking in a deep breath. Sure, I'm starting over with just the clothes on my back. But I've survived an abduction from Earth, a galactic war, refugee ships, and the long journey here. If I could endure all that, I can certainly rebuild one little homestead.

"Shall we proceed?" For the first time, I catch a note of uncertainty in Xarion's tone, as if he's not convinced I'll stay here. His long ears fold forward as his big red eyes watch me.

I didn't realize I had a choice in this. Thought he was just leaving me here on my own with no say from me. After all, I've already signed the papers—a digital fingerprint that secured my place in the Initiative and said that, yes, I want to do this. I give Xarion a big grin and his shoulders relax, his ears perking up.

"Your communication device is inside. I already had it set up for your arrival. I also made sure clean water and waste removal are both operational. There is fresh food to last you for several sols and credits have been deposited into your account to buy what you may need to start life here. If you require assistance," his gaze skips around the yard, "there are many Raki who do work for hire. You can use the communication device to put up a job post, if you desire. I have already loaded your native language onto the system."

I nod, giving him another smile despite the nerves rising within me. Excited nerves. He continues talking as he watches me dismount not-so-gracefully.

"Policy states that I must remain until you give me the go-ahead to leave. This is usually after you have examined the estate for yourself and find it suitable to remain."

"Oh, okay." I give him another smile as I take my first steps toward my new home.

"Are there any other estates close to this one?"

Xarion blinks before looking over his shoulder and pointing down the dusty road. "There are several others that way, but I can assure you that they are in the same state of disrepair. The New Horizons Initiative is a repopulation effort. None of the estates are in great form."

I release a soft laugh as I reach the house and I stretch my hand to touch the stone pillars at the porch. "Don't worry, Xarion. I'm not having second thoughts."

I can tell, even without looking over my shoulder, that his shoulders sag again with relief.

As I press my hand against the stone, I release a breath as I step onto the porch and push the door open. It opens without a creak, telling me that Xarion must have fixed it or installed a new one. Taking another deep breath, I step into what will be the next chapter of my life.

2

ELEANOR

Xarion left about half an hour after I first stepped into the house. Walking around, I made sure everything seemed okay before I gave him the go ahead and with another bow, he took the two oogas with him and made his way outside my gate. *My* gate.

Everything here is mine.

These stone walls. The land. The animals. Everything.

It's almost too good to be true. Almost too hard to believe.

Grabbing the hem of my dress, I do a spin in the little front room which I know I'll designate as the living room. It's small but it will be perfect for hosting guests. That is, if I make any friends. Who knows, I might be here alone for the rest of my life. I've already made peace with that and the thought doesn't make me feel so hollow anymore. Not like it did after I signed those divorce papers back on Earth.

I sigh, pushing the thoughts away. No use dwelling on the past. All it does is drag you down.

Hands on my hips, I stop spinning, another huge sigh making my shoulders rise and fall as I look around the room. What should I tackle first? I'm tired from the journey, but there's the energy of excitement in my veins. I want to do something. Anything.

I head to the bedroom first. There's a little bed there, about the size of a double bed and it takes up most of the room. Looking at the walls, I know I'll have to buy some kind of compound to smoothen it out so I can paint it maybe. I'm already thinking of what color I want it to be.

I choke on a laugh. A pink house on the prairie. A whoop leaves my lips, echoing in the empty house and I throw my hands up and whoop again. A pink house on the prairie! Who the hell is going to stop me? Tell me it's a stupid idea? No one! If I want to turn this into a doll house and live like a child, I can! If I want to build myself a sanctuary with all the little things I like, I can!

There are no neighbors to judge me. No man to tell me what to do. No one to answer to but myself. The freedom of it all rushes through me like a gust of wind, filling my chest with a sense of possibility I haven't felt in years.

I decide to start with the bed. It's dusty and the mattress is old, but it's a beginning. I strip off the ancient linen and carry them outside, shaking them out in the fresh air. The sunlight is warm on my face, and for a moment, I close my eyes and just breathe it in.

Back inside, I rummage through the supplies the New Horizons Initiative provided. There are basic cleaning tools, some bedding, a new mattress, and even human-like cutlery no doubt made specifically for me. I smile, feeling a little more optimistic. This is going to be my sanctuary, my place of peace.

As I clean, I hum softly to myself. The rhythm of the work is soothing, and before I know it, the bedroom starts to look more inviting. I make the bed with the new mattress, fresh sheets, and a colorful blanket I found in one of the supply crates. It's not perfect, but it's mine.

I move to the main living area next, deciding to tackle the

windows. The view outside is breathtaking, with rolling plains stretching as far as the eye can see. The sun is beginning to set, casting the landscape in hues of gold and pink. I can already imagine sitting here in the evenings, watching the sky change colors as I sip tea.

I watch the sunset for a few moments till the weariness of the day begins to catch up on me. With a sigh, I make sure the door's locked before heading back into the house. The bathroom has a tub! It's a strange shape, circular instead of what I'm used to, but I shrug, filling it up. The water's warm and I strip down and slide in, fingers tracing the intricate patterns along the side as I wonder what species lived in this house so long ago and what happened to them. Despite the disrepair, it looks like a house that was lived in and loved. I hope I can keep it the way they would have liked, preserving the sense of warmth and care that permeates the place. I want to honor their memory, too, by making this house a home once again, filling it with love and life.

The water soothes my aching muscles, and I tilt my head, letting the day's events wash over me. That's when I notice the hole in the ceiling. It's right above the bath, giving me a glimpse of the darkening sky as the sun goes down. Well, that will need to be fixed.

As I relax, my eyes start to pick out other details that need attention. The edges of the window above the sink are cracked and weathered, allowing a draft to creep in. There are patches of mold in the corners where the walls meet the floor, and my skin crawls at the sight of them. Definitely need to get rid of that.

After my bath, I dry off and wrap myself in a towel, stepping back into the bedroom. Some of the floorboards creak when I walk and though I didn't notice the sound before, I do now. I also spot four or five more holes in the thatched roof. Not surprisingly, the boards on the floors directly underneath these holes are the ones creaking. A few even look completely rotted out. If the rain falls…

There are probably even more serious repairs that I haven't even noticed yet. Naked, I let my bits hang out as I head toward the pack of stuff New Horizons left. I grab a robe and shrug it on, biting my bottom lip. I can't get discouraged. This is my project; my fresh start. I don't have to fix everything all at once. I can take it one step at a time.

I find the communication device and bring up the note app. Thankfully, it's simpler than the smartphone I had back on Earth. My list starts to get long in no time and I know I'll have to prioritize the most urgent repairs first.

Only, I don't have a clue how to tackle the roof on my own.

I bite my lip again, squinting up at it. No way I'll be able to climb up there to even patch it with some plastic to hold me over. "And I have no clue when it's going to rain. Shit."

"Getting weather information for your coordinates."

I almost jump and drop the little device. "What now?"

"Clear skies for the next three sols. Mild winds and rain in the next four sols."

"Shit." I stare at the little device. Four days before rain? I bite my lips again, rolling it between my teeth as I stare up at the roof. No way I'm going to be able to patch it when I couldn't even climb on top of an ooga.

I could call Xarion, but his job was to bring me here, not help me restore the place, too.

I sigh. I'm going to need help.

That's when Xarion's words come back. Something about hiring a Kari?

"Um, Siri?" I don't know what else to call the thing. "Google?" I know it isn't Google either. But I've never quite been a technology person. That's why this whole farming thing appealed even more than usual. "Computer?" It pulses, letting me know it's listening, and I swallow down my unsurety. "I'd like to hire a Kari to assist with my repairs."

The device pulses. *"Do you mean a Raki?"*

I blink at it, tightening my robe as I start to pace. What did Xarion say again? They both sound alike! Running one hand through my wet hair, I stutter. "W-whichever one does repairs?"

"The Raki and the Kari both do repairs, if requested."

I shrug. "Just hire one please. I need a Kari to help me with my roof."

"Creating the job ad."

"Oh shit." I stop pacing. "I haven't even checked how many credits I have to use."

"You have one thousand credits."

"Okay…" I start pacing again. "And how much would it cost to restore my roof. Give me an estimate."

"Calculating dimensions, cost of materials, and cost of labor."

I stop by the window, staring out, and a wild tilgran catches my eye. They look like small versions of a diplodocus but with the patterns of a giraffe. I swear it's watching me as it bends its head to steal a patch of hay right from an ooga's mouth. I giggle, some of the tension leaving my shoulders.

"The cost to repair your roof is fifty to sixty credits."

My eyebrows shoot up. Wow…is that cheap or did New Horizons make me rich? Just how much is a credit worth?

"Should I cancel the job ad?"

"No no! Post it. It will probably take a while to find someone and I need this roof fixed pronto."

"Job ad posted."

"Thank you." I know I'm telling a computer thanks but manners feels appropriate anyway.

Now that the job ad's been posted I grin again. It might not be much but I've accomplished stuff today.

Heading back to the bedroom, I flop in the bed, lids low as I stare up into the ceiling. My hair's still slightly wet and I'm still in my robe, but I don't care. I lie like that until sleep claims me, not even hearing the ding of the communication device by my side.

3

ELEANOR

*I*t feels like I haven't slept in years. The bed on the refugee ship had been nothing but a pod in a line of pods. Like sleeping on a train every night. This though? This is bliss. The bed frame may be old—I'll probably have to get a new one eventually— but for now, it's serving its purpose.

I stretch, that thrill from yesterday returning as the sleep leaves my eyes.

It's morning. I can tell from the pink sky outside my window. I stare at it for a few minutes before rising on my elbows. Despite the good sleep, the joints in my fingers protest as I grip the bed and sit upright. Groaning, I take the pressure off them, as I run my hand through my tangled hair. That's what I get for not brushing my hair and letting it dry before falling asleep. But who cares? There's no one for miles to see me. I never knew how freeing it would be to not have to keep up with the Joneses. Never realized how much of my life I'd spent keeping up appearances that didn't really matter.

It took leaving Earth for me to realize just how small and insignificant I was—and how that meant the fact I even existed at all was a miracle in itself. A miracle worth embracing.

Standing, I yawn as I stretch, some of my joints popping with release that makes me want to groan. I need to get breakfast. I haven't fully explored the kitchen yet. This is a good day to do it.

I'm sleepily walking toward the living room when there's a bang on the front door that makes my heart jump up into my mouth.

What the—? That's not the wind. One of the animals then? Xarion?

I don't move, staring at the door like it's an alien when the knock sounds again. Definitely not an animal. Far too heavy and deliberate and somehow, I don't think it's gentle Xarion either. Dude looks like he couldn't even harm a fly.

Panic rises within me. I'm alone. I've got arthritis. And there's someone at my door. How the hell will I fight them off if I need to? Will I have to? They said this was a relatively peaceful planet. As someone or something moves near the window, I catch a glimpse of purple and green, pink and blue. Iridescent scales. Oh shit. Something big is out there and the human in me can't just push my caution away. My gaze drops to the cutlery New Horizons made for me and I creep forward, hand closing around a small paring knife before my gaze shifts to the window again. Not big enough. I grab the carving knife instead.

Three blind mice. See how they run. Except, I'm pretty sure that what's outside my door is no little mouse.

There's a knock again, or rather a bang. Either this intruder doesn't know his strength or he's trying to be intimidating. Either way, he knows I'm here. Why else would some random be knocking on a dilapidated house in the middle of nowhere? Whoever it is knows there's someone inside.

That doesn't set my soul at ease one bit.

I want to stay silent, hoping whoever it is will go away and then I can peer at them through my window curtains as they depart. But then I remember I'm new here and I'm supposed to be making friends. What if it's my neighbor?

But you don't have neighbors, Eleanor! At least, not close by. Shit.

"Who's there?!" My voice sounds almost shrill and the sudden silence behind the door only makes the small hairs on my arms stand on end.

"Zynar." The voice is a deep growl, so incredibly masculine that the hairs already standing on end go ramrod straight along my arm. "I'm here for the job."

I blink, the carving knife faltering in my grasp. "The job?"

The alien, who is undoubtedly a male, makes a soft hum in his throat that reaches me all the way through the door, and I blink some more. Job? He's here for a job?

Oh shit!

Knife in hand, I move as fast as I can back to my bedroom. Grabbing the communication device from where I left it on the bed, I bring it to my face. I must have left my glasses in the bathroom last night because I can't read a thing on the screen.

"Computer, the job ad that you posted, is it still up?"

The device pulses. *"The job ad has expired."*

"What do you mean? Why?"

"The job ad has already been answered. A Kari has accepted your request for labor."

I blink, swallowing hard. Already? "Um, computer, what does a Kari look like?"

The device pulses again. *"Kari. A bipedal race known for their iridescent scales, physical strength, and virility. Originating from the planet Karicek Minor, Kari have been displaced since the war."*

The device pauses, then continues. *"Kari males are known for their exceptional courtship rituals, often involving impressive feats of strength and demonstrations of skill. Caution: Kari males are notoriously persistent when they find their mate."*

I grunt as I glance at the door, heart racing. The male outside must be a Kari, then. And persistent. Great. "Let's hope that persistence works well with getting my roof fixed before it rains in a few days."

When I hear a grunt of amusement coming all the way from the front door, I almost quail. He can hear me?

"Um, just a moment!" I shout in his direction, though, apparently, I don't need to raise my voice at all. I'm still in a robe and I haven't even gone through the clothes New Horizons supplied yet. My summer dress from yesterday is too sweaty to wear again and probably wet from where I left it hanging by the tub. I hurry to my bag, opening it to rifle through for something to wear. I throw on another dress, this one just a plain brown thing that lands just below my knees. No makeshift bra or panties. No time. Hiding the knife behind my back because, first impressions and all that—don't want the guy thinking I lured him out in the middle of nowhere to kill him (but yeah, I still need protection)—I head to the front door.

It unlocks a moment later and I swing it open, pressing a smile to my face.

"Hi! I didn't expect you…so…soon…"

My smile falters immediately. I must not be seeing clearly, or my vision is getting worse. Blind as a bat, I'll need my glasses for more than just reading soon.

Standing before me is a towering figure, easily over six feet tall, with iridescent scales shimmering in the morning light, reflecting hues of purple, pink, and blue. It's so utterly beautiful, almost hypnotizing. The male before me is imposing. Taut muscles. Bulging arms. I can tell he's powerful even though he's standing still. Gaze shifting upward over defined pecs, my eyes widen slightly at the strikingly handsome face before me. High cheekbones, a strong jawline, deep-set yellow and vertically-slitted eyes. A mane of thick green hair frames his face.

My breath catches in my throat. This isn't just any alien; he's like a living work of art. I can see why the device mentioned his virility. He's a different species, but I'm aware of him anyway. Everything about this male exudes pure, raw masculinity. As if he's the type to throw a woman over his shoulder, take her to bed, and make her see stars.

Some lucky alien lady must be getting her dues every night.

Clearing my throat, I realize I've been standing here staring at this male for a good minute. He must be wondering what's wrong with the strange human. "I only put up the job ad last night. I didn't expect anyone to answer so soon."

It's only then that I realize he's staring, too. He still hasn't moved since I opened the door either, and there's a frown on his brow. Those yellow-slitted eyes slide from my head to my feet, then back up, and I'm suddenly completely aware of myself. Suddenly aware of what a tangled mess my hair is, and suddenly aware I was rushing so much I didn't even put on a bra!

"And now my tits are hanging low enough to play jump rope," I whisper under my breath.

When the male's lips curve into a small, almost hesitant smile, revealing sharp fangs, I know he heard me. Good heavens. I could die, but I've got at least another twenty or thirty years left, if I'm lucky, and I plan to live every second of it.

My mortification doesn't ebb, just goes on the backburner as the male before me finally responds. His voice is a deep rumble that seems to vibrate through the air.

"I am here to work," he says simply, but his eyes never leave mine, and a strange little tingle goes through me. I push it away.

It's not the first time that's happened. Not the first time I've seen an attractive male and my body has responded. I still have needs and…urges. I still want to be touched. Still want to be loved, even if the fact sends a swell of uncertainty through me. I haven't thought about this in a while. Promised myself I wouldn't dwell on things like this anymore. I've survived an abduction, slavery, a war, and the rocky start of a new life. I'm alone and will be alone for the foreseeable future. But as another tingle goes through me when the male before me slides his gaze over me once more, I'm reminded of how hard it will be to travel this road I'm taking. God, when was the last time I was touched? The closest I've come to being touched was when someone bumped into me in the refugee ship's hallway.

I call that more collision than connection.

I clear my throat, squeezing my eyes shut. I actually speak to him with my eyes shut as I try to clear my head. "Okay, great. Thanks for checking the ad out. It's about the roof. There are some holes in it that I need mended and I'm hoping it can be done before the rain comes in four days." I finish, popping my eyes back open. He's still looking at me in that intense way even as his head tilts slightly. I fold the arm that's not holding the knife over my chest to hide my pancakes and his gaze shifts to the movement.

Pressing a smile on my face, I wait for him to speak before he takes a step back off the porch and into the yard. Standing in my yard, this male makes the grounds look small. His gaze shifts over the roof, brows furrowing as his hair falls to hang over his shoulders. Hands on his hips, I try not to ogle the way his muscles move as he takes a moment to study my roof.

"I'll need more materials than I assumed," he finally says. It's only then that I notice that out on the road, there's what looks like a vehicle. It's a hybrid between an armored hovercraft and a utility truck. The body is sleek and gray with compartments for storing tools and materials. It hums with a low, powerful energy, and in the back is sitting another Kari just like the one before me.

There are two of them? Can I afford to pay both? I guess spending around ten percent of the money New Horizons gave me isn't such a bad thing if I'm fixing something as important as the roof, right?

The alien turns to his companion and says something in a language the device stuck in my skull doesn't translate. The other one nods, hops out the back, and gets into the transparent cab. In the next second, he's driving away.

I blink, somewhat confused.

"I'll try to save what I can." The alien before me turns and his perfectly white teeth flash with those fangs. "But you might need a whole new roof."

I blink at him again, my arm tightening where I've wrapped it across my chest. Is he trying to rip me off? "No, no. I don't want to change the whole thing. At least, not yet. I just need the holes patched for now."

Setting the knife down on the inside windowsill, I'm stepping out barefoot, the rising sun in my eyes as I walk up to the stranger. God, he's tall. He towers over me so much that when I stand with my back to him, a ripple of...*something*...goes down my spine. I point at the roof. "I counted maybe five or six holes. I just need them patched. Temporarily is fine. You didn't have to send your friend away."

When I turn, I realize I'm much closer to him than I first thought. A lump forms in my throat. There's a scent, and it isn't the scent from the farm or the animals lazily releasing bodily fluids in the fields close by. It's sweet, and it's coming from him. I almost lean in before I catch myself.

The movement of his muscular arm draws my attention, pulls me away from focusing on how good he smells when he points to the roof. "It's rotten. But I will try, little female, to save what I can."

Little female? The term catches me off guard. Little? I've never been called little before. I'm not huge. I'm an average-sized big girl. I huff a nervous laugh through my nose. "I...don't have enough to pay for a whole new roof."

The alien brushes past me, his scent enveloping me like a warm embrace. He's already flipping off a tool from his waist— a laser that reaches the peak of the roof—and I realize he's measuring it. "Don't worry, little female. I don't overcharge."

I go speechless as he grabs hold of a beam and launches himself onto the roof like it's nothing. Once up there, his back turned to me, it's like I'm dismissed. He takes out a device and begins scanning the roof, immediately getting to work. A breath leaves my chest, deflated.

At least he has initiative and I *do* want the roof fixed. If it's more than one hundred and twenty credits then I will just have to pull up my pants and pay him as long as he does a good job. I have to find a way to earn money on my own, anyway.

Arm still folded across my chest, I head back inside.

"My name's Eleanor by the way." But there's no response.

Invisible again, I guess. I don't think he even heard me.

4

ZYNAR

Her name is Eleanor. A soft name that rolls on my tongue.

Eleanor is a strange little female. I've never seen another of her kind before. Perhaps she's new to Hudo III. I'd heard rumors about females being sponsored to live on these plains. I didn't expect a soft little thing like her, though. Maybe a Merssi or even other female species known to prefer a solitary life. This female doesn't give the impression of either.

She's tiny and pale compared to my bulky form. No scales, but her skin is smooth and soft, almost translucent under the morning light. Her hair is a tangle of gold with a few fine threads of silver mixed in. It hangs in a loose wave to land just above her shoulders, framing features so delicate they caught me off guard the moment she opened the door. Even with her having disappeared inside the lodging, the image of her small straight nose, her round, soft jaw, and her plump parted lips are seared into my mind. Her eyes are a deep, captivating shade of blue that looked right into mine, unafraid. Unflinching.

And yet, nothing about her tells me she could ever be a

threat. A prey species then. So why is she on the plains of Hudo III? Alone, it seems, too. Where is her herd? Where is her *mate*?

I remain still on the roof where I stand, listening even though I probably shouldn't. But I hear no other voices inside. Is she really alone? When the door opened and my gaze fell to the little thing before me, for a moment, I forgot where I was and what I'd come here for.

I had no clue what species I'd be working for. Didn't really care. A benefit of being Kari, I suppose. Few species will dare to cause us trouble. I accepted the request to mend the roof, hopped into transport at first light, and headed to the coordinates. I expected a roof with a few holes that needed mending. I didn't expect…this.

A roof so weathered it's barely providing shelter, and a strange new female that caught me off guard.

Small prey species like hers can be easily scared by a Kari like me. But the female didn't seem afraid. At least, not afraid enough. She opened the door, but not without hiding some weapon at her back. I almost chuckle at the memory. She's no fool. She's smart.

I walk on the roof, making sure my footing is sure as I make my way across the small abode. Probably abandoned by a Merssi farmer ages ago. It's small but will make a nice, safe home once all the repairs are made. But it is also old and has been left unkempt for a long time. Most of the treestem holding it together is rotten and the fibers that prevent rain and starshine getting remain only out of loyalty. The strange unexpected female doesn't want me to redo the entire thing? I don't think I'll have a choice. I cannot with good conscience do subpar work.

As I pass one of the holes in the roof, I crouch and stick a digit in. It goes right through and I grunt, marking the spot as dangerous. And there are more just like that. I'm just about to rise and continue my survey when I catch movement through the hole.

The little female is within.

I stop moving. I should turn away but curiosity has me freezing there, watching her.

The garment she wears sways as her hips move, the hem brushing against her smooth legs. She heads out of sight and I hear her muttering something. Flipping off my language implant, her words float into my brain in their original form. "Needtochecktheoogas andwalktheperimeter, seehowbigthis- placereallyis whilethishunkworksonmy roof." It's a sing-song way of speaking. Almost like an avian chirping.

Endearing.

But it's not a language I've ever heard before. Not even close. She's from somewhere far, far away from the Hudo star system.

She appears again and my core-beat gives a hard thump, a soft growl developing in my throat as she lifts her colorful strands high on her head and sort of rolls them together, revealing her neck. There's something mesmerizing about the way she moves, a grace that has me still staring when I should have already looked away. Under usual circumstances, I wouldn't have paused to look at all. But I'm caught unable to look away as I watch the strange creature move within.

She has no wings but when she walks she flutters, her steps light and airy. The garment she wears swings. The tendrils on her head sway.

Like an avian inspecting a bloom, she peeks into things placed on a table within the lodging. Poking here and there before fluttering to another section.

It's captivating.

I continue to watch, my eyes tracing the line of her neck down to her shoulders, the gentle curve of her shoulders. When she turns my way, there are strange transparent things in frames balanced on her nose. Those weren't there when she greeted me at the door. They restrict the view of her blue eyes and I detest them immediately, but as she adjusts them on her nose, I find myself transfixed again. They don't take away from her beauty; no, they give another view of it.

Beauty?

Hmm. I hum low as I watch her. Too low for her to hear.

It's been a long time since I've found any female beautiful or even mildly interesting. But this strange avian without wings… she is. Undoubtedly so. Though I don't know exactly why. Despite that, I cannot deny that this little female is beautiful. Very beautiful.

Grabbing what looks like a strange bowl I soon realize is a head covering when she places it on her crown, she heads to the front door and disappears from my view.

I shake my head to clear my thoughts, her disappearance enough to push some logic back into my brain. It's a new day. The *start* of a new day. There's much to do and I'm already so easily distracted? Varek will return soon with the materials I need and I must be ready to make the most of the time that will follow. By the end of this sol, I can have the roof recovered, safe, and ready for the little female.

Rising, I continue my survey, constantly aware of every sound the little female makes now outside of her abode. She's being quiet. Just little hums here and there as she walks around the lodging. When I get near the edge of the roof, I catch her once or twice, touching wild plants growing freely in the yard. It takes a moment for me to realize it's not just random plants she's touching. It's the blooms. Pops of red, yellow, and violet among the dark syleen weeds and orange grass-feed. At one point, she leans in, brushing her nose against one of the blooms and I shift closer to the edge, watching her. She's behaving like an avian again. She seems particularly attracted to the blooms, as if they give her some kind of pleasure by simply existing.

Strange new *liora*—a fitting name for such a female like her.

I watch as she moves from the blooms over to the remnants of a well. She peeks into the dark hole before turning her focus to the old, retired tilling machines resting beside it. Just from the way she pauses then walks around them it's clear she has no idea what they are or how they work. But she will need them to till the ground for her crops. There is no other way to do it.

When she walks off and promptly disappears into the tall grass-feed, I stand tall, my brows furrowing.

That field needs to be tended to. Anything could be hiding in it and the female's so tiny…

I don't know why a breath of relief makes my shoulders less tense when I see her headgear bobbing through the grass as she makes her way toward the perimeter fence. A small smile threatens at my lips, a brow quirking as I watch the headgear move. A *liora* indeed.

She starts at one end of the fence, taking her time, head bobbing as she walks. It's the only thing that tells me where she is, just that bit of her headgear that tells me she seems to be checking the perimeter.

I forget my task as I watch her go. A few oogas lift their heads to look her way before ignoring her again and her laughter reaches me on the wind. She says something I don't understand and I curse myself for forgetting to switch on my implant again.

"—note to self," she says loudly, the implant picking up her words as it starts firing again. "If I find a snake, try not to scream like a little girl and scare the big, strong alien working on my roof. Are there even snakes out here? Shit. I didn't ask Xarion."

Another soft huff of a laugh brushes through my nose.

This little female is…entertaining. But who is this Xarion? Her mate? I snarl before I can catch myself and the sound momentarily brings me to my senses. This female is unknown to me. Why should her having a mate cause any reaction? But it does. Again. Right there. The simple thought makes me want to snarl once more.

I run a claw through my mane, brushing the filaments away from my face. Clearly, I have not had enough mealbars today. I only growl and snarl for no obvious reason when I'm hungry. I make a mental note to take a few extra bars with me next time. Meanwhile, my gaze still tracks the female. If she has a mate, why is he not guarding her? Helping her? Tending to the things she needs? Why has he left her here to deal with all this when he knew I'd be arriving soon? Is he so careless as to leave a Kari alone with his little soft *liora*?

I chuckle at the thought. 'Tis only in jest. We Kari only care about what is ours.

When the female reaches one end of the perimeter and begins making her way back up, I force myself to continue my survey. She'll be able to see me now and her impression must already be shaky. No need to make it worse by staring at her as she approaches. I feign intense focus on one part of the roof, even though I'm only listening to her movements. I hear when she comes through the broken-down gate because it creaks and then struggles before it slams shut. She'll need someone to help with that too and I can already tell that with this many holes on her roof, her flooring must be damaged inside. Plus, there's her field and all the other work this farm needs. That's a lot of labor, and it's more than one person can handle alone.

This Xarion, or whatever his name is, needs to do better.

A shiver goes through my scales as I sense her close. When I turn she's directly below, squinting as she looks up at me. My attention heightens on her face.

"Hey, everything alright up there, um, Zynar? Hope I got that right. I'm not good with names so pardon me if I've butchered yours."

Intriguing. Her phrasing is strange.

She said my name perfectly. Better than some other species

can. And still, like the brute I am, the mischievous part of me responds instead of the part that's supposed to be an upstanding citizen. "Say it again for me, so I can know if you said it correctly?"

"Zynar."

Gods. I've never heard my name as a song before.

When I don't reply she blinks, a slight furrow on her brow as she adjusts the lenses on her face. "Did I get it right?"

"Perfectly," I purr, unable to stop my voice from dropping lower. Frakk me, this is unexpected.

Her cheeks warm a peculiar red and I wonder if I'm mistaken and she has scales that change color too. There's a sound she makes in her throat as her eyes drop from mine for a moment before they pierce me again. "Is everything going well with the roof? Do you think you'll be able to fix it over the next few days?"

The next few sols? Ha. I'm almost insulted. I open my mouth to tell her it will only take me a single sol to finish work like this, but something stops me. Something holds my tongue and the upstanding citizen is gagged as that other part of me responds again.

"A few sols…perhaps." Where the frakk am I going with this? Why lengthen a job that won't take me much time? I have no clue.

"Great!" She perks up. A soft early wind blows across her face, playing in the golden strands that have escaped to frame her face beneath her headgear. "Well, please let me know if you need anything. I haven't made breakfast yet. Actually, I'm about to make it. If you'd like a cup of tea…"

Tee? What is this tee? I'm tempted to ask her, but it's unusual to be offered sustenance on jobs. As a matter of fact, it never happens.

"Or coffee?" But then she mutters something about probably

not having any of this thing called koh-fee. "Either way I can give you something hot to drink. Sound good?"

No, it doesn't, but I hesitate to say this. The star is rising. The dawn is not cold. My gaze shifts to her form. Possibly her thin skin does little to keep her warm despite the heat Hudo's star brings. And, perhaps if I reject her offer, I will offend her despite that a hot drink sounds like torture.

I should decline.

"I appreciate your kindness," I say.

Fool.

"Okay, great." She smiles at me, fine lines framing her eyes that make me want to lean closer to soak in the warmth of her truly genuine joy. Suddenly, that hot drink doesn't sound like torture at all if she will smile like that again. She pauses, her skin getting redder and I realize she must be waiting for another response. Perhaps I wasn't clear.

Lifting two fingers, I give her the Kari salute, tapping my fingers over my core-beat that's thrumming in my chest. She must take it as enough because she makes that sound in her throat again before she disappears into the little abode.

I stand there frozen, a tingle going over my spine. The lodge falls silent, save for the distant hums of the creatures in the grass. I'm almost tempted to slink over to that hole and spy on her again. But even *I* have boundaries I know not to cross.

With a confused growl in my throat, my gaze sweeps over the roof once more, assessing the task ahead. It's a big job, but not impossible. For this pretty *Liora*, I will make sure it's done right.

5

ELEANOR

I stand with my back pressed against the front door, my heart beating far too hard for my own good.

What was that? I felt like a schoolgirl talking to the hot guy from the football team while all the other girls looked on, bewildered. Here, it was oogas and tilgrans watching from the distance. Calm animals, those oogas. I don't know what to think of the tilgrans yet. I was scared to go too close to the perimeter fence because one had ventured near. They're massive up close.

Pressing a hand over my heart, I breathe out slowly, even as my heart still thunders in my chest.

The hunk of an alien, Zynar, looked at me as if I had his entire attention. God, I haven't felt my heart beat like this in so long. It's almost alarming, and I pull out one of the chairs at the table and sit down to steady myself.

Glancing upward, I can hear the faint thumps of his boots on the roof as he moves. He's obviously from some predator race with those eyes. Maybe that's what this is. Fight or flight. My body's scared of *something*.

I sit there for a few more minutes, my heart slowly calming down as I listen to Zynar work.

This is so stupid. *Eleanor, you're out of your mind.* He has to be what? Like thirty? Thirty-five, tops. I can never know, though. These aliens don't age like humans. Nevertheless, he's certainly not my age group and certainly, most definitely, has a woman out there somewhere. Young males like him like playing around. Party and do whatever they want. Have as many women as they want. They're not looking for anything serious. Not that I'm looking for anything serious, either.

I'm not. I'm not looking for anything at all! I didn't come to this planet for romance. I put that behind me a long time ago. I thought that was clear. Possibly, I need to remind myself that men, romance, and everything that comes with relationships are things I can do without.

I frown. I'm getting ahead of myself. Maybe the suddenness of these sensations is what's putting me out of sorts. Back on the refugee ship, I was surrounded by aliens and this never happened. Most of them didn't look like beings I'd ever get in bed with, but there were a few humanoids and I didn't feel a thing. I thought I was dead inside. Or perhaps it's because none of them ever looked at me like *that*. Like I was something entrancing. Something…desirable.

And maybe that's why I can't help but dream. It doesn't hurt to dream, right? As long as nothing happens, I can dream all I want. I might even dream about those yellow eyes tonight. The warmth in his gaze is a memory I'll keep for a little bit, even though I know he must look at all the ladies like that. He's a tradesman after all. Customer service and all that.

I sit for a few more moments, listening to the soft thumps above me as the alien continues to survey the roof. A soft smile comes over me before I huff out a deep breath and stand. Dreams. Memories. Lost hopes. That's all this is. Time is moving and if my walk around the grounds was anything to go by, I have a lot of work to do. No use in sitting around dreaming about things that will never happen. The work isn't going to do itself.

Rising, I head into the little kitchen. Everything within it is strange—the stove, the oven, even the placement of things. Strange, but not impossible to figure out. When I'm settled in enough I'll try baking some cakes. For now, I'll keep meals simple. Judging from my little chat with the roofer, this place might need more extensive repairs than I first thought. That means the thousand credits New Horizons left might not be enough after all. I have to be smart with my spending.

There's a little kettle Xarion set up, thankfully, and I put it on the stove. After more tries than I'd like to admit, I get the fire going. Taking fresh mugs from the supplies, I grab crackers too and tea flowers. I make the cups of tea in no time and set the crackers on saucers. There's no butter and I wonder briefly if ooga milk will be able to create the stuff. They're like cow-hippos after all. I'll have to check one day. Can make my own butter and even sell it too, if that's the case.

More plans come into my mind as I place the food on a tray and step outside, walking a few steps into the yard before turning to look up at the roof. I spot him immediately. The color of his scales is hard to miss. Using that same measuring tool attached to his waist, he sends the laser along the thatched roof, the device extending and retracting with precise movements. He disengages it and it disappears without a sound before he uses something that looks like chalk to create an X on the roof fibers.

My brows shoot up. There are about ten Xs just on this front part of the roof that's visible. I'm staring at them, realizing slowly that it must be where the holes are, when Zynar turns around.

His gaze finds me immediately as if he knew I was already standing there. That delicious misplaced tingle spreads through me again.

"I brought tea." I smile and his gaze shifts to the tray balanced in my hands. "Are those…"

"Weaknesses," he says, gesturing to the markings with one arm. He doesn't even look at the roof. Those yellow eyes are glued to me. "In these spots, the beams supporting your roof are…inadequate."

Oh no. That really doesn't sound good. I thought it was the roof fiber alone that needed changing. "What do you mean? They're rotting too?"

"Yes." His gaze shifts slightly as if his eyes are traveling over my face. "They need replacing."

I bite my lip. Shit. "How much will that increase the cost? The computer told me around fifty to sixty credits for patching the roof. I didn't budget…" I worry my bottom lip. I didn't take time to do a budget. Not yet. But the roof is important. If I don't have a roof over my head, I might as well sleep in the field with the oogas.

Zynar watches me. "It will require more supplies…more time…"

He must see the uncertainty rising within me because he continues. "Do not fear, *Liora*. I've already contacted my siblingkin, Varek. He will return with everything we need."

Great. *Liora*. So he *did* hear my name. Only he's forgotten it.

I don't correct him. Doesn't matter, he'll be gone in a few days anyway. Instead, I press a smile to my face. "What about the cost…"

He smiles and it catches me off guard. He really is beautiful. The more the sun rises, the more it plays over his scales, sending purple, blue and pink back to me.

"I do not overcharge."

"So not more than sixty then…" My eyes narrow playfully and Zynar barks out a low laugh. That catches me off guard, too, and I press my lips into a line before smiling back. "I'm joking. I know it will cost more than that, but I'd like a quote, at least, so I know what to expect."

He gives a slight tilt of his head in affirmation.

"I have tea. Come before it gets cold."

He's quick to move. One moment he's on the roof, the next he's standing right before me, the earth beneath my feet vibrating with the power of his descent.

Did he just jump? From the roof?

My eyes are wide, hands shaking a little from the sheer adrenaline and power that seems to have sent a delicious tingle from my soles right up through me.

Muscles flex before my face, awakening that girl within me some more, and I blink a few times to clear my head.

"I'd invite you inside but..." My words trail off because at that moment his ears flick at my words. They're like elf ears but pointing toward the back of his head, pink-tipped and with a purple hue. "But it's a mess in there..."

"I am fine here." There are two stumps in the yard where mighty trees must have once been and he moves over to sit on one. His attitude is so nonchalant, so unbothered, that it takes some of the tension from my back. I sit too, liking the fact that he's fine with not being fussy or formal. Already he seems like the simple type that doesn't care about getting dirty. Figures. He does hard work for a living.

I take a moment to just feel the cool breeze blowing around us. It's been a long time since I've played host. This almost feels like I'm pretending, but I push away the feeling, adjusting the tray on my lap as the soft wind plays with the steam coming from the mugs. I'm having morning tea with an alien. I'm almost civilized.

Handing the alien one of the mugs and some crackers, I take the rest for myself.

We sip in silence. Or rather, I sip while Zynar blinks at the tea. I suddenly realize it might not be something he's used to having. Or, probably, that he doesn't want it at all.

"Oh, you don't have to drink it if you don't want to." Mortification fills me. "It's totally fine if it's not to your taste."

But then he takes a sip. The scales on his brow move upward, his eyes widening slightly.

"Hot," he finally says.

I choke on a mortified laugh. "You're supposed to take small sips and blow on it first."

I demonstrate, heat filling me as his gaze drops to my lips watching as I blow on the tea and then take a sip. He follows my movements, humming a low tone in his chest that sends a vibration across my skin. I clear my throat, rubbing at my arms and he watches me do that, too.

"It is good," he finally murmurs.

I smile again before focusing on sipping more of my tea. "Yeah, it's good. Not like the tea I'm used to. This one uses actual petals from edible flowers."

My gaze shifts to his hands holding the mug. It looks like he's holding a kid's toy for a tea party. That's probably what this feels like to him. I get the distinct impression he's doing this only because I offered. He's a stranger that doesn't owe me a thing, but at least he's being sweet about it and I can't help the little bit of happiness it brings me. Just doing this, feeling normal after feeling displaced for so long, is healing a bit of me inside.

I watch as the alien sips the tea, my focus snapping to his lips. He's even eating the crackers too. That firm jaw works as he chews and swallows, the muscles in his neck adjusting as he eats.

It's hard not to stare, even despite my reservations and the war inside my head. It's like having a display of pure masculinity right in front of me. One that doesn't seem toxic and riddled with conditions. If I was brave enough, if I hadn't sworn off men, I'd actually, maybe flirt with him.

God, I'm shameless. Flirt? He's in his prime, and I'm...well...not.

Trying not to stare at him directly, I settle for glancing at him every now and then. He's incredibly sculpted. His face, his shoulders, his arms, his abs. Every single part of him. How is it possible for one man to look this good? This perfect? Where I come from, people go to great lengths to look like he does. Gym, steroids, surgery, you name it. Maybe it's his species? Maybe also the hard labor.

And his color... It's like looking at a canvas meant to invoke pure and utter awe and peace.

His long green mane rustles in the breeze and when my gaze shifts up to his, I realize he's staring at me. Probably been staring at me the entire time that I've been ogling him. My heart does a little stutter that makes me almost choke on a cracker. That's what I get for staring so shamelessly. Luckily for me, he doesn't say a word.

But now that I've caught him looking at me, I'm completely aware of it. We sip in silence, only the occasional sound of an ooga baying or the sounds of the breeze in the tall grass breaking the silence. And every few minutes when I dare to look over, Zynar is watching me. And not just watching me either. Even in my limited experience with other beings, aliens, I can tell he's not looking at me like he's wondering if I'm food. If I'm sentient. Not looking at me like I'm ugly or disgusting either, like some of those aliens would do back on that refugee ship. He's looking at me in a way that sends a strange shiver right through me. As if there's nothing else around us and I'm the only thing he can see. Despite the swaying grasses in the fields, the animals grazing, the beautiful pink sky and sun, I'm his sole focus. My heart does a strange little thump that makes me completely aware of every inch of my skin.

I thought his looks earlier had depth, but the way he's looking at me now, his eyes hold me pinned in place. I wonder what he's thinking. Probably about the laugh lines around my eyes or the few gray hairs starting to appear. The last few years haven't been kind to my body. Age and stress have taken their toll, and I'm not the woman I used to be. I look at my hands, fingers a little shaky around the mug, and wonder if he notices the age spots from too many years spent gardening in the sun or the way my skin isn't as firm as it used to be. Does he see the tiredness etched into my face, or does he see past that, to the woman who's trying to rebuild her life from scratch?

Of course, he doesn't. How could he? Most of my own kind don't, or don't even care to. As soon as you can no longer bear children, it's like the world ceases to care about you anymore. It's probably the same here. Probably the same everywhere. It's only nature.

Again, I thought I was past this.

Zynar's still staring and I take a bite of a cracker and sip my tea, pretending to be oblivious even though the tiny hairs at the back of my neck stand on end. All these years of confidence I'd built up teaching at the community college back in my town on Earth seem to go out the window and I can't open my mouth to ask him what's caught his attention so much. Too afraid to know. Too afraid to find out what his truth might be.

Oh, Eleanor. What has happened to you? You've lost a lot but you haven't lost it all, have you?

I clear my throat, the alien's eyes still on me as I force my attention on the swaying orange grass. I'm as alien to him as he is to me. For all I know, he's wondering what this strange, obviously-out-of-her-element thing is doing here on his planet. As far as I know, humans are rare, having only been trafficked by that horrible race called the Tasqals. Perhaps Zynar's wondering which planet I originated from. But when my eyes shift over to his once more, I find his gaze is steady, thoughtful, as if he's trying to figure out something else. Like what makes me tick. It's unsettling, but also…thrilling.

"I…do not want to intrude." His voice breaks the silence and although it's pitched soft, it still brings my alertness up one thousand percent.

My complete focus shifts to him. "Yes?"

Zynar's gaze drops immediately to my lips. "What brings a soft female like you all the way out to the frontier plains of Hudo III?"

There it is. See? Nothing untoward. But first 'little female', and now '*soft* female'? Ha. When have I ever been called *that*?

"I could ask you the same question. A farming planet doesn't exactly seem like prime territory for a big, strong male like yourself." Now, why did I say that? I want to take back my words when the alien before me suddenly flexes one thick arm and my eyes trace the motion. A lump forms in my throat that has nothing to do with the dry crackers.

"Repairing homesteads and working the land with my siblingkin is in my blood. We Kari were built for such labors."

"I see." It's all the words that manage to come from my lips.

"But you have yet to explain your own situation, little *Liora*. This seems hardly the place for one so delicate and…unaccompanied." It almost sounds like a question. Like he's fishing to find out if I'm single. Is he? Surely, he isn't.

Conflicting emotions play within me. Do I really want to tell him I'm single? That I'm all alone out here on my own? I don't know him. I don't know anyone. I might be human and new to this world, but I'm not a fool. I've been around long enough to know it's not safe for women in basically every part of the universe I've lived in so far.

Plus, I don't even know this male. I met him like six seconds ago.

Biting my lip, I say fuck it and finally reply. "Let's just say I needed a fresh start after my…previous circumstances went awry. The New Horizons Initiative offered me a chance to start over, to make a life for myself here. Though I know they're keeping track of me and everything I do." I add that last bit for an ounce of safety, letting him know I'm being monitored so he doesn't think I'm entirely alone.

Even though I'm not. Xarion probably doesn't give a fig about what happens to me out here.

Zynar seems to consider my response, but he doesn't pry and I'm thankful for that. When he responds, I'm happy he takes my answer for what it is. "I see. I must have your new homestead set to rights swiftly then. It would sully my honor to have such a rare flower resting exposed to the elements."

The compliment disarms me and I smile, something warming within me even as bells ring in my head that this is a road I've forbidden and put warning signs all over. "You're too kind. Though I fear my petals may be growing a bit withered these days." I joke, taking another sip of the tea.

He makes a sound in his throat, almost like a purr that vibrates through *me* instead of *him*. It makes me hold the tea too long in my mouth and I almost choke again when his gaze skips over my skin. "Hardly, little *Liora*."

I swallow down the tea and smile knowing he's being polite. But then he leans a little closer, his nostrils flaring slightly in a way that makes me feel like he's smelling *me*. "I'm an excellent judge of beauty...*Eleanor*."

So, he *does* know my name. I can feel myself blush. Shit, I must look like a freshly plucked tomato. Before I can reply, Zynar rises fluidly to his feet, positioning himself with the sun at his back. His body casts a shadow over me, making that lump in my throat swell. As he sets his empty mug down on the tray in my lap, it puts him close enough that his scent wafts right through me again. I almost close my eyes and inhale deeply, stopping myself just moments before doing so.

What the hell is wrong with me? Remember the path you

mustn't tread, Eleanor? Remember that you've been down this road many times before and it always ends in a crash at the end of the ride? Yes? Remember that? Shit, woman, you almost died after the last one.

Repeat after me: Men like to flirt, but they always desert.

"I should return to my preparations before my siblingkin arrives with the materials. Though…" Zynar's voice pulls me from my internal battle and when I focus on his eyes again, this time, his gaze brazenly trails over me, sending goosebumps and tingles all across my skin. It's a helluva thing when your mind screams one thing but your body does another. "I would not object to sharing this 'tea' with you again…if you are willing."

My lips part slightly, my eyes widening. Now that, I didn't expect.

I manage to give a small nod, speechless.

Zynar rewards me with a quirk of his brow and a flash of fang. "Excellent."

Good god, his gaze skips over me again.

My mouth goes dry. Is he…*flirting* with me?

I watch, feeling flustered, as Zynar grabs the beam with one hand and leaps back up onto the roof with an easy, powerful grace. My cheeks still burn like I'm sitting too close to a furnace.

Part of me wants to downplay his words as just meaningless flirtation that comes naturally to his kind. But another part of me, despite the war in my brain, preens at the attention. His brazenly roaming gaze sets my skin tingling in a way I haven't experienced in years and a part of me weeps at that fact while another part of me lights up like a Christmas tree.

As he moves about on the roof, muscles rippling beneath his iridescent scales, I can't tear my eyes away. This male is utterly at ease with his physicality, his strength. So different from the human males I remember.

I take another sip of the floral tea, more to occupy my hands than anything. Zynar glances down at me again and I quickly look away, staring sightlessly into my cup as I try to regain my composure.

6

ELEANOR

I try to busy myself with the house. I push the hot hunk of an alien from my mind and focus on what I came here for. The first thing I do is take out the things that are too broken to use. Small pieces of old furniture I can lift, and other little things. There's a large wooden box I think used to be for storage. It sits off to the side of what I'm going to call the living room, but it's far too large and heavy for me to even shift. I stand staring at it. I might have to break it apart little by little and take away the small pieces one by one, but just the thought of hammering on anything when my hands ache so easily makes me clench and unclench them at my side, trying to think of an alternative.

Lifting the final small broken stool, at least that's what I think it is, I take it outdoors. The sun beams down on me immediately, making me aware of the sweat on my brow as I squint at the difference in light. The hover-truck is by my gate again and I catch Zynar standing with his brother. Together they unload a row of beams, each taking one. Both shirtless, their muscles ripple as they work. It's like watching a show put on just for me. They talk to each other as they work and though they almost appear identical, I can tell them apart just by the hair and build. Zynar is slightly thicker, his hair an inch or two longer. This is only confirmed when he looks over his shoulder and spots me. He grins, flashing fang, and my cheeks warm. Gods, they're both attractive, although there's something about Zynar that makes my eyes linger on him. Setting down the stool in the pile I made, I wave. His brother pops his head up and spots me, too. He stares and I swear I hear Zynar growl. With a sharp chin to chest, the brother greets me.

I return the greeting before forcing myself to turn around and head back into the house. I can't just stand and stare at them.

Work, Eleanor. Not gawk.

Time passes and I hear them talking as they work together bringing materials closer to the house before it goes relatively silent again. I'm busy moving things out of the way when I hear the dull thumps of Zynar on the roof. There's a creek and then a whooshing sound like straw breaking before light suddenly pierces right through the ceiling. I squint, my eyes adjusting to the glare as the hole above me gets wider. Bits of debris fall right inside and suddenly Zynar and I are face to face.

He freezes the moment he sees me, and those intense yellow eyes seem to suck me right in.

"Ah," I try to break the tension. "I'm being a silly goat, aren't I? I can't work in here while you're fixing the roof."

"I don't know what a goht is, *Liora*, but you are anything but silly."

God, more compliments. More than I've ever received in such a short space of time before. I try not to react but my skin heats anyway.

Glancing at the things New Horizons sent and then at the floor, some of the debris has already fallen on them. If it's any indication, the whole floor will be filled with dust, dirt and straw soon.

"Right." I bite my bottom lip, running my hands through my hair as I create a ponytail. Glancing up at Zynar, he's still frozen there watching me. "Just wait a sec!"

Moving as quickly as I can, I get the old linen I'd aired and bring them back inside, covering everything important that I can. Hurrying into the bedroom, I rip the sheets off the bed and turn the mattress on its side. I'm huffing by the time I make it back to the hole Zynar made, my entire body aching, too.

"Okay." I give him a thumbs up but he doesn't seem to know what it means. Of course, he doesn't know what it means. "You can go ahead now." He gives me a slight bow like his brother did, chin to chest, that gaze of his tracking me as I head out of the house.

Outside, the soft wind brushes against me, rejuvenating me a little. Guess I'll have to focus my efforts on the yard then.

Heading over to the pile of things I'd taken out, I turn to look up at the house. I expect to see his brother there with him, but Zynar is alone. He rips at the roof material, bringing up the tightly woven straws section by section. And section by section, the rotten beams holding the roof together are revealed.

I press my hands akimbo at my sides. He was right. The entire thing needs replacing. Even with my inexperienced eyes, I can see that. So much for trying to patch the thing. I watch as he continues working, a steady pile of rotten debris growing at one side of the house.

He's efficient and fast, I can already see that. He moves with the strength of at least three men, tearing at the roof with his bare hands, no tools needed. When he glances up and catches me shamelessly watching, I have the decency to wave before forcing myself to turn around and getting on with my work.

I have no gloves, but I suppose I can do something easy. It's not like there's a rush to get everything done within the first week of being here. I can take my time.

With that, I sidestep the pile of crap I'd started to make

unwisely in the center of the yard, and head over to the side where the main lodging is fenced in. There are wildflowers and there are weeds. Guess I can start here.

For the first few minutes, I make good progress. The variety of flowers just in my yard alone is astounding. If I had my tools, years of teaching about plants and how to grow them could help me identify the species—or at least, make my own names for them since they're definitely not from Earth. But I could at least decide how best to cultivate them. I grin, gaze shifting around the yard. It's like my personal Eden, each bloom offering a promise of what this land can become.

I gather the seeds of a few of the flowers and the shoots of others that are growing in the wrong place, reminding myself to pick out a good spot for a garden later. There are several with thorns though, and I weed around them. I work hard, but soon not even my hat's good protection from the heat or the ache in my legs from stooping so long. Good god. Taking my hat off, because it doesn't seem to be helping one bit, I set it on the ground and kneel on it instead. It's foldable, so I don't worry about destroying its integrity as I put my weight on the thing. Now in a slightly better position, I resume my work with renewed gusto.

I work fast, glancing up at Zynar as he works too. He's so efficient, I wonder how much he really has to do on that roof that it will take him a few days to complete. Even as I glance over my shoulder, he's almost done clearing the entire front side of the roof away. It pushes me to work harder and I lean into the rhythm we have. The sounds of him ripping the roof, the resulting soft crash of rotten fiber on the pile he's making mixed with my soft grunts and the growing pile of weeds at my side. I'm so into it that I make one terrible mistake.

"Ah!" It's the sudden pain that makes me stop. I don't even truly realize what's happened at first. Not until pure red blood runs down my hand as I lift it, wincing as I see a thick thorn at the end of a deep wound in the center of my palm.

I cut myself.

"Well, butter my butt and call me a biscuit." I clutch my hand, trying to keep the blood from dripping everywhere. Do I even have a first aid kit in those supplies? I'm staring at the wound, applying pressure to my wrist and trying to think fast when a shadow suddenly looms over me. I'd have thought it was the clouds if that sweet, intoxicating scent didn't waft into my nose a second later.

Before I can move, Zynar is at my back. He kneels immediately, his thick thighs closing me in as he comes in close behind me. The unexpected closeness makes me freeze. Tingles erupt in my belly, the pain in my hand fading to the background as the heat of his chest presses into my back and the warmth of his crotch spreads across my behind. Sudden images of us, naked, in this same position flash through my mind. I'm now frozen in pure horror at where my mind has immediately gone.

Zynar reaches around me with both arms, closing me in even tighter in his embrace as he gently takes my injured hand between his large ones. I'm utterly engulfed in his personal space, cocooned by hard muscle and the dizzying aroma of his masculine scent.

"Let me see, sweet *Liora*," he rumbles, the vibrations traveling through where our bodies are flush together. I catch myself trying not to lean back against his warmth as he carefully examines the thorn embedded in my hand.

This close, I can feel the power thrumming through his frame, like a great tautly-controlled force of nature. I'm almost overwhelmed by the sheer physicality of him surrounding me so utterly. Arousal stirs low in my belly even though there's a meager fight within me to resist it.

"So soft," he murmurs, frowning at the wound.

I don't know if it's a criticism or an observation. I'm

suddenly unable to think with him so close. Too close. This isn't appropriate. I'm his employer. Wouldn't this be frowned upon? Do those rules even matter when you're on Hudo III? Does it even matter?

"Hold still," he rumbles, his voice vibrating through me. His touch is surprisingly gentle as he takes one finger to the thorn. I hiss. "You've got a nasty flesh tearer here. It's in deep."

His breath is warm against my ear and I can't breathe. "It's nothing," I murmur, but the sting in my palm tells me otherwise. Leave it up to me to injure myself on my second day of being here. Hopefully, New Horizons isn't using me as a test dummy to see how other humans will fare on this new world. I don't want to make them think we're not up for a new life. A new home.

Zynar grunts, bringing my attention back to him even though I'm trying to focus on anything but him. Like the rise and fall of his chest against my back as he breathes. Or how he's fit around me so well it's like we've been in this position before and it's second nature now.

I have to remind myself that he's not human and him wrapping himself around me like this is probably not strange to him. Shit, if this was on Earth and my roofer did this, I'd be thinking he wants to take me to bed. It's unnecessarily close. If I even move my hips a little, I'm sure my behind will be rubbing against his cock.

"Look at me, pretty Liora." Words that make my gaze shift up to his, my heart stuttering a beat. Why's he saying those things? Calling me pretty when it's been clear most aliens think my kind is hideous. I wasn't even called that back on Earth where I supposedly belong.

My brain takes this opportunity to bring up a memory I'd rather forget. Me standing in front of the full-length mirror in our bedroom, smoothing down the fitted red dress I'd bought. My ex-husband walks by, adjusting his tie. Doesn't even glance at me. I push away my disappointment. He's distracted. This is his big night, after all. This isn't about me. Tonight, after years, he makes partner. And so I push my disappointment away, hurrying from the mirror as I hear him call my name down the stairs.

"Coming!" I remember shouting. Stepping down the staircase, I felt like a queen in that dress. I couldn't help it. I had to ask. "How do I look?" He barely glances at me. In fact, he grumbles. Frowns. Appears annoyed that I'm distracting him.

I push away the disappointment again. I remind myself tonight is his night. But then, at the party, some young blonde waltzes by us. Vivacious. Skin glowing. In her prime.

"Patrick!" she beams, coming to a stop. "Congratulations!" Her gaze shifts to me and she smiles. I return the greeting even though my darling husband doesn't even attempt to introduce us. I have nothing against the pretty lady. But her face is a blur because all I remember seeing is that we were wearing the same dress. All I remember seeing is how my now ex-husband's eyes lit up.

"Oh, Rachel." Hunger rises in his eyes. Eyes that haven't looked at me like that in so long. "You look absolutely *divine* tonight."

She blushes, doing a small curtsy as her date comes by her side.

"I can see why you'd say that, Patrick," he says, eyes twinkling as they land on me. "After all, our gorgeous women have impeccable taste."

Patrick had looked at me then, as if only just noticing what I was wearing. His eyes flickered with irritation, a subtle but unmistakable shift. He gave me a cursory glance, the kind you'd give to someone who'd just spilled wine on your shoes, and then turned his attention back to Rachel. "Well, isn't this just…something," he said, his tone flat and dismissive. "Rachel, you look stunning."

The compliment hung in the air, a stark contrast to the cold shoulder I was receiving. Patrick barely spared me another look, his focus entirely on Rachel. The moment was a clear reminder of how far apart we had drifted, how invisible I had become to the man who once couldn't take his eyes off me.

The disappointment I'd been pushing down all evening threatened to choke me. The rest of the night was a blur of polite smiles and forced conversations, each one a reminder of how invisible I felt. And just like my hand right now, my heart bled.

Because at that moment, I realized this wasn't just *his* party. It was mine too. I'd been there by his side for *twenty* years. Two decades spent being his support. Being the one to go to his boss to apologize for his rotten behavior. Being the fool who believed in him when others didn't. I'd been there in the shadows, being the rock he needed.

It was *my* party too.

I'd been called gorgeous that night in a sort of backhanded way, but it wasn't enough. I'd spent years in the background, supporting a man who didn't see me anymore. That night, as I watched him fawn over Rachel, I realized how diminished I'd become, and how much of my identity I'd sacrificed in the process.

But now, I'm here on Hudo III, with the most attractive male I've ever seen telling me I'm *pretty*.

Why? Why is he calling me that and why's he calling me *Liora*? I want to ask those questions even though the answers might not be ones I can bear. But as I look up into those slitted yellow eyes, every part of me ignites. Zynar holds my focus, his gaze engulfing me like I'm about to be consumed. He distracts me enough that when he suddenly pulls the thorn from my palm, I barely make a sound.

"There," he whispers, his gaze shifting over my face, almost as if he's documenting my features again.

When he suddenly brings my wounded hand up to his lips, I don't react fast enough. At first, I don't react at all. Zynar's mouth closes over my palm and I feel his hot tongue on my skin.

I finally jerk in surprise, reflex causing me to pull my arm toward me, but he holds it fast, tongue swirling over my palm in a way that makes my spine tingle.

"Zynar," I manage to whisper, my voice trembling. "W-what are you doing?"

His eyes meet mine, intense and unwavering. "Kari saliva has healing properties," he explains softly, his lips brushing against my skin. "It will help."

I can barely breathe as he continues, the sensation both strange and oddly soothing. But underneath that soothing swirl, is a bolt of electricity going to a place that hasn't been touched by anyone except me for a long, long time. His touch, his proximity, everything about this moment feels surreal.

I clear my throat, clawing for some semblance of the intelligence God gave me. "You don't have to," I whisper, but he simply shakes his head.

"I'm the only male within your proximity. Unless you have a mate hiding somewhere in that lodge…"

I blink several times, shaking my head as I do. "A mate? Like a boyfriend? A husband?" I give a nervous laugh. "God, no. I don't have a mate. Not anymore."

A purr sounds in his throat, so deep, I feel the vibrations across my back.

"Good."

Good?

"It's my duty then to ensure you are unharmed." His voice a deep rumble. "And I want to."

He wants to…

His words send a shiver through me, and I find myself

unable to look away from his gaze. There's something in his eyes, something I can't quite place, but it makes my heart race.

When he finally pulls back, my hand feels warm and tingles where his tongue touched. Not a drop of blood is left, just an angry red wound. Zynar's golden eyes flick to mine, a smirk playing on his lips. "You're braver than most," he says softly.

I can't even answer. I don't know what to say, and so I try to brush it off. "It's just a scratch."

He makes a sound in his throat like he doesn't agree. "I've seen males quiver at the sight of this much lifeblood." With a swift motion, he reaches into a small pouch at his waist. "Let me bandage this for you."

I nod, a mix of embarrassment, gratitude, and something else swelling inside me. His fingers are deft as he wraps a clean bandage around my hand, securing it with surprising skill.

"Thank you," I say, my voice barely more than a whisper.

Zynar smiles, a small, almost hesitant flash of his fangs that makes him look surprisingly gentle.

"You're welcome, Eleanor," he says. I don't miss that he uses my name this time, which only makes the moment feel more intimate.

He helps me to my feet, the cloak of his body disappearing and leaving me curiously cold. I brush my hands over my arms, wincing slightly from the pain in my palm as I stand on shaky legs.

Zynar pauses there, his hands lingering on mine for a moment longer than necessary. His eyes lock onto mine, the intensity in his gaze making it hard to breathe. "You must be careful, Liora," he murmurs, his voice a low rumble. He turns his head, surveying the yard. "Leave the weeds, I will take care of them."

My eyes widen. "What? No. That's—" I shake my head. "That's fine. It's fine, really."

"When the star goes to rest. I will clear the weeds."

My mouth falls open but he's already heading back toward the house. I sputter. "Y-you don't have to. I couldn't possibly ask—"

"You didn't ask," he says, pausing to look back at me, his eyes glowing with a promise I can't quite decipher. "I want to help. Rest now."

My breath catches at his words, the tension between us thick and palpable. Is this what that computer meant about Kari males being persistent? As I watch him launch himself up on the roof again, ladder be damned, his touch lingers like a ghost on my skin.

It's a path I'm tracing with my fingers without even realizing. The moment I do, there's mounting horror? Chagrin? Anticipation? I'm not sure which. All I know is that there's a tingle in my belly, warmth in my veins.

I'm attracted to the male working on my roof.

I've been here a single day. Good god, Eleanor. You should be ashamed. Attracted to a male because he's being nice? Where have my standards gone? Not to mention it's a male I can't possibly have, and now my heart is beating double time just at the memory of his touch.

7

ZYNAR

I might be interested in the female.

No. I *am* interested in the female.

I watch her from the corner of my eyes as she stands for a moment, watching as I go back to my task.

I rattled her. Could feel her core-beat stutter and restart as I pressed into her back. Bold of me, but I couldn't resist. Couldn't help it. The moment I scented her lifeblood in the air, I was off the roof and by her side. The little whimper I'm sure she didn't realize she uttered pulled me in. All instinct said I should care. *Protect.* Soothe. Leaning in, she smelled like the fresh air that rises at dawn, and her golden filaments? Soft, like the finest threads of silk from Karicek.

Her body's so small. Softer than I could have ever imagined. She fit right between my thighs and I almost groaned at the sensation of her there. I shouldn't have; it was far too close. Far too inappropriate. She could end the job contract for my lack of boundaries. Some prey species don't like to be touched—too scared of our claws. Some don't like to be spoken to—too scared of our fangs. I'm glad she seems to be neither of those, and yet, I pushed my luck.

What drove me to do so? Only the gods could tell.

I'm overly aware as she moves, walking slowly around the yard. She can't go back inside the lodge and she can't pull at the weeds anymore. I wonder what she'll do. As I continue clearing the roof, the debris piling up high on the ground, I try not to stare at her as she makes her way around the lodge. There's an outbuilding several lengths away from the main abode and she heads there. When she disappears inside it, I catch myself just before I whine.

The fact it almost escaped from my throat has me standing still for a few moments.

Growling at myself, I focus on my work. What the frakk is wrong with me this sol? Thank the gods Varek isn't here to see all of this. The other job he's doing should last the entire sol, too, but if he was here, he'd bop me over the head. He's the level-headed one. The serious one. The one that gets the jobs done fast and moves on to another, always keeping busy. And I'm the one always matching his pace.

Because we strive on these preoccupations. Fixing homesteads is an easy way to distract from other things missing in our lives. No real home. No mates. We didn't have to stay on Hudo. We could travel the stars, but orbits of doing that only underlined one thing. Something's missing and lives of adventure only filled that gap for a short time. Now, on Hudo III, we keep busy by fixing other beings' problems.

It's honest work. Hard work. No time for the mind to wander then.

But when a strange little female appears from nowhere, knocking my focus back, the mind begins to wander to things it shouldn't.

My core-beat is steady now, only picking up a strange thrum when the female is near. My core-rhythm as silent as it's always been. But I can't deny that the little female has me wondering about that one thing that has haunted me and every displaced

Kari since the war. Our core-rhythms are silent because there's no *kahl*, no destined mate, to sync with.

For the majority of us, we Kari have no home.

Lifting my head, I glance down the dusty road. Not a thing but the soft breeze disturbs the grass-feed growing on either side. It's so quiet out here, I'd think I'm the only one within my immediate proximity. Not even sound comes from the female in the outbuilding she disappeared into.

Clearing the last of the rotten fiber off her roof, my gaze shifts to the outbuilding again, brows furrowing at the silence. Should I check on her? Would that be going too far? What if she gets hurt again?

The sight of her blood flowing down her arm had made alarm run through me. I'd brought her flesh to my lips without even thinking. The way she looked at me...the way her lips parted slightly, her cheeks flushing a delicate pink. It had been hard to pull away.

I should ask her what species she is. Where she came from. I don't want to pry, but as the hors pass, more questions arise in my mind.

More clicks pass until I'm simply balancing on her rotten roof beams as I stare at the outbuilding. I should go check on her. Maybe ask her some more questions about herself. Figure out why there's suddenly an itch within me that needs to be scratched.

But I am simply here to work. Nothing more. I'm not supposed to interact with the employer more than necessary and I've already broken that rule in the few hors since being on this farm.

Still, an uncertain energy rises within me and I step closer to the edge of the roof, ready to jump down and go make sure the female is alright. I'm just about to do it when the large doors to the outbuilding swing open and I see her pulling a rotten bale of grass-feed behind her. She huffs, the bale obviously heavy from being soaked through with moisture. I frown, the tool I'm using hanging in my hand as I watch her.

"Need help, Liora?" I'm about to hop down, but she shakes her head.

"No. No, I'm good." She huffs again and the urge to assist makes it difficult to stand still. She's working hard again despite the wound in her palm. She pulls the bale a few lengths from the door, head tilting my way. There's a slight smile on her lips and it sends a tingle through me before she turns and heads back inside the outbuilding.

A growl rumbles in my chest. She's hired me to do a job. I should focus on it, and on it only.

Repeating this in my head, it keeps me sane as I finish preparing the frame of the roof. Stripping the entire thing takes a few hors, mostly because I spend half the time listening and watching for signs of the little female. Working underneath the hot star, I get the job done until the star starts to make its descent across the pink sky. All the while the female works, too, and I try not to keep track of her in the corner of my eye. Adding the waterproof membrane over the roof, I secure the brand new beams that will hold the weight of the new roof fiber. I'm adding the last bolt when I hear a soft voice down below. Hers.

A tingle goes down my back immediately, one I think will go away but only increases when I look over the edge of the roof to find the female standing down below.

"Looks good!" She smiles up at me and my core-beat skips. "Waterproofed now, right?"

I give her a slight nod, not trusting what will happen if I open my mouth.

There's a smudge on her face, dirt, maybe mud, and her swaying garment has streaks of the same mud all over it. For hors, I glimpsed her as she cleared out the outbuilding. From the items she's taken out, I can tell it was used to house animals.

Maybe oogas or some other kind of large grass-fed thing. More than once, I wanted to tell her not to bother, that I can get to it when I'm finished with the roof, but the last thing I want is to make her reconsider hiring me. It's clear that just like me, she wants to keep herself busy and the last thing I want to do is make her turn me away.

Frakk that. I didn't want to intrude because I feared I would do more than intrude.

"Waterproofed and ready for new roof material," I finally answer her question with words.

"Good," she blinks at me and even in the dying light, I can see the rosy color rising in her cheeks. "You haven't had lunch yet, have you? Or dinner. I haven't seen you take a break."

Is she about to offer me food again? Another purr rises in my throat. I've been getting increasingly hungry, but not for sustenance.

She glances up at the sky. "It's getting late. Maybe you should stop for today?"

"Varek will not return for several more hors."

"Ah." Her cheeks warm some more. "Well, I mean, you're welcome inside while you wait for his return." She's inviting me inside her abode? So trusting. But even though I'd never harm her, I'll have to decline. It's bad enough being in a wide open space and unable to take my eyes off her. Inside there, with four walls surrounding us, she'll dominate my senses and I might do more than scare her slightly.

"Inside isn't really clean with all the debris," she continues. "I've just cleared the essential areas so I understand—"

She jerks a little when I pocket my tool and leap from the roof to land before her. I grimace and I'm about to apologize when I notice those blue eyes are glued to my arms, moving slowly to my chest, at the same time that her throat moves. Behind her lenses, her eyes are wide.

"It's better if I wait here, Eleanor. The dusk is pleasant." I try to keep my tone neutral, but the way her name rolls off my tongue feels too intimate, too familiar.

She nods, a bit flustered. "Right." She squeezes her eyes shut for a moment. "Right. I'll bring you some dinner, then. It's the least I can do, having you work all day."

As she turns to head back inside, I catch myself watching the sway of her hips, wondering what lies beneath that thin tunic she wears. I shake my head, trying to clear it. It's no use. The thought of my claws ripping the tunic to shreds rises in my mind. Would she be soft all over? Pale all over? Would she sing my name in that way she does if I run my tongue all across her skin?

While she's inside the lodging, I pace, trying to focus on anything but the way she looks, smells, and the memory of her warm, soft skin under my hands. Looking off into the fields, I take a deep breath and head within them, brushing the tall grass out of the way as I go. Maybe if I'm not so close to her abode I'll clear my head. Clicks pass and my core-beat finally stops rising. I'm in the center of the field, petting one of the lazy oogas when I think I hear my name. Tilting my head, I look over my shoulder when I hear it again.

She's calling me. Is she finished already? I never thought it would be that quick or I wouldn't have walked all the way out here.

When her voice sounds far too close I realize she's followed me out here into the field.

The moment she breaks into the small clearing the oogas have made, her eyes meet mine and my core-beat falters again.

"Thought you ran away." She chuckles.

"I would never." My words make her gaze dip and I realize she's carrying a tray with two receptacles on it. I reach for it, giving it a steady hand as she murmurs muffled gratitude and looks around.

"Not much place to eat out here," she whispers, cheeks growing warm again.

I glance down.

"There is only the grass-feed beneath our feet and the sky above us." My gaze shifts back to hers. "It's beautiful."

She is. Not the grass or the sky. *She's* beautiful. But I can't tell her that. Not again. I've crossed the line too many times already and I'm starting to like this little female. She caught my attention from the first moment I set eyes on her.

Eleanor nods, gaze shifting to the grass and with a small huff through her nose, she sits, stretching her legs out before her.

"I guess this is okay," she breathes. "God, I haven't had a meal like this in years."

I sit beside her, balancing the tray in one hand. It smells good. Some kind of stew. "What do you mean?"

Her gaze darts to mine quickly and she licks her lips before pulling them into her mouth. Her eyebrows rise and her eyes go distant as she reaches for a receptacle on the tray, blowing at the steam before taking up a strange, small scooping device.

"Well…I guess…it's been a long time since I've felt free enough to simply…have a meal on my back lawn." She shrugs again, but I don't miss the note of sadness there. Wistfulness. It makes Eleanor's petals droop. I don't like it. And it's my fault for prying.

"It's been a long time for me, too." I say, hoping the words help rather than worsen the situation.

Some light returns to her eyes as her gaze shifts to mine. "Really? How come?"

She seems more alert now, as if she wants to learn about me and it makes a nice little vibration move through my core-beat. Reaching for my own scooping device, I take my bowl and put a bit of the stew into my mouth.

"Mmm," I groan, not even bothering to disguise the depth or rumble of my voice, "so good."

Through my peripheral vision, I sense Eleanor watching me with slightly open lips. She's completely enraptured and that part of me that's certainly not an upstanding Hudoian citizen rolls my tongue over the scooping device, emitting another moan from my throat.

I hear when her breath stops. It takes everything within me not to slide my gaze to her and do it again while staring directly into her eyes. Because at this moment, I'm wondering what every bit of her skin tastes like. What she would feel like if I ran my tongue over her instead of this scooping device in my grasp.

She makes that strange sound in her throat again before she forces a laugh, blinking as she points her gaze forcefully to her stew. "Really? I didn't have much time to prepare. It's pre-made, and I assumed…" Her gaze shifts shyly to me. "With the fangs that you're a carnivore? Omnivore, at least? That you eat meat."

"It's perfect." Not the stew. *Her*. Each click that passes, she becomes more intriguing. So soft. Even her personality. What's a sweet thing like her doing without a mate? My luck, I guess. Their loss.

"Carnivore leaning." I answer her question, my gaze shifting down her form.

She shivers under my scrutiny, and I can see her struggling to keep her composure. With shaky fingers, she lifts her scoop to her lips, sipping the stew. Her little tongue darts out to clean her lips before she dips the scoop and repeats the action. The tension is palpable, a taut string ready to snap.

"I guess that's good to know," she murmurs, trying to focus on her meal.

I should focus on mine too, but frakk the stew. I want to ask her if she knows what I'd really like to taste? That it's been on my mind from the moment she opened that door.

But I don't know her species' mating rituals. I should not court her when there's no indication that she is mine—just this unignorable fascination that's growing with each click.

I can't take my eyes off her as I finish the stew. Surprisingly filling, I set the empty bowl down on the tray and fall back against the grass. Eleanor gives an amused huff through her nose as she watches me rest with my arms behind my head. Above us the sky grows purple and the distant stars begin peeking out.

"It's been a long time since I've eaten like this because Varek and I usually get our meals from the taverns. Meat, fresh dough, and drink, before we head back to our quarters. I do not usually eat under the stars," I answer her first question, gaze shifting to her as she finishes her stew, too.

She sets her receptacle down before glancing at me, her bottom lip curiously being eaten by her own mouth. Her nose crinkles in the most endearing way before she shrugs and mutters something about "fukking it"—whatever that means— before she falls back onto the grass as well.

From this angle, the mounds on her chest are even more prominent each time she takes a breath.

A soft giggle rises in her throat before her gaze shifts to mine. "This is nice."

"Mm." Not even a word. I cannot speak. Here, in this light and so close, her skin looks even more enchanting, almost as if the dying starlight is giving her an embrace.

"This must be usual for you, though," she whispers. "A calm life like this on Hudo III?"

I don't answer for a moment, just watching the stars with her. She's wrong. My life has been anything but calm, but would she be scared of me if she knew the truth?

"You know nothing of the Kari?" I hedge.

She hums a sound in her throat. "Apart from the fact you're good at fixing roofs, no." There's a soft laugh in her throat and I find my lips curling in humor, too.

"For most of us, life has never been calm. Not until now, at least. We've fought in wars. Many wars. I have only lived this calm life on Hudo III for the past...ten orbits."

I sense when she shifts. Feel her focus on me.

"You've fought in wars?"

"More than I can count." And the memories haunt me. But I don't tell her that. I don't tell her that inside every Kari she'll find here on Hudo III is a gaping hole that can never be filled. "The Tasqals made sure of that."

I hear when she inhales sharply and through my peripheral vision, I watch her shoulders rise and fall.

"The Tasqals..." she murmurs. "I know them. Somewhere up there," she points at the stars, "is Earth. One of those dots."

There's that note of sadness in her voice again and I watch the light in her eyes slowly die. The excitement being ripped away by some memory that's haunting her. I'm drawn to it. Drawn to some urge to comfort her.

"Erth?"

"Yep..." A deep exhale. "My planet. What was once my home."

"Do you miss it?"

She shrugs. "Not really. My life was over anyway. Those brutes that abducted me might have traumatized the shit out of me, but I think, in the end, everything will work out for the better."

Abducted? Frakk.

I'm a qrakking fool. I don't have to ask. I don't *want* to ask. The thought that this delicate little bloom might have been a victim of the Tasqals is enough. Their kind is hated across the galaxy for their crimes. What they did to us Kari...what they've done to so many others...is unforgivable.

Without realizing this *Liora's* a victim of the same race that had me and Varek fighting when we were only chids, I've now awakened memories she must have tried hard to push away. Idiot!

"Do you like it here?" she whispers. "On this planet?"

"It is a nice place. Peaceful, mostly. Especially all the way out here."

Eleanor smiles, her gaze distant. "Good. If you're anything to go by, the residents are quite nice." Her gaze shifts to me for only a moment before she does a sort of strangled laugh. "I'm sort of banking on this whole new home thing to work out."

But even though Eleanor is saying positive things, her voice has changed as if she's holding back much more than she's letting on. Even a clueless Kari like me can see that and I have the sudden urge to learn each and every one of her secrets. To maybe even tell her some of my own.

I'm caught with that thought when something wet escapes from her eyes. Water. And before I realize what I'm doing, my claw is near her jaw, scooping up the strange expulsion on the tip of one digit. She winces away slightly, surprised, before she pauses, wide, watery eyes on me.

"What's this?" I peer at the water, moving closer to her.

Her eyes shift to my digit before she squeezes them shut. That only pushes more of the water out.

"God," she whispers under her breath. "What's *wrong* with me today?"

"You're leaking."

"Not leaking just…It's okay. It's nothing." She shakes her head.

"It seems like more than nothing." Something makes my scales ripple. An uneasiness I've never felt before. As if this water is particularly offensive to me. I do not like this. Whatever it means, I do not like this water.

"*Liora*, I might have only known you for a single sol, but…"

But I want to know her more? That I would sit here for the entire dark cycle just listening to her tell me about her life? Her experiences? Her everything? Good and bad?

I can't say that. Those are words reserved for a mate. One a displaced Kari like me will possibly never have. And yet, there is the urge to say the words, anyway.

Eleanor's eyes open and they pierce me. "You're kind," she whispers. "Very kind."

I hate that despite these positive phrases, there is pain hidden there.

"It's tears," she whispers. "Happens when a human is sad."

"Human…" I whisper. I've never heard of her species before. But most of all, I have made her sad with my prying.

"I apologize," I rumble, wiping more of the water away. She's frozen in a strange sort of way as my digit brushes against her cheek, cleaning the liquid away. She's watching me. Hardly breathing. And there's a strange look in her eyes. Sadness. Hope. Want?

My movements falter at that last one. Could it be?

Does Eleanor…*want* me?

I pause, the moment charged, when her gaze falls to my lips. This close, there is little space between us.

Her breathing stutters, hardly there, and I get the sense she's waiting for me to do something.

But what?

My gaze shifts over her face, the digit moving to wipe away the smudge on her skin as my focus moves to her little plump lips. Her tongue shifts over them then. Slightly parted, they're moist and enticing this close.

She wants me to do something. My scales shift again, a ripple going across my skin as my core-beat picks up pace. The moment feels frozen, as if I'm walking on tense air itself. Her every breath is mixed with mine and time stands still.

Nothing moves, not until the grass-feed suddenly parts. My claws extend from where they're retracted as I turn, aware of Eleanor's sudden gasp at my movement.

But it isn't an intruder. Just someone who couldn't have come at the worst possible moment.

"Varek," I growl at Varek as he steps into the small clearing.

"Oh!" Eleanor sits up too fast. The receptacles and tray tumble in the grass. She scrambles for them as if we've been caught doing something inappropriate, and I growl at my brother again, this time flashing fang. He quirks one brow at me, unperturbed but clearly confused as Eleanor's cheeks grow as red as the color of her blood.

"Hello!" She has the tray balanced on one arm now and is brushing hay from her hair with the other as she makes that funny sound in her throat again. As she adjusts her garment, her gaze shifts to me only briefly before she pushes her lenses higher on her nose. "I guess it's time for you to go!" She gives me a little bow, moving quickly. "Thanks for keeping me company for dinner. I'll see you tomorrow for the roof then?"

When she glances at me again, she blanches because I'm still glaring at my siblingkin. Frakking bad timing. It's with great effort that I force my annoyance away enough to face the *Liora* in our presence.

"As the star breaks the dawn."

She gives me a brief nod. Gaze shifting to Varek, she gives him another slight bow before hurrying back through the grass-feed. It swishes in her haste as she makes her way back to her lodging.

As soon as she's out of earshot, Varek snarls back at me. "What the frakk was that about? I was looking everywhere for you and the strange female. I thought you both fell in that well since you were nowhere near the lodging."

"She's not *strange*." I'm standing and in his face a second later. "She's...different. *Special*." His brows lift higher. "And you were supposed to come in *three* hors."

"Do you not see the star's position, brother? I'm on time."

With a growl, I pull out my communicator, eyes widening slightly as I check the time. He's right, of course. Varek is hardly ever wrong when it comes to time.

"Fine," I grunt, turning my face to the sky and running my hands through my mane. "I apologize."

"Care to tell me what that was all about?"

"No," I growl, brushing past him, my focus on the little lodge as I walk back through the field.

Varek follows behind me, his confusion thickening the air around him. "What's going on, Zynar?"

There's a light within the little lodge but the door's closed and there's no sign of Eleanor. She's hidden herself away.

"I...don't know," I murmur, something pushing me onto the little porch and to Eleanor's door. I stop just outside it, my fist hanging in the air as I contemplate whether I should pound on her door and apologize.

But apologize for what?

Inside, my core-beat wails. The last time I felt like this, it was when Varek and I found the wreckage with our mor. This unsettling feeling, like a part of me is being ripped in two. That I must fix—whatever this is!

I didn't do what she wanted me to do and Varek came before I could figure out what that was.

With a defeated sigh, my fist falls, and I step off the porch.

Varek's gaze bores into my skull.

"Let's go, brother."

He glances back at Eleanor's place before heading with me back to our transport.

"Everything okay?" he asks, and I realize I'm being sour with him for no reason. He's always been by my side. He's everything I have. The closest thing I have to home. He deserves an explanation, too. But how can I explain what I don't even understand?

"All is well," I reply.

In all my orbits, this has been the most confusing sol of my life.

And I need to figure out why.

Varek nods, chin to chest, but his gaze shifts back to the little lodge. I know this isn't over. He'll ask me to explain again, but later, when I'm hopefully not so sour about what just transpired.

As Varek starts the engine and heads back to the town, I take out my communicator, pulling up the search.

With unsteady movements fueled by something I can't name, I type in the one word that might give me all the answers I need.

"Human."

8

ELEANOR

I wake to zero sound. Not the low hum of the refugee ship. Not the chatter of other females who'd been rescued by the Restitution. Not the screams that haunted me after we were all attacked by the Tasqals. But also not the sound of my alarm blaring from my bedside clock either. Not the sound of my neighbors cutting their lawn. Or the sound of my cat at my door demanding I rise and serve her breakfast, or else.

I wake to quiet.

My gaze shifts to the window. To the pink sky and the morning sun streaming in.

I'm on Hudo III and it's peaceful here.

I blink at the view, my brain slowly coming back online as I stretch and release a slow breath. With a groan, I sit up, grimacing.

It feels like I slept with a metal pipe across my back. Every bone underneath my skin is annoyed. But when I'd gone to the bedroom the night before, I'd realized with sorrow that the mattress, now inflated, is much heavier than it was when I'd put it on the bed. Back then, the small pack it was delivered in only weighed about forty pounds. I could move it. Now on its side where I'd pushed it to protect it from debris, it's like a wall stuck between the bed frame and the actual wall. I can't maneuver it in the narrow confines of the bedroom.

Whether that means I'll be sleeping on the large storage box for the foreseeable future is unclear. Maybe I won't be smashing the thing to bits after all because it will be my new bed.

A hard, uncomfortable bed Goldilocks would definitely not approve of.

I rise, rubbing sleep away from my eyes as I head to the bathroom. Bits of debris crunch under my feet as I go, and although I'd gotten most of it out of the house, working until late into the night, there's still a lot of cleaning left to do.

I wash my face and that wakes me up a little more as I grab my toothbrush and get my teeth clean. It's more like a hard cotton swab infused with mint, but it works. Finished, I head to the front door, gaze shifting to the roof membrane above me—a stark reminder that Zynar will be returning today.

As my hand closes over the doorknob, I let out a slow breath. He probably isn't here yet. It's early morning, but when he arrives, what will I say?

I'd hurried away last evening, heart in my chest beating too hard, tingles all over my body. I'd wanted him to kiss me. I'd come *so* close to actually letting him do it. If his brother hadn't suddenly appeared, I'd have let our lips touch. Heck, I might have initiated it myself.

I don't know if it's shame or anticipation that even fills me now, but I have to…I don't know…I have to get rid of it, right? There's no way this works out well for me. Getting entangled with the first male I see will only leave me heartbroken and feeling even more alone than I already am.

I'm bigger than some silly crush! Because that's all that this is. A crush. A harmless, unexpected crush.

The moment I pull the door open, pep talk making me a little more confident, is the moment I step outside and all that confidence just…disappears.

Because before me is a yard I didn't have when I went to bed yesterday.

"Oh…my…" I step off the porch, feet hitting the ground as I turn in a slow circle, my eyes wide.

All the weeds, every single one of them, are gone. The tall grass that was in some spots is gone too. I can see the slightly reddish earth beneath my feet and my heart cracks a little when I notice something else. The flowers are still there. All the wildflowers stand tall, unhindered by grass or weeds.

"How…"

"Good dawn, Liora." I jump a little at the sound of the deep voice above me. A delicious shiver goes through my entire being as I turn and look up to see Zynar standing at the highest peak of the roof. My eyes widen even more and I see, rather than hear, his soft, deep chuckle. "I didn't mean to startle you."

He's doing more than frickin' startling me. My heart's doing the cha-cha and picking out wedding china while my brain screams for some semblance of sanity.

"Hi!" Where have my words gone? There's a lump in my throat that I swallow down, all the memories of the evening before coming back like a wildfire. My skin heats. My whole body responds as my breath picks up. Everything I said to myself before I opened that door is forgotten. "Good morning, Zynar."

He grins at me, flashing fang, and makes his way down a central beam. His balance is exceptional as he reaches the edge, and crouches there above me. Fiddling fish sticks, he's gorgeous. It's the closest we'll get if he doesn't come to the ground and even then, it feels too close. As if I can feel his breath against my skin.

There's a twinkle in his eyes as he watches me. "I am ready to work."

I clear my throat, blinking as my cheeks warm. Glancing around the yard, I shake my head in disbelief. "It looks like you've already started working. I didn't expect you to…"

"Get rid of the weeds?" His voice is a deep rumble that sends the question like a vibration through me. "I do what I say I will do, *Liora*."

Why do those words sound like they have more weight than they should?

I turn in a slow circle, little shivers going across my spine and just under my skin as I turn my back to him. "You did it all."

"I did not want you to hurt yourself again. Syleen weeds are notorious for rending flesh, and yours, Liora, is far too precious to bleed."

I face him again, blinking to clear my thoughts. His words warm me. Make me feel special when they shouldn't. Do all Kari speak like this? Are all Kari this…intoxicating? I'd ask his brother, but like yesterday, he's not here again.

"Thank you, Zynar." I give him a smile. "I appreciate it."

He jerks his chin to his chest before rising from his crouch. In one hand, he flips the tool he's been using, something with a curved double hook on one end, before he tilts his head at me. "You can rest, Liora. There will be no more holes in your roof for many, many orbits to come."

I smile again, gaze shifting to the roof. It's only then that I see he's begun adding the roof material back. A type of thatch that binds together. It's the color of pine, and gives just that section of the roof that's done a new vibe.

Nodding at Zynar, I hurry back inside the house. I know I'm escaping, but each moment in his presence is making me lose my head. When have I ever been this blatantly attracted to a male before? I mean, men are a bit shit and it's better to do without them. But here on Hudo III, it feels like that realization is beginning to no longer apply.

Now inside the house, it's quiet again. Only when I head over to the kitchen do I hear the faint scratches where Zynar's adding the roof material.

I bite my lip, gaze shifting to the mugs and kettle. I could make tea.

No. I won't survive if I go back out there. Not now. And so I hide away. I work on cleaning the house. I work, and I watch. Little by little, I can see the thatch being applied as Zynar works. He makes no sound. Apart from the soft brushing of the fibers being applied and sporadic knocking coming from his tool as he pushes the fibers into place, there's no other noise.

At one point, I hear when he jumps off the roof and the sound of his boots as he nears the door. I freeze, heart pounding against my ribs as I lift my head from where I'm scrubbing the floor and listen. But nothing happens. He stays by my door for a few minutes, and then his boots sound again and he's gone.

I release a breath of relief even though, at the same time, I'm scolding myself for being so foolish. I'm hiding away like a child.

Hours pass and I clean out debris until the floor and every surface is spotless. By the time I'm done, I'm exhausted, tired, and hungry.

I look toward the door. Zynar must be hungry too.

Squeezing my eyes shut, I rise and head to the kitchen. Preparing one of the pre-done meals is easy and I have quite a few supplies that Xarion left. I don't have to worry about food. At least, not for a while yet.

I decide to do sandwiches. Or, at least that's what I'm calling them. They look like little packets of sweets. Like those gummy burgers kids would go crazy for on Earth. Once I take them out of their packages and place them on plates, they inflate into doughy, meat-filled sandwiches.

Taking the plates, I put them on a tray. I'm at the door when I stop again.

Gosh darn it, Eleanor. What the hell are you so afraid of?

I don't know, but my heart is beating double-time.

I force a breath through my nose. I can do this. He's just a man. Well, not a man. He's an alien male—oh crud, I'm derailing myself again. Let's go.

Balancing the tray on one hand, I open the door and come to a stop as the tray is crushed onto a rock-hard iridescent chest.

"Zynar," I breathe. Ski-boop! There goes my heart again.

"Hello, *Liora*. I was just…" He makes a sound in his throat as his gaze falls to the tray pressed between our bodies. Neither of us moves back to give the other space.

Zynar runs a hand through his green mane and I follow the movement with my eyes, throat getting dry by the second. So this is what people mean when they say they're thirsty. It's a parched kind of feeling. I want to drink, but it's not water that I want.

"*Liora*…I…" When his brows furrow slightly my eyebrows lift. Is he rattled? So I'm not the only one then?

That only makes another thrill go through me.

"I thought you might be hungry," I start. When his brows furrow some more I hurry on. "And since you did the entire yard for me, saving me days of backbreaking weeding, I can't possibly not do something in return." I point at the tray with my chin. "It's a meat sandwich."

His gaze falls to my lips and his throat moves before he pulls his gaze to the tray.

"I…thank you, Liora." He steps back finally, gaze shifting to the tree stumps we sat on last time.

"Zynar." I swear I see his scales shiver slightly at the sound of his name. "Let's eat inside. It's cool in here." Plus, maybe I can control my thoughts if we have some semblance of formality.

He turns to face me, his throat moving again, and I wonder

if he has a recurring lump like I do. Smiling up at him, I turn and head back into the house.

"Don't worry. It's all clean." My gaze shifts to some items I still have to get rid of. "Mostly." I cringe. "Excuse the mess."

I set the tray on the table and turn to face him, only to find he's directly behind me. That lump in my throat rises with my brows. Tilting my head back, because that's the only way I'll be able to look him in the face, I try not to show how flustered his proximity is making me.

I knew this room was small. The entire house is. But Zynar inside my space makes it even more obvious. There's suddenly no room, only him.

He shifts slightly, reaching around me to pull out a seat. "For you, Liora."

I'm caught off guard. Never in my life would I think I'd have an alien pulling out a chair for me, but here I am. I sit, thankful my shaky legs don't have to hold my weight anymore. My eyes are wide dishes as Zynar walks to the other side and takes the seat in front of me. Even the chair looks dwarfed in his presence.

He watches me now, like a hawk, and I clear my throat. Reaching for the plates, I set one in front of him. "Oh, drinks! I forgot drinks!"

I stand abruptly and his gaze follows me, pausing at my chest and honing in before I spin and head for my supplies. It's only while in the kitchen that my chest tingles where he was looking at me. My breasts. Oh God, he was looking at my breasts.

Immediately, heat coils in my core.

I grab the drinks. Cylindrical things like beer, but I'm sure it's either juice made from flowers or fruits. I return, set one before him, my hand briefly touching his. An electric tingle shoots across my hand and I see his fingers twitch, too.

The silence is deafening. I can't even glance at him because I feel his heavy stare on me. So much for thinking straight by being civilized. It's even worse now that he's swallowing up all the space.

"Sorry about being so absent today. I was trying to get inside here clean." Lies. I was trying to hide away from him. But he doesn't need to know that.

"You have done a commendable job, *Liora*." His tone is so deep, so dark, that my gaze shifts to his. My heart does that ski-boop thing again.

Silence descends again and I realize that, unlike humans who get so uncomfortable with silence, it isn't the same for the Kari. Zynar seems perfectly content simply staring at me. As if he could sit all day before me, just…taking me in.

"Zynar…" There's a purr in his throat again at the sound of my voice. "Why do you call me that?"

"Mm?" That purr increases even as he tilts his head slightly as if he's not sure what I'm talking about. It's almost as if he's not aware of the deep rumble. As if he's not really focusing. His gaze could eat me up and that makes me think of him *actually* eating me up. Gods, what would that feel like?

There's a sudden throb between my legs, a little bud waking up, and I clamp my thighs shut.

"Liora," I whisper. His gaze heightens on mine then, as if I've just said a keyword, a passcode to something secret and consequential. "Why do you call me that and not my name? What does it mean?"

"Mm," he purrs again.

"Is…" I clear my throat because the longer he stares, the hotter I get. It's hard to focus and I try to remind myself that just like other aliens I've met so far, he may simply be staring because I'm so different from him. "Is it like a polite term? A… cultural thing?"

His gaze is on my lips as if he's consuming each word that leaves my mouth and I get another revelation that it's exactly what he's doing. All this time I've been getting jitters from the fact his gaze keeps shifting to my lips means absolutely frickin' nothing. It's not because he wants to kiss me. He's from another species! Another culture! He probably doesn't even know what kissing is!

I could groan. Like I've thought, I've been such a fool.

"On Karicek…" he begins, that rumble in his tone pulling me in. "A liora is a little avian. Soft. Delicate. With wings that move so quickly, they appear invisible. It flutters around blooms and other things it finds interesting. It is…of the most beautiful things one can witness."

Soft…delicate…beautiful…

I blink at him, his words slowly seeping into my brain. "Little avian?" I whisper. "Little bird?" My heart does several ski-boops. "You've been calling me—" Oh God, I could choke on the emotion swelling in my chest even though this probably doesn't even mean a thing to him. "You've been calling me Little Bird?"

His head tilts as his gaze lifts and I realize he was consuming my every word again. "Yes, *Liora*. That you are."

I don't know what to do with this information. What I should say or how I should respond. The air suddenly feels weighted around us and I forget how to breathe.

Little Bird. It's endearing, almost too intimate, and I can't decide if I'm thrilled or terrified by the depth of it.

"It's…a beautiful name." I try to brush off the nervous thrill going through me with a soft smile and Zynar watches my lips shift. Clearing my throat, I take up my sandwich and take a big bite. With my mouth full, I can't talk. That means I won't say something stupid like the words bubbling in the back of my head.

Stupid things like how I've never been given a pet name like that by anyone before. Not by old boyfriends. Not by my ex-husband. And certainly not someone I've had a crush on, like him.

As Zynar takes up his sandwich and takes a big bite too, he finally leans back in his chair, thick shoulders rolling. God, why doesn't he wear a shirt? Would it even make him less distracting?

"The kalui storage," he suddenly says, prompting my gaze to his.

"Hmm?"

With one finger, he points to the large storage box I slept on last night. "Will you be keeping it?"

"Oh, I…" I take a moment to chew, frowning as I stare at the box. "I wasn't planning on it. But I might have to, at least for a while."

"Why is that, Little Bird?"

Oh my God. Now he's using my language. That makes it even worse. Heat warms my cheeks and I clear my throat. Taking another bite of the sandwich, I try to calm myself. "Until I get my bed ready again." His brows furrow and I hurry on. "It's a whole thing. My mattress is toppled and I'll have to find a way to get it back on. Till then—"

Zynar's suddenly rising. With one last bite, he finishes his sandwich, and my eyes widen slightly as I glance down at mine. I still have ninety percent of mine left. Well, I guess lunch is over. Something in my heart drops a little and I realize that even though this is unexpected and confusing, I'd been hoping to spend some time with him. Maybe to convince myself this is just harmless attraction. Setting my sandwich down, I force a smile on my face as I look up at him, standing to see him out the door. But Zynar's not facing the door. He isn't even facing me.

I'm given the view of the tight muscles in his back as his gaze shifts around the room.

"Where you sleep," he takes a few steps forward, "it is here, correct?"

Yellow eyes find me as he looks over his shoulder. With one arm, he's pointing directly at the bedroom.

"I, uh, yes…"

He's off after that, heading directly into the bedroom. I rub my hands in the hem of the tunic I'm wearing before hurrying after him. I'm at the door when my eyes widen into round pools because Zynar is in my bedroom, filling it completely. I can just see over his shoulders as they flex and bunch before he lifts the heavy mattress and sets it back on the bed frame. Eyes wide, I can only stare at him.

Shifting it into place, his gaze slips around the room before his eyes find me again.

I'm speechless.

"Thanks. I…" I what? I don't even know what to say. It felt like it weighed a ton to me but he lifted it like he was lifting a biscuit.

"Now you can sleep well, Little Bird."

Oh crud. Is he going to use the English phrasing all the time now?

He comes toward me and that fight or flight thing kicks in again because my heart's thundering in my chest. I step back and he passes me, heading straight for the storage box at the side of the living room. With a crouch and a heave, it's in his arms.

My mouth falls open but sense soon comes and I'm hurrying past him to open the door. I'm speechless again as he takes the thing out and brings it to the pile of stuff I'm planning on getting rid of.

There, he frowns again.

"What is it?" I'm caught in a sort of awe and confusion. Thoughts I'll have to dissect later all threaten to rise and come to the fore.

"You will rear oogas?"

I blink a few times. "Well, yes. I suppose."

His gaze shifts to the barn I was cleaning out the other day.

"This box will be good for storing bagged feeds for your animals."

My eyebrows lift slightly. "Will it?"

I can hear his words, but all I can think about is the fact he's lifting the box again as if it weighs nothing and he's heading toward the barn with it. Balancing the large box on one arm, he flings the barn doors open with the other. He grunts something, probably not impressed by the interior, before the door swings shut and he disappears. When he doesn't immediately come out, I find myself following after him.

Inside the barn was messy, still is messy, and I walk in to find Zynar turning in a slow circle, gaze roving everywhere. When his head tilts and he looks at the roof, worry springs inside me.

"What is it? Is the roof bad as well?"

He makes a long sound like a hmm.

"The roof needs patching in several places. The beams supporting it have some rot that needs to be replaced. The walls could use reinforcement, and the floor needs to be leveled and cleaned. The doors should be repaired to close properly. You'll need proper storage for feed and tools, fencing for the pasture, and ventilation for the animals. The water troughs are cracked and should be replaced, and the grass-feed storage," he points above us where there's a loft, "needs new supports."

My heart drops, a part of me feeling suddenly overwhelmed. "That sounds like…a lot…"

Zynar's gaze shifts to mine and he takes two strides before he's standing in front of me.

"It is…" he murmurs. "These farms aren't usually managed by one individual."

"They aren't?"

He steps closer, gaze shifting over my face. "I can help you."

I gulp. Hard. I almost ask him in what way but it's clear he's talking about the labor. Though, if he comes any closer, I may put myself into labor.

"I couldn't." I shake my head. "It's far beyond what I hired you for and—" And, well, I can't spend all the credits New Horizons provided on hiring people for repairs. I'll have to do some of them myself. It will only take me a long, loooong time.

I've always wanted to live the DIY life. Guess I have that opportunity now.

My breath hitches as Zynar suddenly reaches down and grabs my hand. I try not to react as he immediately presses my palm against his pecs.

Don't react, Eleanor. Don't do a thing.

I feign confusion. No, I don't feign it. I *am* flippin' confused even though I like it. His scales are like silk. Smooth and not filled with ridges like I expected. Underneath my palm, his muscle jumps and I resist the urge to tighten my palm and grip his chest.

"Feel this?" His tone drops.

"Mm mmhm?" I swallow hard.

"Look at me, Little Bird."

Oh shit, I respond to the command like a little flower opening up to the sun. I can't breathe as Zynar leans in. His scent envelop s me. Those slitted yellow eyes are all I can see, and I'm suddenly thrown back to the day before when I'd been desperate for him to kiss me. To make me feel alive again.

"Feel that?" His muscle jumps again and I make that same mumble of affirmation because my throat is no longer capable of forming words. "I am Kari. We strive on this. Let me work. Let me help you."

"It's not just the roof though..." I whisper. "There are a lot of things that need to be done."

Zynar purrs underneath his breath and I feel the vibration against my palm. "Are you doubting my skill, Liora?" he purrs. "I can assure you, I am highly competent." He leans in closer. "And a great learner."

I almost choke on my tongue.

I want to nod. I almost do. But this is supposed to be *my* project. My new start in life. My new independence. Seeing this place rebuilt with my own hands while healing that part of myself that's broken and needs rebuilding, too.

I'm supposed to be the alien on this farm. I'm not supposed to *get* an alien for the farm.

But that's a stipulation I've put on myself. A restriction no one but Eleanor Tabitha Taylor has created. What's wrong with getting help when I need it?

"Put it on the tab?"

"Tab?" Zynar's too close. There's barely any space left between us.

"Yes, my middle name is Tabitha, so technically, I'm a Tab. Might as well make use of it." What is wrong with my mouth? Why am I talking and what am I saying? Dear God, I am what my students would call lame! I clear my throat. "A tab's like… like a bill?"

He doesn't answer, only moves closer.

I take a step back, only for my calves to bump into something low on the ground. I look back. It's a tool that looks like it's for manually tilling the soil. When I look back up, Zynar's right before me and the look in his eyes stops my very breath.

"Zynar…"

"Last sol, Liora. I offended you."

My brows furrow, some of the tension clouding my brain dissipates. "What?" And then I realize what he's talking about. My cheeks flame. "Oh! No. No, you didn't."

Zynar takes another step forward and I step back, not out of fear, but out of pure adrenaline. My calves bump into the tool again and I almost fall if strong arms didn't suddenly wrap around my waist.

I hang there like that, his arm wrapped around me as he leans in, my heart thundering in my chest and a whistle going off in my head like a steam engine coming down the tracks.

"I spent all night reading," he whispers, gaze shifting to my lips.

"Reading?"

"Learning…" His voice is so low, and his complete focus is still on my lips. "As I mentioned, Liora…I am a good learner."

My breaths are little pants. I try to clear my throat but nothing happens. "Wh-what were you learning about?" I whisper now.

"Humans."

I stop breathing. Zynar doesn't continue. Instead, his gaze shifts up from my lips painfully slowly. Moving over the arch of my nose to my brow then to my hair before dropping back to my eyes.

The intensity in his gaze makes me shiver.

"Eleanor," he murmurs, his arm still firmly around my waist, keeping me balanced. "I don't want to offend you again."

"You didn't—" I start to say, but he interrupts me, his voice a deep rumble.

"I could feel it."

When he says that, his chest moves under where my palm's still pressed against him and my focus moves to the spot. My breathing picks back up as I stare at him.

Is his color different? His scales were more purple and blue, with dashes of pink, weren't they? Right now, they look pinker. I'm distracted when another rumble goes through him.

"Little Bird," he whispers. "There's not much information on your species in any archive."

I release a short laugh through my nose. "That's because we're not supposed to be here. None of us are supposed to be out here. At least, not yet. I'm afraid, Zynar, you won't learn much about us that way."

"I found one archive. Cultivated by a rebel named Kyro. Through his research...I did learn...one thing," he murmurs, voice getting lower and I become aware he's still balancing me on his arm. That I'm still tilted back and he's holding me against him. But it's the sound in his voice that catches my attention.

"You learned something?"

"Yes. And I would like to show you."

9

ZYNAR

The mouth touching is a strange practice. One I'm not sure how to apply successfully, but the moment my lips hit Eleanor's, her entire body stiffens and so does mine.

We stay there for clicks, not even the sound of our breaths disturbing the air as we stare at each other. But even though I have no clue what I'm doing, I'm sure this is the right practice. I'm sure this is what I was supposed to do last sol. This is what my Liora wanted.

Something passes in her gaze as she looks up at me, frozen in a sort of panic that keeps her still even though her core-beat thunders in her chest. And in mine, my core-beat does the same.

I increase pressure a little, pressing my lips against hers some more and Eleanor's eyes flutter closed. Her lips open slightly and I almost fall to my knees to roar a battle cry of victory. She's opening to me. Accepting me.

It's more than I expected and I purr without inhibition, pulling her tighter against me as I open my lips and do every-thing I read on that research archive last sol.

I slip my tongue to touch her lips. A groan rumbles through me immediately. Eleanor tastes like the sweetest sucre from the

Isles of Madora. When my tongue slips past her lips to meet her own, I hear the softest little moan that makes my cock harden immediately. Eleanor grips me, blunted digits digging into my scales as I press her tighter against me. I don't mean to do it. Don't mean to push my tongue farther into her mouth. Don't mean to let my arms stray from where I'm holding her firmly against me. But like a storm ripping me from where I've been planted, my tongue delves into her mouth and her moan travels right into my throat, making me purr harder.

Her body melts against mine. I feel the roundness of her behind as I grip it and fasten her to me so she doesn't fall. The softness of her entire frame.

When her tongue meets mine, rolling over it, playing with it, I almost fall to my knees again.

Something happens within me. Like a lock being broken. My core-beat stutters and something new blooms deep inside.

The contact intensifies, our tongues dancing together in a primal rhythm that's so intimate it's now immediately clear why this act is noted about her species. Eleanor's hands slide up to my shoulders, clinging to me as if I'm her anchor. The heat just underneath her skin spreads through me like a raw connection that goes beyond words. Every brush of her tongue against mine sends waves of electricity through my body, igniting a fire I didn't know existed.

Her taste, her scent, everything about her is intoxicating. I want more, need more, but I also want to savor this moment, to let it stretch into eternity. Claws pulled in, my digits roam over her back, feeling the delicate curve of her spine, the softness of her skin. She arches into me, pressing closer, her body melding with mine.

This is more than mouths brushing against each other. This is a dance of desire. I'm suddenly aware of her...completely. The fact her entire being seems perfect for the most carnal of acts. She's so soft against me, like something that should always be protected, and still something in me wants to flip her around and pound into her with thinly controlled thrusts. My cock hardens almost painfully, pressing into her and I hear when her breath hitches the moment she becomes aware of it. But there's only a momentary pause before the movement of her tongue against mine continues.

This...is bliss. The world fades away. Hudo III ceases to exist, leaving only the two of us in this perfect, suspended moment. It's only me and this Liora. This Little Bird. *My* Liora. Because after this, I know I want her even more. I want this sweet, enticing female to be mine.

The emotions, the thoughts, everything rises within me all at once.

It's probably why I don't hear the sound of the intruder. Probably why I don't realize we're not alone until something shifts in my periphery.

A voice sounds and Eleanor freezes, breaking the contact of our lips. I growl, eyes flashing as I turn my attention in the direction of the door. There stands a Saffion, his ears immediately folding back the moment his gaze lands on us. On *me*.

"Oh dear," he mutters.

My Liora is hot but she grows even warmer the moment her gaze focuses on the Saffion in our presence. "Xarion?"

"I did not mean to intrude on your...mating act." He adjusts the cuff of his garment, gaze dropping away from us. "I attempted to contact you via your comms, but there was no reply. I ventured out here in case you were in some form of trouble but—" His gaze slides back to us and I glare at him. His ears fold back even flatter against his head. "—But it appears you were...otherwise occupied."

Eleanor slips from my grasp and I curse the gods. First Varek and now this Saffion. Her cheeks flushed, Eleanor straightens her tunic as she steps away from the tool on the ground and, in extension, away from me. "Xarion, this isn't—"

Ah, so this is the male she'd mentioned before. The one that brought her here. What does he want? Is he, perhaps, interested in Eleanor? The thought only makes my core-beat become unsettled. Just like last sol when I couldn't figure out what I'd been supposed to do and everything felt threatened, so it does again.

"This isn't..." Eleanor glances back at me, cheeks still that beautiful color, and I catch the uncertainty in her gaze.

"—necessary to explain," I cut in, my voice a low growl. Stepping closer to Eleanor, I ache to pull her against me once more, my protective instincts flaring. "Are you here on business, Saffion?"

Xarion's ears twitch nervously. "I was concerned for Eleanor's safety. But I see she is well...attended to. Is that correct, human? Or do I need to contact the guards on your behalf?" He adjusts his cuff again, gaze shifting from me to Eleanor and back. I don't miss the way his feet are planted despite the flattening of his ears. Saffion aren't a confrontational species, but this one looks prepared to come to Eleanor's rescue if she even suggests she's in trouble.

My respect for the male goes up a notch even though he's just threatened to get me arrested.

Eleanor blanches before taking a step closer to the male. "No, Xarion, I'm perfectly fine." She gestures to me. "This is the male you advised me to hire."

The Saffion's ears perk, gaze shifting to me and then back to Eleanor. "I advised a Raki, not a Kari. Raki are much better suited for the repairs you need here."

Eleanor releases a breath. "Yea, well, I mixed up the names. The computer told me that the Kari are skilled laborers and Zynar here has been quite efficient. The roof is halfway done."

The Saffion's big eyes narrow only slightly. "Yes. I did notice that."

Eleanor beams at him. "Right. We were just..." She clears her throat. "Did you need something? Is there something I forgot to sign?" There's an almost unnoticeable tightening of her shoulders. "Is everything alright? With New Horizons, I mean? They haven't changed their mind, have they?"

I stand taller, her words making me pull my gaze away from her to the male before us. Changed their mind? Is she worried they will take away the home they've given her?

The one called Xarion shakes his head. "Nothing of the sort. I just wished to inform you that a Raki has agreed to assist you in your repairs of this estate." He gestures wildly at nothing in particular. "Since you're the first settler of the initiative, we hope for everything to go smoothly. New Horizons will cover the cost of the repairs."

The air stills, my world slowly peeling back like old plaster stuck on a wall.

"If you accept, the Raki will be here on the next sol. He will also tend to the farm and make it ready for basic crops."

"What? Really?" Eleanor's surprise can be heard in her voice.

No, Little Bird. Reject the offer.

"Affirmative," the Saffion continues. "I must apologize for the delay on this. We are still refining our processes on the Initiative."

Eleanor turns to look at me. "I guess I won't have to bother you with all my monotonous tasks." She gives what sounds to me like a nervous laugh.

"No." I've never before wanted to stay longer than needed on any job. But in this, I am resolute. Something is telling me I need to stay here. Near to this Little Bird. "I'll do it for free," I growl.

In my periphery, Eleanor's eyes grow large and before me, the Saffion tilts his head in confusion.

"I don't understand," he says.

"What do you mean?" Eleanor whispers.

"I will get the farm ready. The roofs, the outbuildings, the field, the crops, the main lodging, and the yard. I will do it all. No charge."

The Saffion's ears perk higher.

"What? No." Eleanor is shaking her head. "Zynar, you barely know me. I couldn't ask—"

"I'm offering." Standing tall, I cross my arms, eyes on the Saffion. He works for one of those government departments. He won't resist a deal like this. In fact, saving credits for his precious department to invest in other things will probably look good on his performance record. "The Raki may be cheap, but they are lesser skilled and slow workers. This will be no cost to your department *and* I will do a better job." Arms still crossed, I flex my muscles just because. "Whatever she needs, I will do."

Eleanor's eyes bug out and she's suddenly before me again. Her hand touches my chest and electricity sparks from the spot. When I shift my gaze to hers, there's confusion warring with surprise in her eyes. But underneath all that, there's a note of something I recognize. Hope. Maybe because I'm feeling it right now, bubbling inside me. Hope for something new.

"Are you *insane?*" she hisses underneath her breath.

I chuckle softly. "Never been more sane in my existence."

Eleanor looks confused. "Don't you have other jobs after mine? I can't let you cancel them to work for free! That's absurd! Plus, this will take weeks to complete. Maybe even months. Who knows if it will take a year. I—"

I grin down at her, uncrossing arms. With one claw, I cover the hand she still has pressed to my chest. "There's a lot to do and I'm not finished here yet."

"Yes, there's the roof but…" I can see the spark of something in her eyes, but she's fighting it. She's shaking her head, a frown on her brow, and I could grin at her defiance. She's stubborn. Got some fire in her. The only reason I don't show my pleasure in her spark is the fact the Saffion is still here watching our exchange, and this, whatever it is, is new. Fragile. I need to tread with caution, though every click in the Little Bird's presence feels like I'm steamrolling down a hill, doing things I usually wouldn't do.

"What do you say, Saffion?" I tilt my focus to the other male.

Eleanor turns to look his way, too, eyes still wide.

"Is this Kari…" The Saffion pauses, watching me. "Is this Kari of threat to you, Eleanor? Just say the word and I will get the guards to remove him from your estate. Forcefully, if need be. They are known to be a persistent, obstinate species."

My eyes narrow, but the male isn't deterred. My respect for him goes up a little more even though he just told Eleanor I'm like a wild tilgran that needs chaining.

"No, Xarion, don't do that. He's no trouble. He's been great. But that doesn't change the fact that he can't just work here for free. That doesn't sit right with me."

"How about I charge you a small fee?"

She looks up at me, brows slightly furrowed now. "A fee? Yes. How much?"

I have no clue where I'm going with this but as the clicks tick by, the more the plan forms in my mind. "Labor for sustenance and board."

Eleanor's brows dive. "I have no problem paying you, but that doesn't sound like a fair trade."

The Saffion seems surprised. "You would accept this Kari's offer?"

Eleanor nods, facing the Saffion. "Yes. I would. An offer we can both agree on."

The Saffion's ears perk up and he hums a tone in his throat. "This would work well. The Kari are a displaced species like yourself."

Eleanor spins to face me, those brilliant blues of hers searching mine. A myriad of emotions I cannot name swim within them. "You lost your home?"

I tilt my head slightly in affirmation and when her eyes

widen in horror, I know she has the wrong idea. I can't, however, explain now. This is all heading in the right direction, in my favor. If I open my mouth and tell her the truth, I might lose to the stupid Raki this Saffion will bring in to replace me. I'll lose her. If I leave this farm now, what reason will I have to return that won't come off as me pestering her. She might become afraid and ring the guards herself.

"Word of your partnership would be good news for the Initiative. This positive turn would increase funding to place more of your kind on estates like this." I can tell the Saffion is thinking out loud. His words make Eleanor spin to face him again.

"Wait a minute there, Xarion. You're telling me that if I allow Zynar to work here, you'll put in a good word that I'm making ties with the local community? Is that what you're saying? And that this will help more humans into homes here on this planet?"

The Saffion nods without hesitation. "Affirmative. My department is committed to the success of the Initiative. The more you integrate, the easier it will be for us to bring more refugees in."

She stares at him for a few moments, her eyes still wide. It's clear this is an important development for her. Without even asking, I can tell she cares about the others of her kind who have lost their homes as well. My Little Bird has a gentle soul.

After a few moments, she releases a breath. "Yes, Xarion. Of course. I'll discuss payment with Zynar and arrange things privately, but yes. A thousand times, yes."

"Very well." The Saffion does a flourish so grand that his ears almost sweep against the dirt. When he stands tall again, he adjusts his cuffs. "Then I will be in contact. Please have your comm close at all times."

Eleanor nods and we both watch as the male disappears outside the door.

When it's clear he's gone, I make a sound in my throat. In the deafening silence between us, it sounds like thunder and I catch the moment Eleanor becomes suddenly aware we're alone again.

Her shoulders tighten, and her breathing stops to the point I wonder if she's still taking in air.

I take a step closer, hoping we can continue what was interrupted, but the moment is gone. Eleanor spins to face me, but doesn't meet my gaze.

"I—I should go get my comm and check my messages," she says.

"Liora—"

"We also need to talk about this new contract. We can just pretend you've stayed here and done the work. You don't really have to. It doesn't matter." She forces a smile. "Not if it helps others."

"Li—"

"I'll talk to you about it all later, okay?" She glances up at me only briefly before she's hurrying away. Watching her go, my core-beat becomes unsteady at the same moment that another hum begins in my chest. Another rhythm right underneath my core beat that I've never felt before. It's faint, but as soon as it onsets, a flood of panic rushes through me as I watch the Little Bird go. The panic is so fast, so sudden, that I grip my chest, forcing myself to breathe.

I've done something wrong again. Overstepped, most likely. Can it be fixed though? I'm not so sure. None of the literature on humans explains how to navigate this.

10

ELEANOR

I'm pacing in the house when I hear Zynar return to the roof. I bite my lip, my heart thundering in my chest before I bring my fingers to my lips, brushing over the shadow of his touch that still lingers there.

His kiss was electric. As if it powered all the dying neurons in my brain and set me alight. My body trembled. I wanted to grip him. To press my body into his. To *feel*.

Running my hands through my hair, I release another breath, gaze shifting to boxes of more supplies Xarion must have left before he found us in the barn.

Gods. Will Zynar be staying here now? Did I just agree to have a stranger living with me on the land? And what was his deal? Why offer to do all this work for free? What is he getting out of this?

I run my hands through my hair again, gripping the roots tight enough that I feel the pressure.

What's his endgame?

I hate that there's a new rhythm to my heart, or maybe I love it? All I know is that every time I hear him moving either on the roof or on the ground, something swells within me that makes my heart beat harder.

It's only been the second day, and yet I feel like I've been teased for months on end. I can't carry on like this. I need boundaries and I need to reevaluate myself.

I put myself to work within the house, using my swirling thoughts as backdrop to the chaos around me. By the time the sun's going down, I've now cleaned the cupboards and packed away everything Xarion bought. I've put on a new tablecloth and the house actually looks livable. I've conquered something, at least, but there's that one thing that's been on my mind since I walked out of that barn.

As the sun drops lower, turning the sky a dark purple, I know I need to face him.

Throwing the door open, I step outside. Hopping off the porch, I look up, heartbeat unsteady. But he's not there. Did he leave and I didn't hear him go? Walking around the house, the muscles in my chest feel tightly pulled together. The moment I see him on the gable at the rear of the cottage, I inhale sharply, my shoulders slumping in relief that shouldn't feel this good. He spots me immediately, his fingers pausing where he's tucking in one last bit of roof fiber.

His gaze flicks to what he's doing only briefly before he secures the roof fiber with one hand and uses his tool to tuck it in with the other. Bolt applied, he rises and looks at his work before his gaze turns back to mine. My heart flutters as he hops off the roof, tucking his tool away before he steps back and looks up at the roof with me.

"All done, Little Bird."

My heart does a flutter again and I squeeze my eyes shut. Alright, that's it.

"Zynar…" But his words cut me off.

"Before you speak, Liora. I must apologize."

My lashes flutter, breath caught in my throat. He's going to apologize for what? For volunteering to do backbreaking labor, for sure.

"I should have allowed you the choice of hiring that Raki. I overstepped."

I can only stare at him. "That's…you don't have to apologize for that. It's not like you didn't give me a choice."

His head tilts slightly, gaze slipping from my eyes to my lips. My whole body heats at the memory of his kiss. I decide to just go for it. What's the use of beating around the bush? All it does is confuse the gardener.

"Zynar, what happened in the barn, it can't happen again. Especially if you'll be working here for a while. That kiss was…"

Beautiful? The best thing I've felt in over a decade? The thing that has my heart beating, my skin flushed, and me feeling young again?

"Kees?" he whispers.

I squeeze my eyes shut again. He doesn't understand. "When we ki—" Ah, how do you even describe that? "When we… brushed mouths together. When our tongues…" I roll my hands to communicate etcetera etcetera because if I utter the words, I'm only going to get lost in the memory and forget the purpose of this.

"You didn't like it?"

Oh heavens.

I open my eyes to stare at the ground before looking up at him. "You're my employee."

"That means you didn't enjoy it?"

"I—" I stammer now. "I didn't say *that*."

"So, you *did* like it." He beams now, his gaze brightening, and I realize now that worry had been clouding his eyes. God, I'm doing this all wrong.

"Regardless," I clear my throat, "it can't happen again."

Zynar frowns now, turning to face me fully. The breeze brushes past us and his scent comes along with it, swirling around me and making me dizzy. Something has to be wrong, I've never reacted to a male like this before. This is new and, admittedly, confusing.

I thought I'd already figured out life. Why, oh why, is it still throwing curveballs at me?

"Why not?" He takes a step forward and I take one back, holding my hands up. All that does is press my hands against his chest. He rumbles something deep at the contact but he stops advancing. "Why stop something that we both enjoyed? Something we both liked? I do not understand, Liora."

I shut my eyes again. "Because…" Well, isn't it obvious? Do I have to spell it out? And then I realize I do. He's not human. He can't understand my emotions without an explanation, and even human men struggle with that, anyway. "Because we hardly know each other."

"We can get to know each other. I would like to get to know you, Liora."

God. This is hard.

His words call to a part of me that's been wounded for so long, even the possibility this might be something real scares the life out of me. And the rejection if it's not? The ultimate heartbreak…I…I'm a coward. I can't.

"We hardly know each other," I say, meeting his gaze. "I just want to be honest—I'm not looking for something casual. If this is just fun for you, I understand, but I'm at a point where I need something real and meaningful…or nothing at all. I hope you can understand that."

His brows furrow slightly as he digests my words.

"So, if you're going to work here, I think we should keep it professional." I drop my hands from his chest and outstretch one for a handshake instead. It stays suspended in the air like that until Zynar crouches before me. He meets my gaze as he presses his lips to the center of my palm. Electricity erupts from the spot, and I have to stop breathing to prevent myself from inhaling sharply.

"I will heed your concerns, Liora," he whispers, those yellow eyes boring into mine. "I read in the literature about your species' mating habits. I understand. But…"

"But what?" I ask, my voice barely a whisper.

"But I am not playing games, Eleanor. I have no interest in games. I am interested in you."

Fiddlesticks.

He rises and places another kiss on my hand, his touch brushing my skin in an unexpected softness that sends a tingle right through me. Smirking, Zynar steps away. He points to the roof, a twinkle in his eyes.

"All done, sweet bird." Then he salutes, tapping two fingers to where I think his heart must be. "I will see you at the start of the new dawn. We will have tea and you can tell me what you want me to do. I will do anything you desire." His eyes darken even as he steps away. "Anything."

My throat is a desert as he leaves, and I'm only vaguely aware that his brother appears at the side of the house. He salutes me too, but I'm stuck staring at them like a frog in the middle of a lake on a lily pad.

Somehow, I feel like I didn't just set any boundaries at all. Somehow, I feel like I just challenged the Kari. Challenged him to pursue me when being pursued is the last thing I want.

Or is it?

THE NIGHT IS QUIET, and as I sit in my bed at the late hour of what I think is nine PM, I can't get Zynar out of my mind. I toss and turn, the memory of his kiss, of his touch all culminating into a snowball that's gathering mass as it rolls downhill.

Reaching for my communicator, I stare at it.

The notifications for missed calls from Xarion are still there, but I have no idea how to clear them. And then there's the whole thing of having to create a budget and plan. I spend a good portion of the next two hours making a plan. The handy computer onboard the device is helpful with the lists and estimates. I'm thrown back to the days I used to have to draft large documents and presentations for the community college and didn't have a device as powerful as this.

When I'm finally finished, I have a simple plan of what needs to be done to improve the farm and the potential cost. It's a lot. A helluva lot, but I relax against my pillow with a new sense of determination. What's it been? Three, four days here now? I've gotten a lot done, considering I only just arrived.

I even have…

Him.

Taking a deep breath, I tell the computer to show me the job ad and explain how I should transfer the payment to Zynar for the work he did. He truly did a good job. The roof fiber is neat and well-aligned. The true test will come when the rain falls, but I doubt there will be a problem. Even if there is, it's not like it will be hard for me to find him. He seems intent on returning here.

I clear my throat to still the tremor at the center of my chest.

"Right." I stare down at the little device over the rim of my glasses. "Now, how do I send the credits?"

"The job must be marked as completed by both parties before payment can be transferred. Would you like to mark the job as completed, Eleanor Taylor?"

"Um, yes. Yes. Please do."

"Done."

I wait. Seconds pass that turn into minutes. "Has the payment been transferred or do I have to do something else?"

"Payment has not been transferred because Zynar of the Korruk line has not marked the job as completed."

"Oh."

"Would you like to send a ping to Zynar of the Korruk line?"

"Um, sure, I guess." I shrug. A ping must be like one of those pokes you do on Facebook. Just a little notification.

I'm wrong.

This is why I hate technology. Because my comm device suddenly turns into a dark screen before it shifts and I'm staring at what looks like a light in a ceiling. I bring the thing closer to my face. "What the…"

A low rumble makes me freeze, eyes wide when the image shifts, and I see purple and pink scales before Zynar's face comes into view. Live.

"Zynar!" My heart stops and if I had more sense I would scramble to cut the feed to hide my embarrassment because 'ping' apparently means 'call'.

"Everything alright, Little Bird?" He grins and my heart stops a second time. Pretty soon I'll be pronounced dead if this keeps up much longer.

"Um, yes. Sorry to be calling you so late. I just…the roof's not finished?" I put on my most businesslike, customer-service, polite heiress voice. "I thought it was."

"It is." He nods, and even through the device, it feels like his gaze is eating me up. I resist the urge to blush and probably that doesn't help because I feel my cheeks heat anyway.

"The computer says you have to also say that the job is completed so I can transfer the credits I owe."

"You're going to let her pay for it?" I hear another voice say just as Zynar's gaze shifts to someone out of view.

The device blurs as it's pulled out of Zynar's grasp, and I hear him growl right before Varek's face comes into view.

His brother grins at me, and I realize it's the first time I've seen him smile.

"Hello, Varek!"

"Hello, Liora."

"Don't call her that," Zynar growls. Varek grins wider. His fangs look as thick as my pinky fingers each. When the device is grabbed again, the tension in my shoulders relaxes somewhat and I chuckle. "Sorry, Little Bird. He is being a pain in my—" Zynar clears his throat. "Sometimes he's desperate for attention."

Varek's voice sounds far, as if he's moved away, but I hear him anyway. "I'm not the one with a hard cock just from taking a ping."

For the first time, I see Zynar squeeze his eyes shut in what I can only presume is embarrassment, simply because I do that same thing all the time. But Varek's words echo in my ears and I can only stare at Zynar, not sure what to say. He's turned on? Because I called?

Zynar makes a sound in his throat as he opens his eyes again and this time, when his gaze lands on me through the screen, his pupils are dilated.

"Pardon me, Liora. I seem to be having some trouble focusing." His gaze dips and I look down at myself, seeing that the tunic I'm wearing to bed has a plunging neckline that seems to have drawn his attention.

That tingle within me that I've been trying to ignore rises into a high crescendo.

"But I will not act on it," he whispers. "As promised."

I bring a hand up to my throat, rubbing it awkwardly as Zynar watches me.

"Do not worry about the job ad," he says, "I will take care of it."

Nodding, I swallow hard. "Okay. Sounds good." I clear my throat again, the heat in his eyes making me aware of every bit of my body again. "I guess I'll see you tomorrow, then?"

"As the star creates dawn," he answers.

I swallow hard again. "As the star creates dawn."

Zynar's voice drops. "Rest well, Little Bird."

I nod, words failing me, right before the screen clicks off and the call ends.

I melt against my pillow, staring up at the new roof.

I told him I wanted to keep it professional, didn't I? So why is my heart still beating so hard? Slipping a hand down my belly, I close my eyes as my fingers skip over my thighs. With a release of breath, I bring my fingers in, brushing over myself underneath the sheets.

My whole body erupts in tingles. Not because I've touched myself. No.

But because I imagined that my hand wasn't mine, but his.

Because I imagined the person touching me there wasn't me but Zynar. That his deep rumbling voice was in my ear, his dilated eyes engulfing me as he touched me and told me how beautiful I was. How much he wanted me and how much we were destined to be together.

I touch myself until tension leaves my body in a shattering moan. Lying there in the aftermath, I could almost sob into my pillow. Because all that's a dream.

Reality is never nearly so accommodating.

11

ELEANOR

I'm awake early. Probably ingrained from not completely ever feeling at ease on that refugee ship. I rise. I stretch. My gaze shifts to the window and it's pink sky and sun. A calm day, as seems to be usual here. I smile but then my gaze shifts out to the living room. My smile falters. My breath comes a little unsteady. Between my thighs is a slight stickiness from my explorations the night before and now, like the lingering residue, comes awareness.

He'll be coming back today.

I rise, adjusting my night tunic before reaching for my glasses where I'd left them on the windowsill above the bed. I slip them onto my nose before grabbing the communication device. Doesn't seem like there are any new notifications. I take it with me anyway as I head to the bathroom to wash up. There, I stare at myself in the mirror, droplets of the cool water running down my face.

I have no idea what's going to happen today. Am I even ready for it?

I dry my face and move back to the bedroom to change my clothes. It's nothing flamboyant, just a brown tunic and closed-toe shoes—the regular outfit it seems New Horizons has sent multiples of. Dropping my communicator in my pocket, I head for the door. My hands close over the knob with some trepidation, my ears perking for any sound outside. It's silent out there. I don't even hear the soft wind.

Gathering my guts, I pull the door open.

The yard is quiet. Nothing stirs, only a few flowers whose stems sway in the breeze. Stepping off the porch, I turn and look up, but there's nothing on top of my new home apart from my now perfect roof. Zynar isn't here.

I don't know why some disappointment swells within me at the fact. Despondency rises like a little cloud around me.

I shouldn't be disappointed. Why am I? I've only known him for what? A few days? Zynar doesn't owe me a thing and if he chooses not to turn up, that's fine.

Squaring my shoulders, I push the sad thoughts away. *There's work to be done, Eleanor.* Like focusing on my task for today. Taking out my communicator, I bring up the list of things I need to get done. The barn, for one, needs recovery. I can't move the animals from the field till I have a proper place for them to stay.

I head there, the large doors closing behind me with a loud creek. Here in the shadows, it's hard to tell what I should work on first. Even though I'd done a lot of work already mucking things out, there's still so much to do. I get to work, trying to figure out the tools lying against one side of the wall. I get handsy with a few and find one that's great for pulling down the vines that have found their way inside.

Work pulls me in despite that, for some reason, I keep glancing at the door, every little sound making me pull my head up from the work I'm doing. I curse myself, brows furrowing. I told him I wanted to keep things professional, didn't I? And when he comes, *if* he comes, this will be a business deal. No more flirting. No more hot looks. And definitely, no more kissing.

If he helps me, I can help other humans. And that's more important than some crush that's probably not going to go anywhere.

I finish with the walls and finally get all the stalls clean. Exhausted, I head back to the house, gaze shifting to the front gate. Still alone. I become hyper-aware of how quiet everything is. No boots hitting my roof. No soft shuffling of roof fiber as it's pushed into place.

I'm as alone as I ever was supposed to be. And that should be fine except there's still that unnerving little sliver of disappointment threading through my thoughts.

I take a few minutes to get a cold drink and a moment to sit down. I like the silence. It's soothing. At least, it never bothered me before. It's bothering me now. Curse this—this unsettled feeling just underneath my skin. I want to pace. I even pull out my communicator at one point, staring at it. Should I ping him? No. I shouldn't. If he doesn't turn up then I simply contact Xarion tomorrow. Tell him the Kari fell through and that he should send the Raki instead. Even the thought makes a strange sour feeling develop in my chest.

I don't want to do that. Not really.

But actions speak louder than words and I know that to be a fact of life. I've lived it. If he doesn't turn up then he's exactly what I've thought him to be. Someone who I shouldn't get hung up on. Someone who I shouldn't let past these walls I've built up, despite that his presence has had me asking questions I shouldn't have been asking in the first place.

Grabbing another drink, I take a few more moments to rest and then I'm right again. I step outside in the sun once more. After adjusting my hat, I place my hands akimbo. My gaze shifts from where it lingered at the front gate for a moment too long to the animals in the field. If I'm to move them to the barn, they'll need food. I'll need to cut some of the grass and bring it in. Then I'll need to herd in the animals too.

Glancing at the front gate again, I curse myself one more time before I head back to the barn. It takes me far longer than it should to find a tool that can cut the grass. There's nothing like a grass cutter or anything. Just strange devices I have no clue the purpose of. I settle for a wicked-looking thing that looks like the Grim Reaper's scythe.

"This will do." My voice echoes in the still barn. I head back out, adjusting my sun hat. My eyes still drift to the front gate.

He's not coming. All that talk yesterday and he's not going to turn up. It figures. This is a lot of work for someone who won't be properly paid. It's a labor of love and will only be fruitful to me, not him. I curse myself for even anticipating his return. When I'm in the field, dragging the scythe by my side as I pass two resting oogas, I hear a ping on my comm.

I flip the device out so quickly, it almost slips from my hands. I curse myself again. I'm acting like a teen! And I keep saying that but I have no other frame of reference. The last time I acted like this, I was in high school. I was in love. Looking at the screen, I see there's a new notification. I select the message.

"Job rejected by Zynar of the Korruk line."

I blink at the words, repeating them in my head. Job rejected? It can't be the job he already did because, well, it's already done. He can't reject it when the roof is already finished. My nose wrinkles as I bring the device closer to my eyes as if that will create some understanding in my brain. Is it the new job? The new contract? Did he or Xarion initiate something I was unaware of? I try to navigate on the little device, trying to pull up the job ad being referred to, but soon give up, my shoulders drooping.

He's truly not coming, is he.

Disappointment shouldn't be so swift or nearly as painful.

I stare at the ooga beside me who flicks his little hippo-ears.

"I shouldn't have gotten my hopes up, should I?" I whisper. The ooga ignores me. I talk to it anyway. "Yeah yeah, I know what I said. I know I said no relationships. Men are shit and then they split, and whatnot. But damn it, I also know what I felt." I sigh as the ooga continues to ignore me. "Something I shouldn't have felt," I whisper, staring at the grass though not really seeing it. "I know. I know better than this."

I force a smile, lifting my head as one of those tall tilgrans ventures close. It's standing right where I want to start gathering the hay and I frown at it. "You're not going to trouble me, are you…Bob?" I don't know why I name the thing. It just feels appropriate. The tilgran simply chews as it watches me and I sigh. This place is safer than Earth in most respects. I've nothing to worry about. And so I move to the spot where I wish to start gathering the hay. With struggling arms, I lift the scythe and swing, my eyes widening as it cuts down a swathe of the grass in that single arch.

"Well, I'll be a monkey's uncle!" I stare at the blade. I thought it was rusty! "This thing's sharper than my wit on a Sunday morning." But it's heavy too. I struggle to swing it again, sweat rising on my brow but I soon get into a routine. Lift. Swing. Rest. Lift. Swing. Rest. Lift. Swing. Try not to fall on my ass. Rest.

I'm on my fifth swing or so when I suddenly hear a growl at my back. A shadow looms over me mid-swing and I cry out in alarm as the blade comes around. Purple and pink scales reflect in the light as a strong arm closes on the handle of the weapon, stopping the deadly swing with just a second to spare.

My heart lurches in my chest as I look up and there he is. I don't know whether to scream or slump against him in relief. I want to do both. Instead, words choke from my mouth in dismay.

"Zynar?!" *He's here?* "I could have killed you!"

He has the nerve to chuckle. "I'm tougher than you think,

Little Bird."

His chest is against my back and I can smell his scent again. That sweet smell that's like honey mixed in with perfume. Personal space, anyone? My chest heaves as I suddenly find it hard to breathe in his proximity. Pressed against my back, he's still holding on to the scythe, his arm curled around me where his hold on the weapon is just by where I'm still gripping it.

"You're here," I stutter. " I...thought you weren't going to come."

"I am true to my word." His gaze shifts to the grass I've already cut then back to me. A frown on his brow. "You shouldn't be out here doing this."

I frown slightly, too, trying not to highlight the fact he's pressed against me like this. But mostly a bit annoyed. Annoyed at myself because there's a miniature me in the center of my chest doing the cabbage patch dance. He's here, and it shouldn't make me this happy. I'm practically suddenly glowing. "You don't think I'm capable?"

"Ah, Little Bird. I think you're more than capable." Did he just lean in? His voice is lower. Deeper. I can feel his breath on my neck and it's sending shivers down my spine. "But just because you can do it, doesn't mean I should let you. That's what you have me for."

I blink several times, forcing a lump that's rising in my throat away.

"Come now, you're gathering grass-feed, correct? I will do that. I had planned to clear this field today, anyway."

"You'd planned?" I whisper, trying not to focus on the depth of his voice or the fact he's still pressed against my back! The hard planes of his chest feel like velvety walls I could just melt against and I'm suddenly reminded of what I did last night. How I'd imagined him while my fingers moved against me. I swallow hard again.

Zynar leans in, his purr near my ear. "I am tardy, Liora.

Varek's fault. I would have walked if it wouldn't have taken longer."

I blow a disbelieving laugh through my nose. "Walked? All the way from the town?"

He makes another purr, and I swear he comes even closer even though he's already pressed against my back. I can't move. And despite my reservations, I don't *want* to move. Fuck me. I'm cooked, aren't I?

"You were waiting for me, were you not?" I'm glad when he doesn't wait for me to answer because my cheeks flame at the fact that he's right. "I won't disappoint you like that again."

I clear my throat. "Yes, well. Let me just finish this here. Then we can discuss what you want to do today."

I try to lift the scythe but it feels even heavier now. I realize it's because Zynar's still gripping it.

"Like this," he purrs, his arm tightening around me. With the slightest insistence from his arm, he shows me how to swing the tool without exerting as much effort as I was. Or maybe it's because he's lifting the brunt of the weight. I do learn one thing, though. Apparently, I was swinging it at the wrong angle. Figures. I'm five foot five and this thing is taller than I am.

A few more swathes of grass cut and his arm relaxes. The sharp end of the tool rests on the ground before us and he eases up. I finally get to turn to look at him and when I do, Zynar's standing there with one arm suspiciously behind his back.

I still can't believe he's actually here. I'd convinced myself this was all a joke. That he couldn't possibly have really meant he was coming here to work, for free basically. And now that he's here...well, that little cloud of despondency is seeping away to be replaced by anticipation. And I really shouldn't be anticipating anything.

When he suddenly pulls something colorful from behind his back, my eyes widen, the handle of the scythe falling from my fingers.

Zynar holds the bouquet of flowers in one fist, his yellow gaze searching, unsure.

"It wasn't entirely Varek's fault why I'm late. I tried to find the rarest blooms that wouldn't die in a sol." His gaze shifts to the bouquet. They're huge flowers, each one about the size of both my fists combined. And the variety, good god. There are some with tiger stripes. Some that seem to change color depending on how the light shifts over them. And some that…

"My goodness, is that one…singing?" I step closer, my heart in my throat, an ache I never knew I had rising to the fore.

Zynar's gaze is locked on my face, as if he's noting my every reaction. "Yes. The wind goes through tiny channels in the petals, producing sound. I was hoping you would enjoy that one the most."

I could cry. I actually could. Flowers. He brought me *flowers*. An alien buying me flowers. How did he…how did he even know I liked them?

"You saw me saving the flowers," I whisper. "When I was weeding the yard. You noticed." That lump in my throat. Those tears. They threaten. They threaten simply because he noticed. But most of all, they swell in my eyes because of memories I forced myself to forget but never really could.

When I look at him, I can feel the tears blurring my vision. I fight them away. "You didn't think it was stupid? Me saving the flowers? A silly preoccupation? A worthless hobby?"

His brows furrow slightly, those yellow eyes still searching mine and even though they're slitted, pupils not round like mine, I can still see the depth of emotion in them.

"Whoever said such things to you, Liora?"

I sniffle, my gaze dropping to the flowers still in his grasp as a sad sort of smile stretches my lips. "A cocky, foolish man who never knew a damn thing."

Zynar studies me for a few seconds, watching as I stretch one hand to brush a finger over one of the petals.

"Your love of blooms is admirable," he finally says. "Why would caring for such delicate things be silly? They bring beauty to these fields. Peace." He gestures to the rolling plains spread out around us. "And they will bring beauty to your home."

A tear slides out with my soft laugh. I'm not quick enough to wipe it away before Zynar catches it. His fangs bare slightly in a growl.

"It is a horrible gift."

"No!" I choke. "It's the best gift you could have given me. Even though I don't deserve it at all. You didn't have to bring me anything."

"I wanted to." There's a depth to his voice that makes me wipe at my eyes before looking up at him again. There, our gazes lock for what feels like time-suspended moments.

I'm in trouble, aren't I.

I'm blinking back a whole train of emotions when the tilgran nearby, Bob, suddenly dips his head over the perimeter fence. He dives straight for the flowers but Zynar is faster. He stretches his arm out of the way before glaring up at the animal. The moment is broken and I pull fresh air into my lungs as I breathe again, wiping at my eyes once more as I watch Zynar and Bob go in a sort of stand-off, both staring at each other. Well, Zynar staring the animal while the stubborn tilgran still stretches for the flowers. Realizing it won't be reaching them, Bob blows a raspberry.

Eyes wide in humorous shock, my hands fly to cover my mouth as Bob dives and takes a lock of Zynar's hair into its mouth instead. I'm tense, hesitating, waiting for Zynar to blow up and get angry, disgusted, but...he doesn't.

"Pesky animal," Zynar grunts, a grin on his face as he lifts his free hand to pat the tilgran's long neck. And it seems the animal was merely eating his hair to piss him off, because the moment Zynar doesn't react in anger, it seems to grow bored. One lingering look at the flowers, it blows another raspberry before it lumbers off to snatch a mouthful of hay from a lazily feeding ooga.

"Bully," I chuckle. I've never seen a creature with more personality. Laughter still on my lips, my gaze shifts to Zynar. He makes a face as he touches his hair, saliva coming off on his fingers as he does the equivalent of an "ew" look.

I press my hands over my mouth again, resisting the urge to laugh, and his gaze shifts to mine.

"You find this funny, Little Bird?" It takes me only a second to spot the mischievous teasing tone in his voice and my entire body comes alert.

"What?" I drop my hands at my sides, my gaze shifting to the tilgran saliva on his fingers then back to him.

Zynar grins, devastatingly handsome, and gestures with his hand. He takes a step forward and I don't know why my heart skips a beat. I take a step back, heart beating harder, just before his lips curve into a devilish grin.

"Maybe you should get some on your mane too, then we can both scold the tilgran together." Zynar grins.

"What? Ew, no!"

His eyes twinkle and I know I must run.

I don't know why, but I do. I turn and I run, a laugh choking from within me.

"What are you doing?!" I scream as I look over my shoulder to see Zynar's actually coming after me, laughter on his lips. He's not even running fast. He's *letting* me run. Catching my eye, he lets out a whoop and laughter chokes some more from my throat.

"No! Wipe your hands off! That's nasty!" I'm still laughing though as I round an ooga to find Zynar's still chasing me. I let out a shriek, laughing more than I have in the last ten years as I cut through the tall grass and curve around another ooga. It's been a long time since I've run. A long time since I've felt pure freedom like this and the wind in my hair. I glance behind me and adrenaline shoots through me, sending my heart up into my throat when I catch sight of Zynar's purple scales not even a foot at my back.

I squeal as his arm wraps around me and we tumble into the soft grass. Breaths heave from my chest as we roll. I land on my back with Zynar above me, laughter still choking through my throat as I try to breathe at the same time.

My lids are low, a big smile on my face as Zynar's face appears above mine. The sun shines through the blades of grass, creating narrow shadows that play over his features. And in that moment, the world slows down. I sober. It's just me and him, complete silence around us. His smile falters as his gaze shifts to my lips and I become aware of the position we're in.

Professional. We're supposed to keep this professional. This doesn't feel professional at all.

He's pressed against me as he balances up on his arms, and as more awareness fills me, I feel the jerk of something hard against my inner thigh. I go still, my eyes widening slightly even as my chest heaves.

Professional? Certainly not.

But Zynar doesn't press in. Doesn't press his hardness against me and blow it off as an accident, even though he could. He doesn't try to make this moment more than it could be. Instead, he eases off me a bit, shifting so he kneels over me instead. I try not to look, but my gaze slides down, anyway. There's a clear tent in the center of his pants. My throat goes dry.

"You're fast," he murmurs.

I blush. "Oh please. I haven't run like that in years."

Wiping away the tilgran saliva in the grass, he hands me the bouquet with the other hand. I only notice then that the bases of the stems are wrapped. The flowers have roots. I'll be able to plant them. More emotion swells within me.

"Thank you. For the flowers." I take them. I almost say it's been a while since anyone's bought me flowers. That I'd been hearing for years that I had enough in the garden, why on Earth would I want money wasted buying me more. That I used to buy them for myself, but it just never felt the same. But I don't say anything. Somehow, it feels like dwelling on that memory, even bringing it up now, will taint the purity of Zynar's gift.

I bring the bouquet to my nose as Zynar shifts and rises. One hand outstretched, he helps me to my feet.

"I should put them in water," I whisper. He watches me in that intense way as I smell the flowers again and I swear I hear a purr in his chest.

"Yes," he finally says. "I will help you dig holes to place them later." He glances toward the cottage. "And stay in. Make some tea. You can sleep if you wish. It will take me much time to complete the field."

My eyebrows rise and when I open my mouth to protest, he frowns. I slam my mouth shut.

"Alright," I whisper instead. For the first time in a while, I feel…I feel like I don't have to worry about a thing. I feel…good. Like a woman. The way one is supposed to feel when she's taken care of. The sensation is so unnatural, it almost makes nervous anxiety rise in my bones.

Zynar seems pleased with my response, his shoulders pressing back, muscles rolling as he pops the bones in his neck.

I swallow hard, trying to not let my gaze slip to his crotch again before I head toward the house. I can feel his eyes on me and when I look over my shoulder, I catch him watching my ass as I go. I don't know why I sway my hips just a little bit more.

It's not a joke. The hot alien is attracted to me. I saw the proof with my own eyes, and with that knowledge comes a sense of power I didn't expect.

Another thrill goes through me and I find myself smiling probably more than I should.

1 2

ELEANOR

*H*e was serious about working.

Zynar works all day, never taking a break from the hot sun.

I watch him from the window. Watch as he uses the scythe to clear large patches of the grass that he then transports to the barn. By midday, half the field is done and I feel like I'm sitting still, twiddling my fingers. But even as I watch him work, a slow realization fills me. The work he's doing? I wouldn't be able to do even a quarter of it in the same amount of time. Probably would take me months. And the animals? They can't wait months. Even now, my hands ache from just wielding the scythe for such a short time. For this place to come together, I need Zynar's help.

For a moment, he disappears and I stand on my tiptoes, scanning the field outside. He must be hungry by now, but he hasn't come inside once. He's serious about getting the job done. When I came to the house to put the flowers in water, I saw the small pack he left by the door. It looked like an overnight bag and my heart skipped a beat. He really is serious about staying as well.

This is only a contract, I remind myself. Still doesn't help the tachycardia.

When I see him again, Zynar's rubbing Bob behind the ears as the tilgran eats a bunch of straw from his hand. He really seems to like the animals. Yet another difference between my ex and him. I know I shouldn't compare. My only point of reference is a man that hurt me so badly, I felt like a husk by the time I had the guts to end it all. Five years later, and my life got turned upside down again by the Tasqals abducting me from Earth.

Both times, it was hard to see the light at the end of the tunnel. But I'm here now. On this quiet farm. Sitting in my cottage. An alien in my fields.

There's no pretense with Zynar. He sits on tree stumps to drink tea. He doesn't get angry when a wild animal chews on his hair. And he chased me through the grass like we were kids. I smile at the memory, my fingers playing with the skin on my chest, right where my heart beats.

Clearing my throat, I pull my gaze away from the sight as I head to the kitchen. Setting my mug down, I grab three drinks this time and another of the meat sandwiches. Heading to the bathroom, I reach for a towel and take that with me, too.

Walking across the field now that it's mostly cleared of grass is quite different from before. For one, I realize I have many more oogas than I thought, the grass no longer hiding most of the herd. And second, I'm no longer hidden as I walk through it. The moment I step onto the field, Zynar turns to look my way. Tingles go across my skin when he looks at me. Maybe because he stops everything he's doing just to watch me approach.

"I brought you something to eat."

His lids become hooded as he watches me. "Thank you, Liora."

He steps away from the tilgran who seems suddenly interested in the tray of food, dipping toward it. I have to sidestep and make a wide arch, a laugh on my lips. This is what Xarion meant when he said they weren't dangerous, just hazardous. When I look back at Zynar, that hooded gaze is still on me.

"Do you want to eat inside?"

He tilts his head before his gaze shifts to the tray again. "I enjoy eating under the sky with you."

I blush before lowering myself to the ground with the tray. "Here's a few drinks. You really should come inside for refreshments every hour or so. It can't be good for you to be in the sun this long."

When he plops down beside me, my gaze shifts to his only to find he's staring at my lips as I speak. "You were worried about me, Little Bird?"

I open my mouth and close it. It sounds like a dangerous question to answer. I've spent the entire morning watching him through the window and it wasn't out of worry.

"I wouldn't want you falling over and getting sunstroke." I smile.

"You don't want me getting hurt, then." He leans closer, that soft rumble in his tone. "You care about me, Liora?"

"Of course, I do," I smile, before clearing my throat. My cheeks burn. "It's basic decency."

He huffs a soft laugh before reaching for one of the drinks. As he tilts his head back and swallows a few mouthfuls, my gaze skips over his skin. His scales glisten slightly. Sweat, I believe. Before I realize just what I'm doing, I have the towel in hand. When I press it against his shoulder, he freezes but doesn't say a word.

I swallow hard but don't pull away. This isn't professional. I'm breaking my own rule. Standing, I step over to him, dabbing the towel across his shoulders, a lump rising in my throat and something fluttering in my belly at the utter power underneath my hands. Slowly, Zynar reaches for the sandwich and begins to eat. He chews as I continue dabbing the towel, neither of us mentioning what I'm doing, neither of us speaking about it. When my free hand rests on his other shoulder, he stiffens again, a low purr in his throat that makes that little bud between my thighs respond.

I ignore it. God, at least I try to. Using the towel, I wipe away the sweat as best as I can. I'm almost done when he groans slightly as I wipe a particular spot on his shoulder. I'm not sure what it is, so I run my hand over the spot again. It feels tense, hard, and Zynar groans again.

"What's this?" I whisper, my skin hot from all the thoughts I'm trying *not* to think. Poking the spot lightly, my gaze shifts to his face, trying to gauge his reaction. He grimaces.

"Just an ache. Injured that spot in the war. Never truly is relaxed."

"Oh…"

"Muscle is tense." He takes another bite of the sandwich and I watch him eat, a million thoughts in my head. Some screaming at me to stand up and walk away and some more quiet insistent ones telling me to do the opposite.

"I can help you with that," I whisper. He pauses mid-drink, the can in his hand. "I can massage it for you."

Zynar's head moves slightly to the side and I know he's watching me through his periphery. "You would do that for me, Little Bird?"

He asks it as if it's such a big deal. "Yes, of course."

"This dark cycle?" he asks.

My heart rate picks up. "Tonight? Sure."

He nods, chin to chest, and I guess that's settled.

For more minutes than I need to, I clean the sweat off his scales. Even when I'm done, I linger still. "Tell me about the war. You said you have no home?"

He stiffens once more and I don't think it's because of my touch. Setting the can down, he stares off into the distance and I regret asking him something so personal. I really have no right when I'm here trying to keep him at arm's length—although, admittedly, completely failing at it. Zynar's looking off into the distance and I think he won't respond, but then he speaks.

"We were chids," he says. "Varek and I. The Tasqals sent their minions to raid our villages. They killed many. Our por, he died in the first wave. Our mor in the second."

My breath stalls as I stare down at him from where I stand. He's said it all without inflection. I can't tell if he's trying to hide his pain or his anger—or if he's just at that state where pain does one of two things: makes you numb or makes you laugh. Still staring off into the distance, the look that passes through his strange eyes is one even I can comprehend.

Pain. Loss. Trauma.

I stare at him. At this male who seems so happy and self-assured, knowing that right at this moment I'm seeing a part of him that's private. Intimate. Vulnerable.

"Me and Varek…we were alone. We formed a resistance with some of the Restitution rebels who came to help us. But we suffered many losses." He releases a breath, slitted gaze shifting to me. "We have no home, Liora, because they destroyed it. Do you know why?"

A ball of emotion is in my throat as I adjust my glasses on my nose. "It doesn't matter, does it? What they did was wrong."

Zynar's gaze shifts across my face as if he's taking me in before a slight smile stretches his lips. "They wanted to harvest our virility."

I stare at him, a million thoughts rising in my mind at that single sentence. "I …don't understand."

He smiles again slightly, his gaze still shifting over my features. And for the first time, even though I'm aware I'm being seen, that I'm *visible* to him, I don't squirm. I don't want to hide away. I feel like I bloom.

"They used machines," Zynar continues, his voice low, his gaze shifting away from me again. "They captured some of us.

Restrained us. Attached devices to us." Almost absentmindedly, his arm shifts to his lower abdomen. I can't see the shadow of what he's touching. Whatever it is, it's hidden beneath his trousers. "They forced us to produce and release the vital substance they coveted."

Horror fills me. "Oh, God."

Zynar smiles at me, but it isn't like all the times he's smiled at me before. There's no mirth there now. I fall to my knees. Without hesitation, my arms wrap around this big alien's broad shoulders as I pull him into me.

"I'm sorry. I'm so sorry." I knew the aliens that took us were horrible, but the more I learn about that species, the more I realize just how utterly horrible they were. "They took from me too, but it's all over now. We're safe here on Hudo III. This place is a new home for us both."

Zynar is still as hard as a rock, but I feel him slowly melt against me. "For you, Little Bird. You have a new home. And that is a good thing."

I lift my head slightly, brows furrowing. "But not for you?"

He gives me that slight smile again. "Do not fret. We Kari are still happy here."

I know there's more to it, but something tells me I shouldn't push for more information from him. At least, not yet. What he just told me must have taken a lot to say. When I was stuck with aliens on that refugee ship, no one spoke about their trauma. As if mere mention of it was taboo. For Zynar to speak to me so openly tells me he trusts me. Out here, that means a helluva whole lot and I give him one last squeeze.

Releasing him more reluctantly than I should, considering the mandate I gave myself, I hope he can't hear my heart thundering in my chest as I rise. He's finished with the sandwich already and he grabs the other two drinks and stuffs them into his pocket.

He rises too, rolling his shoulders as he looks down at me.

The pain and distance seep away from his eyes. "Thank you, Liora."

I blush. Standing there awkwardly, I nod slightly. He takes a step toward me before he stops and his large hands squeeze into fists before he releases them. With a grin, Zynar heads off across the field. I turn and watch him go, knowing that somehow, despite years of preaching to myself, this alien is slowly breaking down walls and I don't know how.

Heading back to the house, I walk across the field, looking over my shoulder every few strides. The scythe moves with precision as Zynar works, most definitely a thousand times faster than I ever could have. I'll have a proper field soon, one I can till to yield crops. Every day this place is looking more and more like the farm it's supposed to be and it's mostly because of him.

I surprise myself by smiling. That sense of accomplishment I wanted to feel by improving this place myself isn't deterred. It's still there.

Zynar works non-stop for the whole day. At one point, I find myself pulling a chair next to the window again, drink in hand as I watch him work. His movements are fluid and efficient, each swing of the scythe precise and powerful. My gaze follows him, heart beating faster with every stride he takes. The way his muscles flex under the hot sun, the power in each swing…it captivates me.

Maybe I'm staring because he seems less like an untouchable being and more 'human' to me now, if that's possible. His trauma, my trauma, shouldn't do that. Bonding over something so terrible should be wrong, simply because it shouldn't have happened to either of us. But it did.

When he pauses, wiping sweat from his brow, and looks toward the house, our gazes meet. For a heartbeat, time stands still. I feel a pull, a connection that defies logic and reason. It doesn't make sense, and yet it's there. Like a current underneath my thoughts, building, getting stronger with each moment that he's here.

Giving him a wave, I force myself to rise from the seat, suddenly self-conscious of the fact I've simply been sitting there watching him. My gaze sweeps across the kitchen and I stretch, preparing to clean up. There's still the towel I'd used to wipe him down and I lift it now. Within the fibers, I can smell his intoxicating sweet scent. I don't know which devil tells me to bring it to my nose, but I do, knees almost buckling at the intensity of sweet sugar that hits me.

I groan, heart thundering at the response as I stare down at the towel still pressed to my nose. Now why did I do that?

But it smells *so* good. Like something I want to press my face into all the time. I tell myself to put the towel down but my fingers only tighten in the fibers as I inhale again.

"Mm, so good." A trickle of something goes down my navel and bursts like a firework in my groin. My breaths come a little harder and I groan again. I'm sniffing his sweat! *And getting turned on.*

It's a strange sensation being both horrified and horny. Like getting hit by a double H whammy—one part horror show, one part hot flash.

Why does he smell so good? I've smelled him before, each time making me want to inhale deeper, but I guess I've never smelled his direct *sweat* before. I inhale again, and that firework bursts in my crotch, making a tingle go through my privates. I stand there in the center of my living room, towel to my nose, and snort again despite myself. When my entire pussy clenches, I almost fall to my knees with the power of the throb.

I breathe hard, inadvertently breathing more of him in as my eyes widen, thoughts, explanations swirling in my mind. Is this the virility thing he was talking about? The thing the computer warned me of? Is this a sample of what the Tasqals wanted from his race? Good god, his scent is like a drug.

It reminds me of how some plants use chemical signals to attract mates or influence other organisms. Like that lesson I taught my students of how bee orchids mimic the scent of female bees to attract males, or how some plants release compounds to draw in predators of their pests. Trust me to ramble in my own head, but is Zynar's scent the same? Pheromones? My eyes flutter and I can't deny his scent is doing something similar to me, a chemical signal that's impossible to ignore.

It takes great effort for me to pull the towel from my nose, to force myself into the bathroom. I stare at the little basket I set in the corner for laundry. I should set it down here, instead, I can't release it from my fingers. The thought actually sends a panic through me. My heart beats harder, anxiety rising, everything within me telling me that washing the towel is wrong. My gaze shifts in the direction of my bedroom. Am I so crazy?

Before I can talk myself out of it, I hurry into the bedroom and set the towel on the edge of the bed. Turning away from it, I make to leave the room before I stop in my tracks. I turn back around and grab it again. What is *wrong* with me? I should put it in the laundry bin. What do I do? The opposite. Instead of placing it where logic tells me to, I fold it neatly, but still don't remove it from my bed. Now, before I can get some sense into my brain, I hurry out of the room, that lingering scent in my lungs and a lump in my throat.

I can't be going crazy over a towel. But here I am. The thought of washing it almost hurt.

It's with great effort that I get through the rest of the day. I force myself not to look out the window. Not to track Zynar's every move. I focus on improving the house. I even found a can of plaster, the words on the tin translated using my handy comm device, and I set to fixing the cracks in the window sills and walls.

It takes some of my focus, this work, even though the only thing I want to focus on is the alien working on my farm.

NIGHT DOESN'T COME SOON ENOUGH. By the time the sun goes down, my entire body is buzzing with some unknown energy I've never felt before. I suddenly feel like a teen who is just discovering myself and the world. It's unknown territory where the rules of everything no longer apply.

I'm pacing when I hear him. My heart stutters and I move to the door, ears perked.

He's transporting the last stacks of hay to the barn, and I hear the moment he's finished. His boots hit the worn planks on the porch and my throat goes dry when I hear him right outside the door. I prepare myself to open it, only Zynar doesn't knock.

I hear when he lifts the pack he'd set there by the door and then he pauses. Hesitates.

"Liora?"

Something tingles inside me. "Y-yes?" I try to project my voice so it doesn't sound like I'm right behind the door, even though that's where I'm standing like some creep.

"The field is finished. Ready for tilling on the new dawn."

"Oh," I blink a thousand times, trying to find the words that should be in my brain. "That was quick!"

He chuckles, the deep sound coming to me through the door and making me lean against it as I close my eyes.

"I will see you at first light."

Wait…what? He's leaving? My heart drops and I'm immediately angry and confused with myself. Isn't this what I wanted? Distance?

"Oh…okay! See you in the morning, Zynar."

There's a pause and I think I hear some hesitation in his voice. "Rest well…Little Bird."

I hear when his boots thump as he moves off the porch and I freeze in a sort of confused state. When I shift to the window, eyes shooting to the front gate, there's no waiting transport there. Varek didn't come to get him. Then…

I catch Zynar's back as he disappears toward the barn, his pack in hand. Of course. There's no Varek because he's supposed to be staying here with me now. We're supposed to be working together, building bridges and convincing New Horizons that this thing can work. Zynar's not leaving.

But he's staying in the barn? We haven't sorted out the bed situation yet, but we could come up with *something*. The barn's not suitable for anyone to stay in. Not even the animals. But do I want him inside the house? There's only one room. One bed.

My throat goes dry as I think of the possibilities, and as Zynar steps into the barn, I find myself staring as the doors close.

He's giving me space. Doing exactly what I asked him to do. Shouldn't that make me happy?

It doesn't.

There's a nervous energy still coiling in my gut and I ease off the door, scolding myself only to start pacing again. I should take a bath, calm myself down. Gaze shifting out the window to the field, I see that he did indeed clear the entire thing. About one dozen oogas stretch across the land, some lying on their stomachs and others standing, lazily chewing on bales of long grass Zynar left behind for them.

He's done what he said he was going to do. I'm the one who seems to have a problem doing the same thing. Being professional. Distance. The whole shebang.

I growl at myself as I head to the bathroom. Filling the bath up, I stare at the clear warm liquid, my thoughts still on the alien in my barn. When I strip down and step into the warm water, I release a groan at how good it feels. I'm slow with the bath. Slower than usual. Maybe because my thoughts are still distracted, or rather, too focused on the one thing I'm trying not to think about.

As I tilt my head back against the curve of the bathtub, one hand slips between my thighs. I shudder as my fingers make contact with my clit, a moan trapped behind my lips as I force my breathing to remain steady. I think of him. This time, I'm not ashamed to. I think of Zynar and I think of his scent. Of how good it felt pressing that towel to my nose and smelling his raw, powerful essence. My fingers work, pulling soft moans from me with practiced precision that has me reaching a climax in minutes. Panting, I relax in the bath, eyes cast upward at my new roof.

What am I doing?

Out of the tub, I grab a free towel and dry myself. Back in the bedroom, I plop on the edge of the bed after slipping on one of the simple brown tunics.

My gaze shifts to the towel I'd folded and left on the edge of the bed. My fingers itch to touch it. I grip the bed tighter. I can't. Good God, I *shouldn't.*

I sit there fighting with myself until I suddenly stand. Shoulders set, I glance at my comm unit. It sits on the bed, screen blank, when, like some manifestation, it suddenly lights up. The sound of a ping comes through and I grab the device too eagerly.

I'm disappointed when I see who it is. I answer the ping anyway.

"Greetings, Eleanor Tabitha."

"Hello, Xarion." I press a smile to my face even though that twinge of unreasonable disappointment is still there.

"I am pinging you about the Raki. Has the Kari taken the job?"

I nod. "He has."

"And are you comfortable in his presence? Kari descend

from a predator species and your species, like mine, dwell in herds. If the Kari has threatened you into this contract—"

"Oh Gods, no. He did nothing of the sort." I take a step out of my bedroom, walking slowly to the front door. My gaze finds the barn immediately. "He's been nothing but hardworking... and gentlemanly."

Xarion's long ears sway a little as he looks down and I realize he's in some office at a desk. "Understood. If you are comfortable, I will send the recommendation off to New Horizons and tell them of the efforts you're making. Your integration with the Kari is quite noteworthy."

"Integration...yeah..." I murmur. I want to integrate, alright. I'm just too cowardly to actually go ahead with it.

"Good," Xarion perks up. "Please ping me if you encounter trouble." Then he makes a sound like he's clearing his throat. One that makes my gaze shift to his on the screen.

"Xarion, is there something else?"

"Yes..."

When he doesn't continue, he pulls my entire attention. My awareness piques as I wait for him to continue.

"About the mating act..."

I blink, eyes widening slightly.

"With the Kari..."

My cheeks flush. "I know to whom you're referring. It was just. It was a one-time thing. You don't have to worry about—"

"On the contrary, I would like to encourage you to continue. Breeding with a Kari would be a perfect way to increase the population of the plains. The more individuals that live on the Hudoian plains—"

"Wait, what? You want me to...*breed* with him?"

"It is entirely up to you. Though it would be a great addition to my report on your integration."

I close my eyes briefly, a soft laugh on my lips. "Sorry to disappoint, Xarion, but my baby-making days have long passed."

Xarion's ears flick, undeterred. "Either way, there would be no harm in trying." I think he smiles at me, I can't quite be sure, before he dips his head. "Now, farewell, Eleanor. I am a ping away if you need assistance."

I'm left staring at the screen as he clicks off and the screen goes blank again.

Did he…did he just tell me to take Zynar to bed for the good of the population? I mean, that's as good a reason to do it as any, isn't there? Haha ha ha haaaaaa…Oh God, I'm actually considering it.

My gaze shifts outside to the barn and I pull my bottom lip in between my teeth.

To heck with it. I can at least go out there to see if he's alright.

Slipping on my shoes, I step outside. It's dark now, just the faint outline of the sun on the horizon as I hurry across the yard.

I don't know what the hell I'm doing. Heading toward the hunk of an alien that's dominated my mind because a white rabbit told me that I should bed him? What will I say when I go in there? "Oh, I'm just here because a rabbit told me to."

I groan. "This feels like Alice following the White Rabbit, except instead of Wonderland, I'm stumbling into hot-and-bothered land."

Of course, nothing is going to happen. I'm just going to check on Zynar and see if he's comfortable. Bid him goodnight and then take my ass out of there and to my room where I belong.

13

ZYNAR

This has been one of the hardest sols of my life.

Out there in the field, only focusing hard on the scythe and the work that needed to be done kept me sane enough to not follow the thread of something pulling me toward the Liora.

Frakk, I almost threw down the tool on several occasions, just to venture close to the lodging to ask her some silly question that had nothing to do with the work she needs me to do. And when I looked toward the abode and saw her there watching me? Gods. How I managed to continue working with the tingle of her gaze on my back was some feat. Even now, standing under the cool spray of a water spigot at the far end of the barn does nothing to coil the heat swirling at the center of my groin.

I thought about the Little Bird all frakking sol and now I'm all tense. My lids lower as I grip my rock-hard cock through my trouse. A groan rumbles deep in my throat at just that touch. At just the thought of Eleanor touching me there. Just having her rubbing perspiration from my shoulders had me so hard it was an effort to sit still without adjusting myself. I didn't dare move unless I scared her away.

Taking the trouse off now, my cock springs free, pointing at the wall like a sword. It's so hot, it feels like steam rises with each drop of water that hits it. I set the trouse down to dry before I step under the spray again, washing myself before I lean both hands against the wall before me. I stare down at my cock and then I grip it again. With a slow pump, I roll my fist along my shaft, grunting with the pleasure that shoots through me as I imagine Eleanor's hand there instead.

I close my eyes, imagining her lips. So soft and inviting, they felt like the sweetest sin against mine. How good she tasted in my mouth. I never thought a thing like mouth brushing could ever bring such pleasure, but now that I've experienced it, I can't help but want more. I want her body pressed against mine. Want my claws roaming over her curves. Want to pull her in and make her feel every inch of me. Just the thought of burying my length inside her heat has me grunting. I pump harder, the image of her never leaving my mind.

I imagine cupping the mounds on her chest, feeling their softness and teasing her until she moans my name. Of gripping those hips that sway with a rhythm that hypnotizes me. And then there's the way she smells. Her scent, a mix of her natural aroma and the lingering traces of whatever she uses to cleanse herself, fills my senses and drives me to the brink of madness. It's like nothing I've ever experienced, a heady mix of sweetness and spice that makes my mouth water and my cock throb with need.

I pump my shaft harder, the image of Eleanor so vivid in my mind that I can almost feel her beneath my claws. I imagine her legs wrapped around me, her breath hot against my ear as she whispers my name, urging me on.

My pace quickens, each stroke bringing me closer to the edge. The thought of her wet and ready for me, her body eager to take me in, is almost too much to bear. I grunt with the effort to hold back, to savor the sensation a little longer, but the need is too great. With a final, shuddering breath, I give in to the pleasure, imagining her with me in every moment. Spurts of lifeseed shoot from my tip to coat the wall before me. My shoulders are hunched, each breath harsh and making my shoulders heave as more lifeseed is pulled from within me. I shudder with each pump from my sac until I'm left panting.

Staring at the seed coating the wall, I splash some water to wash it away, only to realize I'm still frakking hard. Apparently, with Eleanor, just once isn't enough. I'll have to relieve myself again. The image of Eleanor smiling up at me while I spread lifeseed all across her belly makes me groan again.

Cock in hand, I'm about to pump out another one when I hear a soft sound somewhere behind me. I freeze, gaze shifting to the outbuilding's entrance as the large doors push open.

"Zynar?" My name as a song. It reaches my ears and I have to resist a moan as my cock jerks in my fist. Eleanor enters the outbuilding, eyes squinted. There is no light in here. I have not yet lit one but I realize now that she doesn't only need her lenses for general sight but that her eyes cannot parse the shadows.

Lucky for me, because just a few lengths from her I stand bare with my cock in hand. I take far too long to move. To cover myself. I stand there, my cock jerking when she calls my name again and everything I've been imagining about the tempting Liora repeats in my mind. Grabbing a dry tunic from where I hung it, I turn off the spigot and wrap the tunic around my lower half.

"Is everything alright, Liora?" I say, stepping from the shadows. I can tell when she sees me. The slight worry that was clouding her gaze disappears as she looks in my direction. Reaching into my pack, I take out a light stick, activating the thing and setting it down near the stacks of bales I'd made to sleep on.

Eleanor blinks and squints, her eyes adjusting to the new light, before they heighten on me fully. "Oh!" Her cheeks get that red color. "You were showering." Her gaze shifts down my frame, sending a tingle right through me and straight to my cock again. In this simple tunic, the way it stands at attention is obscene and so I turn away from her. She'd said she didn't want to engage in anything outside of professionalism and I wish to adhere to that. It allows me to be here by her side and, as the cycles pass, I realize I don't want to be anywhere else.

"Don't worry, you did not interrupt me. I was finished before you entered." Lies. By the looks of it, I will have to pump my cock through the dark cycle just to 'finish' enough that I won't poke her in the eyes at dawn.

"Oh, good." Her gaze shifts to the bales and then to me. "Everything's fine. I was just…just wondering if you're alright out here and if you need anything. A blanket? Water? Food?"

I smile at her over my shoulder. "I am a simple male, Liora. I have all that I need. Not to worry."

She nods. A slight one, barely visible, as her gaze shifts to the bales again. When she looks at me once more, her gaze moves over my back before she makes that sound in her throat as if she's clearing something stuck within it.

"Well, then, I guess I should bid you goodnight then. Unless there's anything you need…" She licks her lips, gaze shifting to mine before, she blinks a few times and looks away.

If there is anything I need? I almost purr.

I know what I need and it's standing not even a good length away from me, dressed in a simple night tunic that would rip so easily it's hardly any protection from my claws. Her. What I need is her.

"Oh!" Her sudden exclamation almost has me turning

around fully. "Your back." Her eyes light up. "I was supposed to help you with that, right?"

I groan. I can't help it. The thought of her touching me right now while I'm in this state is downright electrifying. And yet, I can't resist.

"The knot in your back is still there, isn't it?" She approaches. She's so small, I can just see the top of her head when she disappears at my back. When her soft hand touches my shoulder, a rumble of pleasure goes through me. My cock jerks beneath my tunic, spend seeping from my tip. Frakk, I might just release with just her proximity and the slightest touch.

"Zynar?"

"Mm?" I groan.

"Is it still there? I could help you with it now if you like?"

Temptation at its finest.

"Or it's fine, as well, if you no longer want me to…"

"Oh, I do." I turn, my cock bobbing and brushing against her soft belly. A lump forms in my throat or I would have purred. I watch as her eyes widen and her neck stiffens, almost as if she's trying her darnedest not to look down. I would smile if it wouldn't make me snarl from the pure effort it's taking not to take her into my arms.

So I move. I walk over to the bales I'd pushed into a flat surface to rest on and I lie face-down. The ache of pressing my cock against the grass-feed does nothing to calm the tension swelling within my shaft. As a matter of fact, the friction and pressure only make things worse.

"Ok…that's…" The Little Bird swallows hard but she comes over to me anyway. "This is fine, I guess."

A delicious shudder goes through me as she sets her hands on my shoulders. She begins her massage, moving slowly at first, as if testing things out and learning what to do, before she begins kneading the muscles beneath my skin.

Gods. Possibly I died and this is the promised place where everything is good. I sink into the bale as Eleanor's soft hands work magic. My face is turned away from her and when I turn my head the other way, my eyelids flutter at the waft of sweet essence that's coming from her. Inhaling deeply, I catch a whiff of something I never scented on her before. Something intoxicating that makes my cock harden when I didn't think it could get any harder. Shifting slightly closer, I inhale deep, a rumble going through my chest.

It's *her*. Her essence from between her legs. Nothing else could make me react like that. The thought that Eleanor might be even just slightly affected by me sets my lifeblood on fire.

"Ah, this isn't working."

My eyes fly open at her words, slight panic going through me. Will she leave now? Go back inside the lodge for the dark cycle? But when her hands shift over me I know I must have gotten it wrong. Eleanor braces down on my back.

"I hope you don't mind." She makes a sort of nervous laugh from her chest. "You're just so big it's hard for me to stretch over you to reach the spot."

She thinks I'm big? Strong too, I hope. All sol I intended to show her I can be a good addition for her here on her farm.

When Eleanor grunts and suddenly climbs on top of the bale, on top of *me*, I go still. The heat of her thighs envelops me as she straddles my back. Gods, help me.

Focus on *something*, anything but how good she feels, how soft, and that heat between her thighs.

"Is this too much? I know it's a bit inappropriate and I can get off you if I'm too heavy."

Too heavy? I almost scoff, but I fear any sound or movement will scare her away. Because my Little Bird is of the timid kind. She will approach what she wants, but I must give her time. Space. I cannot rush her. I cannot scare her. I must let her flutter her wings and fly toward me on her own. And just like a plant rooted in the ground, I remain unmoving.

"Please," I whisper because anything else will come out as a growl of pure need. "Do what you must."

She grunts a smile and settles on me. My cock jerks into the bale, more spend seeping from my tip.

Her hands are magic. Just like the mouth touching, when she mentioned a massage, I thought not much of it. I was unprepared. A groan of pleasure escapes from my lips as she kneads my shoulder and Eleanor blows a laugh through her nose at my response.

"Feels good, doesn't it?" She says, and in my mind, it sounds like a whisper. A dangerously delicious whisper. I grunt a sound of affirmation as she continues to knead the knot away.

"Zynar?" She sings my name again.

"Yes, Liora?"

"I know you said something about this planet never being your home…" Her words make me go still again. "But I want to let you know that…I know what that feels like. On the refugee ship, I wondered if I was stuck there forever. If I would ever find a place that I could call home again. A true place. A true home. But then I saw the flyer. I applied and New Horizons contacted me." She stops kneading my shoulders for a moment and I almost protest with a groan. "If I can help with anything, to help you find a home I mean, or help you create one, I will try my best." She starts kneading my shoulders again, but I'm still unmoving. Not because of her touch, but because of what's coming from her lips. "I might not be good with yard work like cutting long grass, but I'm a mean baker. I was a housewife for most of my life and—"

She suddenly stops talking and this time, she's the one that freezes. I shift a little, turning with her still settled on my back so I can look over my shoulder at her.

"Howse…whyvve? The words don't translate, Liora."

Her shoulders slump slightly and she gives me a thin smile, her gaze shifting from mine to my shoulder, but it's like she's no longer seeing me. A memory then.

"It's a word that means I was a…I was married before." She does that smile again. One that doesn't show her blunted teeth but is simply a slight stretch of her lips that doesn't communicate any mirth, even though that should be its purpose.

"Mah-reed?" I push.

"I was someone's mate."

The thought of her belonging to another sends such a rush of possession through me that I actually snarl. I only catch myself when her eyes heighten on my lips. She does that strange smile again. "I know. It's kind of not a good thing, is it."

Not a question. A statement. One that makes her shoulders slump again.

"Where is he. Your…mate." Frakk. I can hardly say the word. "Is he dead?"

Turning with her still on me, she jostles as I settle on my back, forcing her to straddle my abdomen. At another time, I'm sure she would flutter away. This time, she doesn't even move. The weight of her past is too heavy.

A laugh chokes through her, and she covers her mouth as mirth fills her eyes this time. "No. I don't think so, though I used to wish for it sometimes. He's living his life on Earth with his hot new girlfriend."

"I assume that also means 'mate'."

She nods and that strange smile returns. Frakk. Does she miss him? Does she long for this male?

When her eyebrows lift and she begins to answer, I realize in horror that I asked the questions out loud.

"No. Definitely not. I just…" Lifting one hand, she runs it through her golden filaments with a sigh that makes her body rub against mine. Heat coils in my groin again. "I guess I hate that I'm starting over. You know…I feel like I wasted so much time with him. Like…all my good years are gone."

Her gaze meets mine but this time, my Liora doesn't look away. When I lift my arms and settle them on her hips, she doesn't shift out of my grasp either.

"Do you know why we Kari will never find a home?" I whisper, my voice no more than a low growl.

Eleanor shakes her head.

"For Kari, home is not a place. It is not a lodge. It is not a planet. It is a being. Our homes lie with our mates."

She blinks, gaze shifting to my lips and then back to my eyes as she considers my words.

"You don't have a mate?" Then her cheeks flush almost immediately. "A question I should have asked before I let you kiss me."

I smile, flashing fang as my claws knead her hips. Frakk. She's even softer than I could have ever dreamed.

"I have no mate. My core-rhythm has never sung."

"Your core what?"

Reaching for her hand that's resting on me, I lift it to the center of my chest. "Here. Kari have a core-rhythm here. A vibration that binds around our core-beat. It awakens when we find our mates, binding us to them forever."

"Forever?"

"For our entire existence," I say with pride.

Her digits flex underneath mine, brushing against my skin. "That's a long time."

"And it is all we desire." I freeze again, because those are words I have never uttered. Not to Varek. Not to any other Kari. Not even to myself. "To be bound to our mate forever is all we dream of. She is…home."

A part of me wants to hide away from this utterance. This rawness. But I don't. With Eleanor, opening myself like this doesn't feel like a vulnerability. She won't criticize me. Didn't the first time I showed her a part of me, told her of my past when I don't talk about it to anyone else. Her maturity makes me feel safe.

"I don't understand, Zynar. Why would you think this is something you'll never have? You're kind, helpful, young, handsome, sexy…"

Every word she utters makes me purr a little louder, the sound vibrating in my throat.

"You think all these things of me?"

Her face heats, and she adjusts herself, but doesn't slide her hand from within my grasp. Her heat spreads across my abdomen.

She looks down at where her hand is under mine, her face still warm. "I think you're all of those things."

I purr again. "Just as you are radiant. Your softness. Your beauty. You, Liora, are utterly captivating."

Eleanor's eyes widen slightly, and her cheeks flush even deeper. "You really think that?"

"More than anything."

Her gaze shifts to my lips then and my cock jerks to further attention. I try to angle my hips away from her so I don't poke her in the back. I'm pretty sure this sweet moment between us will be interrupted if she feels my cock prodding her for attention.

When she leans in slowly, everything within me goes still. Even my cock stops jerking. I freeze, breath held as Eleanor leans closer until we're simply a breath apart.

"I know I said I wanted to keep this professional…" she whispers. Her breath brushes against my lips like a promise of what will come next if I can just frakking keep still. "This completely goes against that."

I run my tongue over my lips, breath still held and my entire body heating up like I'm lying on a furnace. I'm captivated as this entrancing female watches the movement as if she, too, is hypnotized. Her throat moves as her gaze shifts up to mine. So close, I see pure water in her gaze—her eyes the color of the coolest springs. I am intoxicated by this Liora. I want nothing more than for her to—

Eleanor leans in and time stills. When her lips brush against mine, almost hesitantly, heat rises in my shaft. I grunt, claw tightening on her hips as she nibbles on my lips. A soft little moan leaves her throat as she sucks on my lower lip. Her eyes flutter closed then but I can't close mine. I can't take my eyes off her. The expression on her face as she brushes lips with mine is almost enough to make me release against my leg.

I grip her tighter, a groan shuddering through me as I open my mouth to hers. It's the first movement I make. When Eleanor doesn't pull away but increases her sucking and licking of my lips I grunt and grip her even tighter. Our tongues brush and I lose it.

My mind fogs with desire, and the only thing I can focus on is Eleanor. Her softness, her warmth, her intoxicating scent. Every touch, every kiss, only fans the flames burning within me.

"God, why do you smell so good?" she murmurs against my lips and my eyes flutter closed, a deep groan rumbling through me when she pulls her lips from mine to nuzzle her face into my neck. At the same time, she rocks her hips where she sits on my abdomen, a thick scent slipping into my nostrils that makes my fangs bare with need.

As she lifts her head to kiss me again, my claws move from her hips, one slipping up her back to cradle her head, digits tangling in her hair. The other slides down to her thigh, gripping it firmly as I pull her even closer. Her moans vibrate against my lips, sending shivers down my spine.

"Eleanor," I murmur against her mouth, my voice thick with need.

"Zynar," she whispers back, her voice trembling with a mix of hesitation and longing.

The way she says my name, it's like a plea and a promise all at once. I can't get enough of it. I deepen the kiss, my tongue exploring her mouth, savoring every taste of her. Her hands slide up my chest, nails grazing my scales in a way that sends electric jolts of pleasure through me. Again she shifts against me, rubbing the center of her thighs against my abdomen. I don't even think she realizes what she's doing. That she could want me this much makes something deep inside me flutter and come to life.

My Little Bird has been chained. Locked in a cage. I want to set her free. I want her to find release and if she must use me to do it, it would be the honor of my life.

I groan, pulling back slightly to look into her eyes. They're half-lidded, darkened with desire, and it's the most beautiful sight I've ever seen. "You're driving me crazy, Little Bird," I whisper, my voice rough.

She smiles, a real smile this time, not the forced one from before. It lights up her face, making her look even more stunning. "Good," she breathes, her hands moving to cup my face. "Because you're doing the same to me."

She pants as our lips meet again. The sensation coupled with her sweet scent filling the air makes my cock swing back so hard it slaps her on her behind. She pauses and lifts her head, her eyes going wide.

No. Oh no no no. I don't want to lose this moment.

But instead of climbing off me like I think she will, my Liora whimpers, a look coming into her eyes that I've never seen before. Her hips shift, the center of her thighs rubbing against me again and I growl, fangs baring in raw, primitive need.

"I shouldn't be doing this," she whimpers. "You're here to work. You're not here for me to have sex with."

My palms slide up her thighs, eliciting a tremble from her.

"Do you want to?" I growl the whisper.

With another whimper, Eleanor gives a slight nod. But I can

feel the fight within her. I can feel the uncertainty. Demons of her past chasing her. The relationship with her previous mate maybe. I can already tell he was a fool to let her go. But even though she's said yes, even though she wants to, I can't do it. Not when she might regret this later.

"Use me," I whisper.

She stops moving. Stops rocking her hips against me. "What?"

"Use me, Little Bird. Take your pleasure. There are no bonds or commitments. No pressure. This is about you and what you need." I let the words sink in, wanting her to understand that this moment is hers, and that I'm here for her in any capacity she desires. "You are in control. Always."

Her breath hitches, and I can see the conflict in her eyes.

"You are perfect, Liora," I growl softly. "Everything about you, as you are now, is all that matters to me. If you want this, I'm here. And if you don't, I will stop. Just say the word."

"Zynar...I..." But she hasn't climbed off me. She hasn't tried to get away. Hasn't tried to stop this. So I hold her at the hips, and I move her against me, making her press her center of her thighs against me as her hot core rubs across the tight muscles of my abdomen.

Eleanor whimpers, hands rising to grip my shoulders as her eyelids flutter.

"Feel good, Little Bird?"

"Mm," she murmurs and her hips shunt in my grasp. So eager. So mesmerizing. So beautiful. My cock slaps her on the behind again and her eyelids flutter up as she meets my gaze.

"You're making me crazy," she groans.

I can't take my eyes off her. Gripping her tighter, I force her down on me, hoping the friction is enough to provide her with some relief. She seems to be craving it, and I know I'm right when she whimpers. Holding on to me, her grip gets tighter as she moves her hips before a frustrated sound leaves her lips.

"Not enough," she pants. "I need more."

My core-beat hammers at her words.

"Zynar...Can I..." She reaches back as my cock slaps her behind again and I freeze, grabbing her wrist before she can make contact. My chest is heaving as our gazes lock—hers searching mine in surprise and mine frozen on hers.

"I'm sorry. I didn't— I thought—" She begins to rise t o get off me, and I stop her with my other arm.

Words fail me.

I've dreamed of this moment, *salivated* over it, and now that it's here, I'm caught in a fear that might destroy it all.

"No," I croak. "Don't move, starshine."

My claw is still wrapped around her wrist and we're still frozen, my chest heaving with each breath, her sweet scent clouding my senses. I'm not sure what to do but I can't let this moment end. Not so soon.

"Close your eyes for me?"

Her eyebrows rise a little but then she obliges. A breath shudders through my frame as my cock jerks and slaps against her again.

"Need more friction, Little Bird?"

She runs the tip of her tongue over her lower lip, the movement like temptation's call, before she nods slightly. "Yes."

"I'll give you more friction."

I shift, angling my hips as I release my hold on her wrist and take hold of her hips. Lifting her off me, I balance her with one arm as I pull my cock from the hastily wrapped tunic and allow it to slap against my abdomen. Pre-spend coats my scales immediately and I take another shuddering breath. The sight of this beautiful female hovering over my hard cock makes another burst of spend seep from my tip. It takes the arms of several gods to resist the urge to press into her center.

I stare up at Eleanor, wanting time—this exact moment—to freeze.

"Alright, starshine. Slowly now."

I help her lower and the moment my hard cock fits in between her thighs, Eleanor goes still, a soft gasp on her lips.

"Zynar, you're…"

"Moving too quickly? I can reposition it if you don't like it there."

"No." She flushes. "No. I mean…you're so *big*." She almost whispers the last word, but I hear it, anyway. It sends a throb through my cock that jerks against her heat. Eleanor inhales deeply.

"You don't want me to see it…" Her utterance is also a whisper and I groan. Not because of her words but because I can feel her heat against my shaft. That sweet scent of her rises and all I can feel and see is her.

"Not yet," I finally utter.

"You don't have to hide from me, Zynar," she whispers. "I know you're probably not what I'm used to, but we're both different from what we're used to. I don't mind."

"Mm," I groan. What gods did I pray to for this sweet bird to come into my life? "I do not wish to scare you away, Liora."

Her eyes flutter open then, but she respects my wishes by keeping her gaze on me. The tunic she's wearing covers most of my shaft, anyway. All that's visible is the sloped head that's still seeping pre-spend.

I groan again. "Look what you're making me do, Little Bird."

She looks between us then, her mouth opening before her tongue slides out and runs across her lips.

"Come now," I growl. "Use me."

I grasp her hips again and force her to rub against my hardness. She inhales sharply, hands returning to my shoulders as she grips me tight.

"That's it, Little Bird. Use me."

Eleanor's eyes flutter as she grinds against my shaft. Whatever it is, the tension and friction is what she needs and I will provide it. Matching her rhythm, I roll her hips as she rides, each slide of her heat over my shaft threatening to make me lose my vision to pure bliss.

When she leans in, I purr. "You smell so good, Liora."

"And you," she pants. "Oh, God." She dips her nose to my neck again, her tongue swiping out to lick the soft spattering of scales there as she groans. "You smell *divine*."

Frakk, I might actually climax if this keeps up.

Eleanor grinds her hips, rolling her core against my shaft till I feel remnants of my spend that must have been dripping down my shaft seep through the undergarment she's wearing. I groan at the thought, and when she lifts her head and presses her mouth against mine again, I know I'm lost.

"More," she whimpers. "I need—" She pants, breaths hard against my skin as she whimpers something incomprehensible.

"Tell me what you need, Little Bird, and I will give it to you." Frakk, I'm not even inside her and her little sounds are making me soak my abdomen. When she releases me, lifting one hand to snake between us, I follow her with my claw.

Her hand stops right at her center and my core-beat stutters. So close to her most private spot. Will she allow me to touch her there? But Eleanor doesn't seem to mind that my claw is following her movements, trying to determine what she needs.

When she pushes away her undergarment, I groan with the pure, unhindered sweetness that wafts into my being. I inhale deeply, taking her in as a flutter starts in the center of my chest.

I follow her path and when my digits brush over the softest bits of flesh I have ever touched, I pray to the gods that this is not a dream. That I'm not alone in the outbuilding, hoping for all this. That I'm really living it.

When two of her digits press into her core, I know that if it *is* a dream, I never want to wake.

But the position is awkward. Like this, she loses the friction on my shaft.

"Let me, Little Bird." I pull my arm out, my gaze going blurry and coming back in at the sight of her juices glistening on my digits. But I've no time to savor them right now. She needs me.

I reach around her instead, sliding my claw underneath her tunic to palm her round behind. She whimpers at the same time that I growl. A squeeze and my fangs ache. I want to bite into it. But that's for another sol. Another time.

Slowly, in case I interrupt her, I push her undergarment to the side.

Gods help me. Her scent is intoxicating.

As Eleanor rubs her core against my shaft, I run two digits over her softness, my lids fluttering as I paint a picture of her in my mind. She's so perfect, even her core feels like the petals of the blooms she adores so much. I groan as she whimpers the moment my digit slides over a small bud. Like the bud nestled within a bloom, she pants and whimpers each time that same bud slides over the ridges on my shaft. I store that information for later, my digits moving down as Eleanor nestles her head into my neck again, inhaling deeply as she slides over my shaft.

When I reach her opening, I replace her hand with my claw, sliding two digits in that makes her stiffen, her chest heaving so hard, I wonder if I hurt her.

But she doesn't pull away. Instead, she says, "Yes."

I seep. My cock weeps.

Her entrance is so small, so tight, it grips my digits like a vacuum sucking them inside her. The unbelievable heat that spreads through my claw as I pump the digits inside her, almost makes me release again. With my free claw, I force her hips to rock and rub that little bud against my shaft as I bring her closer to a climax with my digits alone.

It's sweet torture. Each thrust, I imagine as my own. As if it is my cock entering her, sliding deep into the same heat that grips me now.

"Eleanor," I groan.

"Oh God, Zynar I think I'm gonna—"

"Use me starshine. Take all that you need."

She whimpers into my neck and when I feel her mouth open, her teeth closing around my skin, I spurt. My cock throbs, sending a gush of spend between us as Eleanor screams into my skin. The climaxes catch us both unawares and we're left in a shuddering heap of flesh and spend.

"Sweet Liora."

I slip my digits from within her tight sheath, lifting my claw to the light. Her spend is clear, glistening. I bring the digits to my mouth at the same time that she lifts her head and watches me taste her for the first time.

That strange flutter in my chest heightens, almost as if my core-beat is interrupted. It's in the background of my mind as I lick my entire claw clean, taking every bit of Eleanor that I can get. She tastes like nothing I've ever had before and yet, like something so uniquely familiar.

"You are temptation," I growl.

A breath releases from her making her shoulders sag. With her petals still pressed against me, I feel a throb go through her core.

"Oh, Zynar." Eleanor rests against me, and I wrap my arms around her.

"Don't worry," she murmurs. "I'll get up soon."

"We can stay like this for as long as you like, Liora."

I feel her smile. I feel her joy go right through me. My core-beat skips and that flutter intensifies to the point where my core-beat cuts out for several clicks before crashing, the organ racing.

Never had that happen before, and for a moment, I pause in a sort of scared anticipation. But core-rhythms don't start like that. If my core-rhythm ever sang, I wouldn't have to guess about what's happening. It would be undeniable.

I take a moment to breathe before pulling Eleanor tighter

against me, worried she might squirm away at the fact that my spend is soaking through her night tunic. But she doesn't move. She remains there, letting me hold her. Letting me realize one thing.

This female…

I *need* her. Not just in this moment but in every way possible. The thought of claiming her, of making her mine, is almost overwhelming. But for now, I'm content to lose myself in her, to let her soft moans and sweet kisses consume me completely.

Because if I can't give her all of me, I don't deserve to ask of her the same.

14

ZYNAR

’m awake when Eleanor slides off me and creeps out of the outbuilding. Immediately, loss of her warmth makes the entire building feel cold. Curling in on myself, I open my eyes only the moment that I hear the doors close. I have to force breaths through my nostrils, my core-beat still unsteady and my lungs struggling for air. I blow a small laugh through my mouth. I've heard other beings say it before, but never thought I'd experience it myself. This Little Bird actually takes my breath away. Stretching, my arms and legs splay as I stare up at the dark roof.

That was…beyond anything I've ever experienced before.

Taking measured breaths, I lie like that, trying to categorize what just happened between us. I made her climax. I'm sure of it. Just the memory of her juices on my claws, her taste…oh frakk, I could feast on her for a lifetime.

My cock grows hard now at that thought. Would she allow me to? Would she allow my tongue to bring her pleasure like my shaft and claw did? I shudder at the possibility. Even if she doesn't allow me to enter her, I'm already intoxicated by simply the thought of her taking pleasure from me each sol.

I grip myself again now, cock so hard it feels like metal in my fist, and I pump. My eyes flutter closed, head tilted back as I replay the evening's events. Over and over again, I replay her little whimpers, how her thighs squeezed as she rubbed her core along my shaft, how she buried her face into my neck and scented me... Oh Eleanor, Little Bird... How will I ever leave this farm when the job is done? When she no longer needs me here?

The thought is enough to make my claw slow down, each pump torturously slow as I consider the implications. But then my claw speeds up again. I'll find reason for her to make me stay. I'll work hard. Make her want to keep me here.

I will give my Little Bird all she needs in the hope that she will want me to stay. That she'll see I'm more than just a worker here; that I can be something more for her.

The thought propels me, each pump of my claw bringing me closer to the edge. My mind is consumed by the vision of Eleanor, her warmth, her touch, her scent. The fantasy is almost too much to bear, but I cling to it, letting it fuel my desire, my need, my determination.

When I finally find release, it's with her name on my lips, a growl that echoes through the outbuilding. I fall back against the bale, panting, my mind a whirlwind of emotions. Satisfaction, longing, fear, hope—all tangled together in a knot that centers on one truth: I've never felt like this about any female I've ever encountered. From the very first moment, Eleanor caught my attention.

I...I think I need her as much as she might need me.

Breathing heavily, I clean myself off, each movement deliberate, my mind already racing with ways to prove myself to her. To show her that I'm not just here for the job, but for her. Her human matebonds are not the same as Kari. If it were, she could not be so far away from her past mate. That means her species has a different approach to relationships, one that allows for change and new beginnings. This realization gives me hope. My core-rhythm might never sing, but I will give her my all till my last breath.

I sit up, breaths still slightly unsteady as I stare down with a frown at my cock as it slowly rises again.

I want her.

My Little Bird.

Only fate sent me to this farm. I cannot ignore it.

As the light of dawn begins to seep into the building, I make a silent vow: I will show Eleanor that I am here for her; that I can be the partner she needs. No matter what it takes.

BY THE TIME the sun rises, I'm already in the field.

Oogas mill about lazily, somewhat annoyed that all their grass-feed has been cut down. One bumps me in the thigh with its head and I growl playfully at it before rolling over the bale I'd brought out earlier.

"This should tide you over until I move you and your herd to the outbuilding," I murmur, absentmindedly rubbing a claw across my chest. There's an ache there. Slight. I lean on the tilling machine, frowning as I focus on steadying my breaths. Did I overdo it last cycle? Pulled too much spend from my sac? I've never had to make myself climax so many times to reach satisfaction, and, what's strange is that I still exited the outbuilding with a hard cock. My breaths come a little harder than usual, my core-beat a little unsteadier than it usually is. But I'm hardly paying attention either. My gaze keeps slipping to the lodge, searching for signs Eleanor is awake.

Sweat rises underneath my scales as I till the field when my gaze shifts to the lodge again. The moment I catch movement behind the window, my core-beat goes awry. I stop working, staring at the lodge before I'm suddenly moving toward it, drawn by some invisible string.

I try to think of a reason for bothering her so early. I can perhaps ask for her direction on the tilling. Ask what she wants me to do. Yes. I will do that.

I'm on the porch, my fist formed and hovering at her door when I pause.

My core-beat does that strange thing again. Like a stutter and a restart.

I haven't seen the Liora since she slipped from my arms and crept out into the shadows. What if she regrets what transpired between us?

I knock anyway and I hear sound behind the door immediately.

"Coming!"

I almost groan at just the sound of her voice. I want nothing more than to make her come. It's all that's been on my mind for the past few sols.

The door opens, and Eleanor is standing there. Her hands are covered in white dust that smudges some parts of her tunic. Her hair's slightly tousled, particles of the same white dust in the strands where she's obviously brushed her hair back. She smiles at me, her entire face lighting up as she turns away and hurries back inside.

"Come on in!" She disappears into the meal prep room where a curious scent is emanating from. "I've been up trying to make some meatloaf. The ingredients are different but the little computer's been a real help."

I step inside, my gaze shifting around the room as if I've never entered the space before. Shutting the front door behind me, I walk slowly in the direction she went. When I stand within the doorframe of the meal prep room, I'm caught in two glorious scents.

Her. Undeniably her. And the scent of whatever she's creating. I lean against the doorframe, just watching her flutter about. She looks alive today. At least one of us seems to have gotten some rest.

"It might be nothing like you've had before. Alien cuisine—and I don't mean that in a derogatory way or anything—seems pretty plain for the most part. At least, what I've had. Nutrient bars. Bland porridges. I know it can't all be like that, especially judging from what New Horizons sent me to start with, but I thought I'd try making something you'd probably enjoy eating too." She's fluttering about as she talks. Grabbing utensils. Checking the cookstove. Her gaze darts to me and I see her cheeks warm.

"What is it?"

"Hm?" I blink, easing up off the doorframe.

"You're smiling. Slept well?"

My gaze heats immediately, but she doesn't look away. "I didn't do much resting for the entire dark cycle."

She does that sound in her throat, clearing it, before she shifts her gaze away from mine with a smile on her lips. "Well, me neither."

A purr starts in my throat and I have to fold my arms across my chest before I reach for her.

"Come in, Zynar," she says low. "Don't be a stranger. Wash your hands. The food's almost ready."

I swagger in. Frakk, I've never felt the need to do that before, but this female is making me feel many things I've never felt before. Washing my claws at the sink, I watch her over my shoulder as she pulls two large rolls from the cookstove. The smell is divine and my mouth waters. Turning, I reach over her, caging her in with my arms as I grab the drying towel resting just before her.

The slightest brush of her behind against my groin and I'm suddenly aware of my very hard cock.

"Tempting," I purr.

Eleanor tilts her head to look up at me. "Really? Does it smell good to you?"

This close, every movement she makes causes her to brush against me. I take forever to dry my claws on purpose. "You have no idea how good it smells."

Her smile makes the corners of her eyes crinkle. Reaching for the tray, I balance it in one hand as I allow her to slip out from under me. She gets two flat plates and places the utensils on them before she heads out into the main room where the meal table is. There, she sets the plates down and reaches for the food from me. I watch her, fascinated, as she cuts the large rolls. Sweet flavor fills the air and I'm actually looking forward to trying it.

"Sit. I'll get the drinks."

I watch as she hurries back for the drinks before returning. Her gaze shifts to me with a question, probably because she ordered me to sit. I grin, loving how her brows furrow when she's confused, as I walk around to her side and pull out her chair. Her cheeks flame and she does a little dip of her head before sitting. Once she's settled, I move around to my side.

"Let me," I purr, reaching for the rolls. I handle them with care, not wanting to destroy the meal she so painstakingly made for us as I serve her first.

"Thank you," she whispers, but as I serve myself a short moment later, I find that she's not eating. Instead, she's watching me carefully.

She's nervous? If she only knew I would and will eat anything she presents before me. So, I take a bite of the meatlohf. Probably too zealously, as it just exited the cookstove. I swallow it down anyway, prepared to tell her how great it is even if that's not the case. But I don't have to pretend. Just like everything concerning Eleanor, the meal is good. Mouthwatering. I groan, relaxing into the seat at my back.

"It's good?" She perks up a little, sitting straighter in her chair. "You like it?"

The hope on her face is adorable.

I nod. "I've never had anything like this before. And that's a shame."

I take another bite, not even caring about the heat. This time, I close my eyes and groan. Something swells inside me, interrupting my core-beat. Something warm. It makes me rub at my chest as I chew, but the sensation only increases as Eleanor smiles and begins eating too, taking much smaller more reasonable bites than I do.

I slow down, not wanting to look like a savage.

She glances at me now and then, her throat moving, the tip of her tongue reaching out to lick her lips. When the meal's almost done and I'm sipping one of the drinks she provided, she lifts her own drink too. The drink cylinder to her lips, she suddenly speaks.

"Zynar—"

"Yes, Liora?"

Her cheeks heat. "About last night…" She takes a sip of the drink.

"Would you like to do it again?"

She sputters, drink spewing from her lips as she chokes. My eyes widen but then she's laughing, coughing, holding up a hand to tell me she's okay, and wiping the liquid away.

She clears her throat, taking time to clean herself before she glances my way again. I stop eating, drinking, I'm not even breathing as I wait for her response. But Eleanor is taking her time. She's considering it. Considering her next words.

"Yes." She meets my gaze. My core-beat flutters. She's not looking away. Not blinking. Not hiding from her feelings. She wants me, too.

"Now?" I straighten, ready to rise. My cock's already been ready since dawn.

Eleanor sputters. "No." Her gaze shifts to the outdoors. "We have to get the oogas in. It's supposed to rain today."

I lean in across the table. "Later then. In the dark cycle, after the work is done and we are free."

Her cheeks heat, but a slow smile stretches her lips. There's a glint in her eyes I've never seen before and it makes me rumble at the sight of her like this. She wants me. Holy frakk, she does.

"Later tonight then," she whispers, her eyes on me as she takes another small bite of the meatlohf. I lean back against the chair, satisfied.

This is good. Very good.

1 5

ELEANOR

I've never been more tense in my life.

My entire body is buzzing with anticipation.

Did I just make a sex date?

Yes. Yes, I did.

My first sex date and it's with an alien so well-endowed that I noticed his impressive size even before feeling it, as he dried his hands on the towel. A flutter had gone through me then. Took everything within me not to close my eyes and lean back into him. The pure power in that shaft makes my core tremble. I'm already so needy just thinking about it. And his scent? Good god. I've never smelled a man that made me want to press my face against his skin and just breathe.

Now, as we finish eating, Zynar's watching me like a wolf might watch sheep. The only thing he's not doing is salivating. Those yellow-slitted eyes follow my every slight movement. Each time I swallow, his gaze shifts to my throat. When I open my mouth to eat, his gaze slips to my lips.

The intensity of his stare sends shivers down my spine, making me hyper-aware of every breath I take, every move I make. I'm suddenly being seen, as a woman, an *attractive* woman that's wanted by the male I actually like. Zynar's not hiding that he wants to take me to bed. As a matter of fact, I can tell he's still hard from the way he keeps adjusting himself in the chair.

I reach for my drink, taking a slow sip, hoping to calm my racing heart. Zynar's eyes follow the movement, his gaze almost tangible. Each shift, each look, sends a swell of power through me. Why? Because *I'm* the reason for all these reactions. It's like my whole being is waking up after being dormant for so long.

My confidence rises with each glance, each subtle shift in his seat. It dawns on me that for too long, I've felt invisible, my desires and needs buried under mundane obligation and duty. But now, with Zynar, everything is different. His want, his need, pulls me into the present, making me realize just how much I've *missed* feeling desired. Something so simple. Something craved by simply being human—and I was denied it for so long.

Perhaps it's reckless to let down my guard after so brief an acquaintance. Perhaps I'm a fool. But with Zynar, the more time I spend with him, the more caution seems to slip my grasp. In his presence, all feels right, all other concerns drifting like dandelion fluff on the breeze. Being near him feels...good.

I take another bite of the makeshift meatloaf, the flavors barely registering as I can only focus on the heated gaze fixed on me. Zynar picks at the last bit of meatloaf as if he doesn't want the meal to end, and I smile.

"I can make another for you, if you like?"

"Will you share it with me, Liora?"

I smile again and nod. "I'd love to. It's a date."

His head tilts. "A date?"

"It's like a...hmmm... a date is when two people spend time together to enjoy each other's company. Usually, it's something special, like having a meal or doing an activity they both like. It's a way to get to know each other better."

His gaze darkens immediately. I watch as Zynar pops the last bit of meatloaf into his mouth. "Then this dark cycle is a date, yes?"

My cheeks warm as I nod. "I guess, yes."

Zynar stands and my eyes widen as they fall to his crotch. His trousers are tented like a massive mast is holding them up. He walks around to me, dipping his lips to my ear. "Then I very much look forward to our date tonight, Liora."

That bud nestled at my center throbs so hard, I know I could reach a climax right now if he touched me there. My whole body shudders with something inexplicable as his claw brushes across my shoulder before he heads outside.

I'm left with a throbbing clit and a throbbing heart.

Turning in my chair, I watch as Zynar heads back across the field. He begins herding the oogas together. Far off in the distance, I can see the sky darkening. Swallowing down a lump of need that had begun rising in my throat, I stand and head back to the kitchen to clean up.

As the hours pass, the house remains quiet, save for the occasional chirp of the insects outside. I putter around, wiping down the counters, organizing the pantry, and even taking a moment to gaze out the window now and then, catching glimpses of Zynar moving among the herd. The afternoon wears on, the sky growing more ominous with each passing minute.

I thought the computer said light wind and rain, or perhaps that was my understanding of it. It doesn't look like what's coming will be light at all. Glancing up at the roof, I thank God I had the sense to hire Zynar just a day after arriving here. What would I have done if the rain had come when my roof had been filled with holes?

I'm just done cleaning up when I notice Zynar still out in the field trying to get a stubborn ooga to follow the rest. Stepping outside, I giggle as I head toward him. He seems to be giving the thing a pep talk and when I draw closer, I catch the end of his speech.

"...and if you just cooperate, you'll get extra rations tonight. Deal?"

The ooga flicks its ear, looking at Zynar with what can only be described as mild disdain. Zynar sighs, rubbing the back of his neck, clearly at a loss. I can't help but laugh at the scene.

Zynar turns, jerking his chin at the ooga as he rises from where he's crouched. "This one doesn't want to move."

"Well, the rain's coming. It has to."

Zynar's watching me with that same gaze again. But I'm dressed in a simple brown tunic. I look like I'm wearing a sac and he's looking at me like I'm a buffet and he's starving.

"We'll have to leave him."

My brows shoot up. The thought of leaving the big guy out on the field all alone makes me feel bad. But he's far too heavy to lift and if he won't follow the others, we have no choice.

"Don't worry, Liora. They're herd animals. He will follow."

I gaze at the stubborn ooga for a little before nodding. "Let's get the others in."

Zynar's a great teacher. He teaches me that sound that Xarion did that told the oogas to march. With a branch he cut, he shows me how to herd them in the direction I want to go in and soon I'm doing it by myself. I shudder to think of what I'd have had to do if he wasn't here. There's no handbook for this.

By the time we get the animals into the barn, settling them into the various stalls and giving each set fresh hay, the brilliant pink sky is clouded over. There's a chill in the air now from the sun being blotted out, and I run my hands across my arms. Turning to face Zynar, I watch as he lifts massive bales and rearranges them. There's not nearly enough left for him to sleep on. Not that it was a good place to sleep in the first place. My heart rate picks up at the fact that he'll have to spend the night somewhere else. Possibly with me.

Stepping back outside the barn, a fat raindrop slaps me on the forehead and I duck, using my hands to cover my head as more follow.

"It's coming!" I shiver, hurrying toward the house as quickly as my legs can carry me when an arm snakes around my waist, pulling me backward. I squeal as Zynar pulls me against his chest, his warm breath brushing against my ear as his deep voice fills my auditory canal.

"Why are you running, Little Bird? Don't want to get your feathers wet?"

My eyes almost roll back at the intensity of pleasure that courses through me with just the sensation of him pressed against my back. I feel when his cock throbs, insistent and longing against my ass, and I almost groan. He's been sporting a hard-on for the entire time since the breakfast table.

Rain begins to pelt down as Zynar pulls me against his chest while turning slowly.

"You don't like the rain, Liora?"

I stop resisting, even though I didn't intend to get wet. At least, not of this kind. Choking on a laugh, I squint as rainfall pelts my glasses, making it nearly impossible to see clearly.

"Yes, I do. I just…" I just what? When was the last time I didn't hurry inside from the rain? Run into a building or some other shelter. Used my umbrella to hide away from the raindrops. It was always about not getting my shoes wet. Or my hair. Sometimes I didn't want to get my dress wet and other times it was just because other humans would look at me as if I was crazy if I just decided to walk in the rain with no protection.

But right now? Right now, none of those things matter. They don't even exist.

I relax in Zynar's arms some more as he sways in the rain. When he throws his head back and whoops, the sound echoing then fading in the growing sound of the rain, I chuckle. I press my head back against his chest, and I whoop too.

It's…freeing.

My hair's a mess, but Zynar doesn't seem to care. My tunic is soaked, the thin fabric pressing against me, and I make no effort to hide my body from him. Not after last night. Not after seeing and now feeling his attraction pressing into me. As we turn slowly in the growing rain, I begin to laugh.

I feel alive.

Zynar turns me to face him and it's only then that I realize that he's sobered up. He's not smiling anymore. There is only one expression on his face. Pure, raw, need.

My smile fades slowly as I'm sucked into that gaze, and when I lift my arms he bends slowly, allowing me to wrap them around his neck. We stare at each other then. Me staring into those bottomless yellow eyes and him staring into mine.

"May I, Liora?"

I nod, acquiescing to whatever he's asking for without even asking what it is. When his head dips, his lips brushing against mine, it's with a heat that sears the rain off my skin.

I pant, opening my lips to his as his kiss becomes more insistent. Like a man starved and left to die in the desert, Zynar takes my lips like it's an oasis he never thought he'd see. I whimper, arms tightening around his neck as he lifts me in his arms, wrapping my legs around him with little effort as he balances my weight with a single arm under my behind. He grips it then, kneads the skin, and my core flutters in anticipation.

I'm dimly aware that we're moving. That he's carrying me toward the house. The hard beat of the rain stops as we step onto the porch and then my bum brushes against the hard wood of the door. With one leg, he kicks the door in, pausing just inside to close it with his free arm. All the while, his tongue tangles with mine, making that energy within me rise, that warmth within me extend. That *need*.

I only know we're in the bedroom because Zynar pauses. Just stops suddenly. The bed's in our path. There's nowhere else to go.

With his free hand, he helps me out of my tunic, revealing inch upon inch of my skin. I hesitate, past experiences rearing their ugly heads before I push them away. Lifting my arms, I allow him to remove my tunic. There's no bra, only panties. I'm practically bare before him and my heart strikes hard against my ribs at that very fact.

No one's seen me naked in a long time. Not since I was abducted, at least. Before that, I was always clothed. Even in my own home. To have him look at me now…

My gaze shifts up to Zynar and my heart stops at the look in his eyes.

With a growl, he sets me down gently on the bed, my back hitting the blanket before I brace myself up on my elbows. Zynar slips my glasses off my nose before setting them down. Easing back, he looks at me. His eyes are wide, his pupils blown.

"Zynar?" I whisper, but he doesn't respond. His chest heaves as if his breathing is no longer regular and farther down, his cock is straining so hard against his trousers that I fear it might poke a hole in it. It throbs, jerks so hard that I see the sloped head pulse, a stream of pre-cum seeping from his tip to soak through the material.

My mouth goes dry as I pull my gaze away from his crotch and back to his face. His eyes are still wide, his throat moving. The pupils are so dilated, they don't even look slitted anymore.

He looks intoxicated.

I'm not sure what to make of his response. Zynar isn't moving. I don't think he's even breathing even though his chest is heaving so much.

Zynar's looking at me like no man has ever looked at me before. As if he can see nothing else. As if he wants to consume me. This is levels higher than the intensity of his gaze this morning at the table. Back then, I'd thought I felt like a sheep under the gaze of a hungry wolf. I'd thought that was the extent of his need. I was wrong. So very wrong.

Every inch of my skin tingles under his scrutiny, as if his gaze alone can set me aflame. I swallow hard, trying to steady my breath, but it's a losing battle. The air between us is charged, electric, and I can feel it in every fiber of my being.

"Liora," he breathes my name, and it's like a caress, a promise, and a plea all wrapped into one. The sound of it sends shivers down my spine, and I'm acutely aware of every movement, every shift in the air around us.

Zynar suddenly falls to the floor before me, directly between my legs. There, his gaze scans my body and I get the urge to hide myself again. I won't. I don't. When his arm caresses my legs and he leans in, pressing his face on the inside of one thigh, the growl that vibrates through him as he inhales deeply sends a tremor straight to my center.

"I knew you were soft all over. So incredibly pale and soft. But I never expected this," he growls.

I swallow hard, blinking down at him. "I look strange to you, I suppose." It almost comes out as a squeak.

Both of his claws caress my thighs before moving upward to the slight bulge of my belly. He grips the fat there too, kneads it. *Groans* as he grips my flesh.

My sore pulses. Need swells inside me.

"Not strange. Never strange. From the very first moment I saw you, you were never strange. Familiar, and yet I don't know why." His mouth opens and he nibbles my inner thigh in a way that makes me fist the blanket beneath me. Inhaling deeply again, Zynar runs his hot tongue against my skin. My eyelids flutter at the sensation, at the promise that his tongue might go other places.

"You're beautiful, Liora," he groans, his claws sliding from my belly and down underneath me to cup my ass. There, he grips the flesh with such power, he lifts my hips from the bed. My crotch, makeshift linen panties and all, is presented right in front of his face. Zynar groans, fangs baring as those intoxicated eyes fasten on my pussy. There, he kneads my cheeks, squeezing them together and pulling them apart as he stares at the center of my thighs.

"Will you allow me, Liora?"

Again, I don't know what he's referring to exactly. I nod anyway, unable to form words that won't come out as a moan. When Zynar leans in slowly, his nostrils flaring as he presses his face directly into my pussy, I see stars.

The first swipe of his tongue comes quickly. Almost as if he doesn't want to delay lest I change my mind. He groans at the same time I do and then it's like the chains are broken. Balancing me on both arms, he pulls me against his mouth, a moan rumbling through him and vibrating against my clit as he sucks me through the panties.

My legs go dead. That feeling when your whole body reacts to an intense moment, and you're caught between wanting to move and being completely paralyzed by the intensity of the situation. His eyes are locked on mine, and I can see a myriad of emotions swirling within them—desire, admiration, a hint of desperation. It's overwhelming.

Pleasure rises in my core, my whole being lighting up as he suddenly growls and rips my panties off. Well, I needed new ones anyway. I watch them fall somewhere in the room right before my eyes roll over in my head. Because he sucks. He places his entire mouth over me and he sucks. His tongue swipes out and rolls through my folds before he sucks again, repeating the motion as if he's collecting every bit of my essence.

When his tongue connects with my clit and I jerk with the jolt of pleasure, he growls and murmurs something against me that sounds so incredibly dirty despite that I can't parse what he said. He swirls his tongue on my clit now. Playing with it. Licking it. Slurping. Sucking and even gently running it between his teeth. When I feel the pressure rising, I can't hold on to the bed anymore.

I reach down, grabbing on to his mane of green hair, digging my fingers in down to the root. I wonder if it might hurt him and I almost loosen my grip, but when a moan of pleasure rockets from the pit of his belly, all I can do is hold on as a wave of pleasure crashes through me.

I hold on like my life depends on it, even as my hips shunt against his face with shameless abandon. I can't even control it. My entire body shudders with the intensity of my release. My head falls back, my eyes wide as I stare up into my new roof, the intensity of the climax as strong as the raindrops falling hard outside.

My breath stalls in my chest. My heart doing a strange fluttering thing as I try to breathe again. At the same time, tremors go through my thighs, my legs. I shake, I shudder, as Zynar still laps at me, licking up every drip of sweet nectar that seeps from my core.

I've never, in my life, had a climax like that one. And what's worse, what's bad, is the horrible realization that despite that, I want more. I want him.

I pant his name, trembling hands shifting to caress his jaw. He growls, tongue still swiping at me but slower now. It still sends little rockets through my belly that detonate and shoot fireworks through my entire being.

When he nibbles into my inner thigh, lapping at my skin, his tongue still swirling as he moves lower, I shudder again. Zynar grabs my ass, his mouth opening as his teeth trail over my skin. When he bites down, not hard enough to break skin but hard enough for me to feel his fangs, I shudder again. He's biting my ass, groaning, and the sound and sensation only make me go weak.

My entire body trembles as he laps at the spot he bit into, another rumble going through him as his gaze shifts up to mine. On his lips is a glistening sheen. Evidence of my arousal. I've never seen a more delicious sight.

For the first time in my life, I've had an orgasm that's knocked my socks off and I still want more. My gaze shifts over Zynar's handsome god-like face before moving down his chest. Corded muscles that beg for my hands to explore them flex as he adjusts his grip and rises, leaning over me. My gaze shifts lower, to the tent in his trousers. To the undeniable proof that he wants me as much as I want him.

But will he let me?

Last night, when I tried to touch him, he caught my wrist so fast my heart had jumped, alarm making me go still. He didn't want me to touch him then. Didn't want me to see him. I can't imagine why.

While I pleasured myself using his hard shaft to grind on, the pleasure that had shot through me had been indescribable. There were ridges. Lots of them all along the shaft. I could feel them with each movement against him. Even thinking about them now sends a throb through my core. If he thinks I'll be afraid of those, he's wrong. All his differences, everything about him, are the exact reasons why I'm attracted to him so much. He's damn perfect.

When my gaze slides back to his, I can tell he was watching me stare at the outline of his dick. He watches me like he wants to soak in my every reaction.

"Let me?" I whisper, stretching a hand toward him but not moving all the way to touch him.

He stiffens.

"Zynar," I whisper. "I don't care what you look like." I meet his gaze, letting him know I'm sincere. "I want to please you, too."

A sound rolls in his throat. "You already please me, Liora."

I let out a small, exasperated huff. "Not in the way you really need me to right now."

He shifts, shoulders rolling as he stands up straight. I'm reminded of how tall he is. How he swallows up the space. And just how small he makes me feel. Delicate.

I'm naked on the bed, looking up at a hunk of an alien standing over me with a tent so large it could provide shelter.

Easing up so I'm more upright, I reach my hand toward him again. "You don't want me to?"

"More than anything, Liora. It is all I can think of."

"Then let me." Even to my ears, my voice has gone incredibly soft. Zynar snarls a little, a reaction I'm realizing has nothing to do with aggression but rather him holding himself back.

"I simply do not want to scare you, Little Bird. I want to give you the best parts of me. Always."

His words tear at my heart, making my gaze and my entire body soften. I shuffle toward him, moving until both my legs close in on either side of his. My feet hit the floor as I sit there at the edge of the bed, naked and with an alien between my thighs —only, not in the position I really want him to be. Though, this will do. For before me is something that's rock-hard and just seeping for me.

I meet his eyes again and Zynar's watching me, chin touching his chest as he stares down at me. With the sun no longer shining through the windows, the rain clouds casting gray across the sky, the shadows make him look like something I should be afraid of. Something beautifully tempting but undoubtedly dangerous.

I smile a little to myself. Zynar's both.

"I want to," I whisper, running my tongue over my lips. He watches the movement, his cock bobbing before me so forcefully it almost looks painful being constrained. "Let me. I promise I won't think less of you. I promise I won't run away."

He studies me for a long moment before his shoulders sag. I

almost jump for joy. Joy I've never felt at the thought of having a dick in my face, until now. But Zynar doesn't release himself. He's stiff. Still. Unmoving as he watches me. His chest heaves as he continues to look down at me, the slits in his eyes still so blown they almost look convex.

So I make the first move. My shoulders rise, confidence brimming as I take this into my hands.

I start at his hips. Iridescent scales disappear underneath the waist of his trousers. Clasping him lightly by the hips, I try to figure out how to release his trousers. I run my hands there, feeling his taut muscles even as I get a little cheeky and move my hands around to his ass as well. I grip his butt and squeeze. The ultimate power in his hips makes me almost whimper with the thoughts rising in my head.

I close my eyes briefly, forcing myself to focus as I shift my attention back to his trousers. I see it shortly after. A simple clasp released by a button. The moment I press the button, the pants loosen and begin sliding down his thighs, halted only by the still-hidden cock that's pointing straight at my face. The pants hang there on it like it's a hook.

Gripping the waist of the trousers, I pause, gaze shifting to him again just to make sure he's okay with this. He remains unmoving, shoulders tense, his entire body still as he watches me, waiting. I shift my gaze back down, my anticipation building like that thrum that's starting once more in my core.

Sliding the garment down slowly, my eyes widen with each inch of him that's revealed. My breath hitches. My throat goes dry.

He's huge. As the pants fall and he's revealed, I can't believe this is the thing I'd grinded on the night before. Pink and purple scales splatter at his base before disappearing into dark, smooth purple skin that covers his entire shaft. He's ridged, on both the upper and underside. Small frills decorate the upper shaft alternating between raised bumps that form a line straight to his tip.

He's slightly curved and tapered, the opening of his sloped head seeping clear liquid that stretches and dangles from his tip. He's thicker at the base, the area so thick I'm sure it would feel like a knot. Beneath that, his hanging sac throbs, rising slightly as it tightens at my attention before relaxing again. More precum seeps from his tip.

He's magnificent. My entire body heats at the thought of him sliding deep inside me. I quiver, a pulse going through my core. But then I still. I still because I suddenly see why Zynar didn't want me face to face with his dick. And I suddenly realize why, through all this, he's still standing as if he's holding his breath.

There are scars. So entranced by the difference of his cock to a human's, I didn't even notice them. Not at first. Now I see them everywhere. All over his cock. His lower abdomen. That same area he'd touched absentmindedly while telling me the story of what the Tasqals did to him and his people.

I inhale sharply and scold myself. Fighting to not show a reaction, I don't respond otherwise immediately. I don't want him to think it makes any difference in the way I think he looks. As a matter of fact, it does nothing to deter from his beauty. But the scars, they represent wounds that must have been so painful. They crisscross underneath his skin like a lattice. Deep gorges that have left their mark on his skin forever.

A pain develops in my chest. Hatred for the beings that took me from my planet; the same beings that did this to him. It is difficult to control. But I must, because this moment isn't about them. It's about him. He needs someone to tell him he's not any less because of his scars.

He needs *me* to tell him.

I pull my gaze away from his shaft to look up at him. Those yellow eyes hold mine immediately, searching for any sign of pity or revulsion. I refuse to give him either. Instead, I reach out, my fingers trembling slightly as they hover over the marks.

"These…" I whisper, my voice steadying, "are proof of your strength, Zynar. They don't make you any less beautiful."

He studies me for a moment longer, his throat moving as if he's swallowing hard, weighing my words, trying to determine if they're genuine. It's only then that his shoulders loosen somewhat. He relaxes a little and his cock bobs in the air before me, demanding my attention.

My gaze shifts back to it. "I would like to touch you now," I whisper.

"Please, Liora."

I almost coo.

I start at his base, wrapping both hands around the thick shaft. He jerks in my grasp, a groan emanating through his entire being. He's so silky smooth under my grasp that I slide both hands from base to tip, something akin to desperate need rising within me again as my hands move over the ridges, frills, and bumps toward his tip. There, his precum rises as if milked and I take some in my palm and use it as lubrication as I move back down his shaft.

Zynar grunts, his claws forming fists at his sides as if he's trying to keep his hands to himself. Trying to give me space to do what I want without interruption, coercion, or instruction.

I smile, a pulse going straight to my core as I stroke him up and down. He's so fucking beautiful. I wasn't even lying when I told him he was. Scars and all, he looks like something I want. No. Something I need.

I scoot closer and massage him some more. There's hardly an inch between me and his sloped head and the moment I lean in, the tip of my tongue making contact, is the moment everything I knew about want and need shifts into something primal and all-consuming. Zynar's entire body reacts, a shudder coursing through him at the same time that I pull him into my mouth, a moan vibrating through my throat.

I'm surprised. Shocked. And yet still, I can't stop. I suck, rolling my tongue over his head as I moan again. I'd intended to lick him, take my time, but the taste of him is like a drug. The scent of him like a recipe for intoxication. My pussy throbs, my clit engorging as I suck and there's the urge to slide my hands between my legs and work myself off as I work him.

This isn't...this isn't like anything I've ever experienced before. The taste of his pre-cum on my tongue is like orange marmalade that ignites every nerve ending across my spine. Rocket surges go through me, erupting in my lower abdomen, sending little lightning sparks down to my core. I bob my head, trying to get as much of him into my mouth, down my throat, as I can. The urge to simply consume every drop, every inch of him, overtakes me.

My eyes roll back and I look up at him with lowered lids, a thrill going through me at his expression.

He's snarling, fangs bared, lips pulled back. When my gaze shifts over his chest, down his torso, I catch sight of his claws in my periphery. There's blood, bright and red like my own. It should alarm me. All it does is ramp up this fever within me. Because Zynar's clenched his fist so hard to prevent himself from touching me while I do this. He's giving me space. Allowing me to pull back whenever I want. But, at the same time, he's experiencing such intense pleasure that his claws extended, digging into his clenched fist.

I slow down, pulling my head up from the point where his tip was just at that point in my throat that I could bear without choking. I use my hands now, giving him a slow pump as I gaze up at him.

"Liora," Zynar grunts. "You torture me."

A smile stretches my lips. Seeing the effect I have on him, the raw desire in his eyes, fills me with a heady sense of power. It's intoxicating to know that I can make this strong, fierce male tremble with just a touch, a look.

His breath hitches as I lift one hand and run my fingers

lightly over his abdomen, tracing the contours of his muscles. "Do I?" I whisper, my voice laced with playful innocence I've never had the confidence to use before. "And what will you do about it?"

His eyes darken, a growl rumbling low in his chest. "Anything you want, Little Bird. Anything to make you mine."

His words make a strange tingle go through me. They're serious words. They spell commitment. Why am I not terrified? Instead, the surge of confidence I feel is exhilarating. I lean closer, my lips brushing against his lower abdomen. The scales there shiver.

"Then show me," I murmur, "how much you want me."

ELEANOR

With a primal growl, Zynar pulls back, releasing himself from my fingers as he suddenly kneels before me. He opens my thighs with one singular motion, powerful arms spreading me for him. I gasp. I don't have time for any other response before his lips are covering my pussy again.

A moan barrels through me as I grab the bed. Zynar licks and sucks with fervor, his tongue moving over my inner thighs and every part of me down there, before he growls something about beauty and perfection.

We're moving then, him rising as he wraps both arms around my lower half and lifts me. We climb up higher on the bed before he sets me down and leans over me, pulling me into a kiss that sets my body aflame, every nerve ending igniting with desire. This time, it's my turn to tremble, to be consumed by the intensity of his need. And I realize, with a thrill of anticipation, that this is just the beginning.

"Eleanor," he grunts, breath across my lips. "Do you want to?"

"Yes! God yes."

Zynar growls before looking down between us and pausing. There's a frown on his brow, some worry, even as his chest heaves with unmeasured breaths.

"What is it?" I whisper.

"You're smaller than females of my kind." His tortured gaze meets mine. "I will never forgive myself if I hurt you, Little Bird."

"You won't." My voice has gone hoarse. I can barely speak. "It will fit." And that's more confidence than I should have. Nothing as big as he is has ever fit before. This will be a new experience for both of us. But I guess the confidence he's been instilling in me has transferred to other things, too.

With a grunt, Zynar shifts his hold on me, allowing my back to settle on the bed as he grasps my hips. The first brush of his cockhead against my folds makes my eyes roll back. I grip my breasts, bottom lip between my teeth as I shudder. And, despite the obvious strain on him too, Zynar moves slowly. He uses his leaking fluid to lubricate me before he presses in, fangs bared as he holds himself back, giving me time to adjust to his size, the extent of those ridges, even the sensation of his scars.

Pulling back, he slides in again, working me slowly as my eyes roll back into my head. I can't see anymore. I can only feel. Only feel and hear. The sounds of his soft grunts and growls. The sounds of his harsh breathing. His low moans as he slides back and then forward, carving his way a little deeper within me.

Outside, the rain falls hard, thunder booming. The chaos is all like a backdrop to the sweet storm building inside.

Zynar slides in and out of me so slowly, to the point where it really becomes sweet torture. He works me, making me take him inch by inch, my channel stretching to accommodate him little by little. And when I look at him, that intense stare, his intense focus, is solely on me. He's taking me in, watching my every reaction in the way he usually does, as if each moment is so precious he doesn't want to miss it.

When he finally fills me up, he freezes. Both of our chests heave as I look up at him once more. I squirm, moving my hips, the pressure, the stretch, almost too much. I'm completely filled and the sensation threatens to make me either go limp or go wild. As I roll my hips, moving along his shaft, I start mumbling words that make no sense. Words that are from no language as my whole body ignites.

"Please, Zynar," I beg.

He leans forward, bracing over me, the shift in position pushing him even deeper. His first few thrusts are slow and deep. Each time he pulls back, it stretches me, pulling on my clit before he slides forward again. He curves his back, lifting me onto his thighs as he leans in further. His eyes meet mine, an inch away from my face, as he pumps harder. His breaths come harder too, matching the intense frequency of my own.

As our mouths touch, I sigh against his lips before they crash against mine.

There's nothing else in this universe. Nothing except for him, his intoxicating scent, his addictive taste, and the wet sounds of our mating. His hips move faster, making my entire body jerk with each thrust, and when the heat of his sac hits that space just underneath my core, I know I'm done.

I mumble unto his lips but Zynar's kiss is scorching. I'm about to climax but there's no warning of the intensity. I scream into his mouth, fingers digging into his scales as my entire body erupts with pleasure so intense it feels like there's a tidal wave that rolls through me.

"Zynar, I...oh sweet mercy!" Tears swell and run down my face at the same time that I feel him reach his own climax. He shunts forward, impaling me some more as I stretch to accommodate that wide section of his base. There, I can feel the powerful jerks going through his entire shaft as he releases deep inside me.

I'm crying and I don't know why.

When he lifts his head, Zynar freezes. The blown state of his pupils suddenly lessens as he balances me with one claw while lifting the other to my cheek.

"I hurt you?" he croaks. "Oh gods, I hurt you."

I'm shaking my head, but there are no words. They're choked away.

"Little Bird." I can tell he tries to pull back, but it's too tight. We're locked together like this, the base of his cock too thick and swollen to simply pull out of me. "I didn't mean to—"

"You didn't." I sniffle, lifting my hand to wipe at my eyes. It only makes more tears come. "I don't know why I'm crying. You didn't hurt me. As a matter of fact, I've never..." I sob. "I've never felt so good."

He stares at me for a moment before his gaze softens. He leans down, taking me with him as he turns slightly with me still in his arms. Resting on the bed now, he uses a single digit to wipe away more of my tears.

"You give me the greatest honor," he growls, his shaft jerking at the words.

I settle against him, my face against his broad chest, his scent enveloping me. For the first time in a long while, I feel completely at peace. As if nothing in the world could possibly take this moment away.

Zynar presses his face into my hair, and I hear him rumble with pleasure as he inhales. His manhood jerks again, and my eyes flutter open. It's the only reason I know I'm falling asleep—with a hard shaft still inside me.

"Zynar?"

"Mm Little Bird?"

"You're still hard. Didn't you come?"

"Copiously." There's so much pride in his voice that I huff a soft laugh through my nose.

"But you're still…" I clench my pelvic muscles, tightening around that unbelievable girth, and he groans.

"Don't do that, Liora. Not unless you're ready for another round."

A thrill goes through me despite that my eyes widen. Outside, the thunder rolls and I snuggle closer. I wriggle a little, but there's no way he's going to slip out. Not with that thickened base of his forming a sort of cork.

"It will go down," he murmurs into my hair. "It's only so big because I want you so much."

Another thrill goes through me. "Why does it do that? Why does your base swell?" I squirm again. "I don't…I don't actually think I can get off."

"Do you want to?"

My cheeks heat. Despite everything we've just shared, I blush. "No."

He rumbles something, brushing one claw through my hair before he cradles my skull against him. My eyes close again as I relax. "It's so my spend isn't wasted. So every drop can seep into you and we can create offspring."

His words make my eyes fly open. For a moment, I don't breathe. I don't move.

We haven't even talked about what all of this means yet. We haven't discussed how we will interact after this. But I can't deny that this is more than just sex. That I've never felt like this about anyone before. Felt like this *with* anyone, either. That I want more of this, wherever it leads. Lying to myself, hiding from the fact that my hurt and pain aren't definers for the rest of my life, isn't easy.

I want Zynar. I want all the things he awakens in me. I want life. Love. I want happiness. And…I can give him that. If he wants more than to share a bed with me, I can give him all those things, too. But kids? I realize we're from two different cultures. That he might expect that now we've had sex, kids might occur and he might not even mind. There's only one big problem.

"Zynar…I…I had my period early when I was a girl. I didn't understand what was happening. Thought I was dying. Little girl from the South walking home from school with a bloody dress stuck to her behind. My mother scolded me for bringing her shame. I remember it like it was yesterday. But then, little did I know it was just a precursor to the fact that, I would go through menopause early, too." I pause. I'm rambling again. Giving information I don't need to. But how do I explain this? "I'm not a standard case. Lost my period a year or two before the Tasqals took us. Sorry, I'm rambling." I clear my throat and try to tilt my head backward so I can look up at him. Zynar's holding me so close I can hardly move. Every shift I make only sends a throb through his cock, his knot pulsing at my entrance. "Zynar?"

"Yes, Liora?" His voice sounds deeper, sleepy almost.

"What I'm saying is…I can't have children. Not anymore."

He shifts, his arms tightening around my ass as he pulls me closer to him.

His face nuzzles into my hair and he inhales deeply again. "You smell so good."

I'm sort of taken aback that he doesn't react to what I just said. For years, I thought something was wrong with me. That it had been *my* fault I couldn't get pregnant when it turned out to not be my fault at all. I didn't get the chance to be a mother and the last thing I want to do is prevent Zynar from experiencing the joys of parenthood.

That is if I'm not getting ahead of myself and planning a future that will never occur. I don't know what Zynar wants. This might be a one-time thing, and I have to prepare myself for that.

"When I seeded you, Liora. It was not in the hopes of creating offspring," he finally growls.

My shoulders slacken, tension releasing that I didn't even know was stored.

"I simply wanted to have you. All of you. On my cock. In my mouth. I want to fill you with my seed over and over again." His cock throbs again and I swear he hardens even more. Zynar growls. "I spent all of the dark cycle fantasizing about this."

Fantasizing about me? The thought makes me press against him more, suddenly unable to feel him enough.

As silence envelop s us, we lie there just listening to the rain until I feel his shoulders begin to rise and fall in a steady rhythm.

"Zynar?"

There's no response. He's sleeping and my eyelids are heavy too.

My core clenches as his knot suddenly goes down and a gush of warm liquid spreads between us. It's wet, obscene, and yet I can't say I don't want more. A soft whimper-like moan leaves my lips as I drift off to sleep. I'm sated. Safe.

For the first time in my life, it feels like true happiness has found me.

ELEANOR

*I*t's the indistinct sound that probably wakes me. Something different from the constant sound of rain outside, but also constant itself. Low. Rumbling. Almost comforting, if I wasn't wondering what it was.

As my eyes flutter open, I'm aware I'm still wrapped in Zynar's arms. I'm safe. But there's still that sound and I'm not immediately sure where it's coming from.

My communicator maybe? It's a deep vibration. But when my gaze shifts over Zynar's shoulder, my communicator's screen is dark. It's only then that I realize that noise, that deep vibration, is coming from him. Zynar's chest is humming like the wings of a fast-beating bird.

I stop moving, easing away a fraction to stare at his chest. There's no indication there's any vibration, but I can hear it. I can...feel it. I realize then that it's also hot. Here in this bundle we've created together is suddenly scorching. And his breaths? They're irregular, coming far too hard for it to be regular, especially during sleep.

"Zynar?"

He hears my voice and he grunts, but it's not enough to wake him. He seems out of it. Has he gotten a fever? Oh god, did I overwork him in the field?

"Zynar!" Gripping his shoulders, I shake him and his eyes open. I go still, my own breaths stopping in my chest.

His pupils aren't blown anymore but they've not gone back to normal either. They're so narrow right now that his eyes are almost entirely yellow, the distinction between pupil and iris barely noticeable.

"Zynar?"

He shudders and his chest heaves as if he's finding it hard to breathe.

"Liora," he groans.

Panic rises within me immediately. "Zynar? What's happening? Can you talk? Can you tell me?"

My hands are running over him as I try to find out where's the injury. Was there possibly something I didn't see? Something I'm missing?

His head rolls, dipping forward, and I have to brace it up with my forehead. His lids are low, but he still manages to look up at me.

"Zynar?"

That beat in his chest, that rhythmic vibration increases so loud it's all I can hear. My wide eyes fall to his chest that's still heaving as his head rolls again.

"I don't understand." There's panic at the edge of my voice. Clearly noticeable. I don't even care. "I don't understand what's happening."

Despite his struggle, Zynar still manages to settle me back on the bed as he releases me. His entire body is heaving with the effort to breathe as he stares down at me. He's...pink. Not entirely. There are purple and blue scales, but unlike before where the dominant color was purple, now it's turned to a rich fuchsia. Eyes wide, I reach for him again, but Zynar stumbles off the bed.

"Zynar?"

His gaze slides down my naked form, lingering on my chest and I see when his brows furrow. I'm not sure what to make of his response. Is he regretting this? Is this some sort of post-nut shock?

But even as those thoughts rise in my head, I know that's not the case, because when Zynar meets my gaze again something flutters within me despite that he's acting so strange.

"Varek," he groans. "Call Varek."

He's walking now, stumbling away from me and using the wall as support. It takes a moment for me to realize that he's leaving. I hop from the bed, completely naked, and hurry after him. I hear crashing sounds as he collides with the table before I spot him at the front door.

He's really leaving, but he turns one last time. Looking over his shoulder, his gaze catches mine before he pulls the door open and stumbles out into the pouring rain.

I run after him, stopping just on the edge of the porch.

Maybe it's good we're in the wilderness. Maybe it's good we have no neighbors. I'm in my birthday suit and so is he. I watch in terror as he stumbles against the old well before righting himself and carrying on. He looks drunk but I know that's not what this is. This is something else.

One claw gripped to his chest, he uses the other to guide him toward the barn. I start to go after him before I come to my senses and run back into the house.

Grabbing a linen robe, I wrap it around myself before I slip my shoes on. It takes me just about a minute before I'm out in the rain too, running after him and calling his name. There's no response, and that makes anxiety rise in the center of my chest.

When I try to pull the barn doors open, they don't budge. More panic. More anxiety.

"Zynar?!" No response.

I tug on the doors again but they don't budge. He's barred them from the inside.

"What on Earth?" I slap my hands against the doors, the rain pouring down so hard I can hardly see. "Zynar, open the door. Let me in!"

I'm actually huffing and puffing but in pure desperation, not hunger. My fingers dig into the wood as I hear him groan on the other side of the bolted doors. He's in pain. Terrible pain.

My chest heaves as I look around, but there's nothing I'd be strong enough to lift to break this door down. A back door then? I'm moving before any other thought enters my mind.

The rain soaks through my clothes as I walk around the building. There are no other doors, and hopelessness rises. There is, however, a bit of a plank that's broken, providing a long vertical tear in the otherwise uniform barn wall. I move closer, peering through the hole and squinting, trying to see inside some more.

At first, I don't see him. Everything in there is too dark. All I see is the outlines of ooga butt in the dim light. But then I catch a glimpse of fuchsia. Zynar.

He's stark naked, standing at the far end near the barn doors. He's still gripping his chest before he falls to his knees. My breath hitches.

"Zynar!" He needs help. A hospital maybe. No, most definitely. He looks like he's dying. Did I kill him? With my… Oh my god, did I kill him?

The moment I shout his name his head snaps up. Those narrow slits in his eyes find me like I'm on some kind of beacon. He stares at me across the distance before he's suddenly moving as if given some kind of command. He cuts across the distance much faster than I've ever seen him move before. As if the pain is suddenly gone. Before I know it, he's right before me, staring at me through that single crack in the wood.

My eyes widen at the state of the male before me. He looks exactly like the playful Kari that came to my rescue. Everything except for his eyes. Zynar's eyes are predatorial. His head tilts as he snarls behind the wood, gaze honed in on me. His chest is still heaving with labored breaths that are still not quite uniform. And that vibration? That unique vibration is still there.

When he suddenly inhales, he pulls so much air inside his lungs I can hear it.

A deep growl escapes him a second later as he leans into the wood. My gaze shifts as something else moves and my focus lands on his groin. He's hard. Harder, if that's possible, than before. He even looks larger. My eyes are wide as I shift them back up to him. I have no idea what's happening, but it's clear I have to do something, anything I can, to help him.

Despite the warning signals in my head, I push my fingers through the crack. It's just big enough to fit my entire hand as I reach for him. Fingers splayed, I go on tiptoes to brush my hand across his jaw. He shudders, makes a growling sound, but leans in. I'm almost knocked back by the powerful scent that wafts into my nose. I moan, I actually do as my hand caresses his jaw. Deep down below, my core clenches, his scent seeming like a battery to some kind of new energy that courses through me.

Whatever's affecting him, it's affecting me too.

Zynar tilts his head into my palm, inhaling deeply before he suddenly grabs my hand. I let out a soft yelp. It's not painful, but the suddenness of his grasp makes my heart jump.

With a slow lick, he licks the entirety of my palm, sending shivers all the way through me. He groans, his ears flicking. A strange movement goes through his scales, a shiver, and the vibration increases before he grips his chest again. His gaze suddenly finds mine and I see some of the Zynar I know behind those yellow pits.

He releases me then and staggers away.

"Go, Liora," he growls. "Call Varek. Go now before I—"

A look of horror passes across his face as he staggers back some more. "Go."

"Zynar, tell me what's happening. I can help. I—"

"Go, Liora!" His shoulders heave and I step back. Slowly, he disappears into the shadows of the barn, only the sounds of ooga emanating from the inside and the soft roll of thunder from the skies above.

I turn, my heart in bits as I storm toward the house. I fling the door open, not caring to close it or not as I run to my communicator. My fingers are a wet trembling mess as I activate the screen.

"Call Varek. Call Varek." But I've never contacted his brother before. I don't know if I even have his ping code. FUCK!

"Computer, do I have Varek's contact details?"

"Please specify the designation or ping code of the resident you would like to contact."

I run a hand through my hair, pacing till I find myself at the front door. My gaze finds the barn immediately and it's still locked. Zynar has still barricaded himself inside.

"Uh, Varek uh…" Shit. Fuck. Shit. *Fuck*. I can't remember his name. I've fucked his brother, was basically planning my life with him, and I don't remember his name? What the hell is wrong with me?

"Varek of the Korruk line?" There's hope in my voice as I see the computer recognize my words.

"Sending ping."

The screen flashes and goes dark as I continue pacing. My eyes are wild in my reflection on the device's surface. My hair like a wild bird's nest. When the screen flashes again and Varek's face fills it, a wave of both recognition and trepidation hits me. He looks so much like Zynar, yet he's clearly not. Because Zynar's currently in my barn going through *something*. I have to lean back against the wall in relief and for some support.

"Human female," Varek greets me. "To what do I owe the pleasure of this ping?" Then he growls. "Do not tell me my siblingkin has been caught in some kind of trouble."

I swallow hard. "Trouble, yes. But not the sort you think."

18

—————

ZYNAR

I lean against one of the outbuilding's pillar supports, forcing myself to breathe. My entire body hums as I stare at the doors.

I want to go to her. I *must*.

The vibration rising within me, the rhythm, gets louder as I take the first few steps, an energy rising inside me that no gods can tame. My whole body sings. My whole being is on fire. My every sense alight.

Like a cord leading me back toward Eleanor, something tugs me closer to those doors. Even though I've locked myself in with the last of rational thought, my resolve is quickly crumbling. I have to plant my feet firmly, digging claws into the earth to anchor myself. For I have found my *kahl*. My *mate*. Orbits thinking such a thing was impossible, but here I am, my core-rhythm rising in my chest, binding around my core-beat with such intensity it's taking my breath away.

My fangs ache, my claws extend and retract, my muscles bunch. I'm coiled tight, like I'm about to pounce. The primal urge to hunt, to claim, to rut consumes me. Rational thought slips away, replaced by a singular, overwhelming instinct.

Find her. Take her. *Claim her until she is undeniably yours.*

The transformation is agonizingly slow. My senses sharpen, every sound amplified, every scent magnified. I can catch remnants of her scent lingering by the doors where she'd pounded her fists and demanded that I let her in. And, in my state, I almost did. Now I can hear her voice.

My head tilts and I'm at those doors, ready to tear them off their hinges at just the faint sound of her song. She's on her communicator, all the way in the lodge, and I can hear her. The world narrows to a point, centering only on Eleanor. My vision tunnels, the edges darkening as I stare at the wood as if I can see through it, as if locking onto my prey.

"He's burning up and there's this strange sound, a vibration coming from his chest!" She sounds frantic. *"He ran away from me before I could even check his temperature. I don't know what's going on."* There's a tremor in her tone and I growl at her distress even though I'm the one causing it. I am to make her cry out in want and need, not in sorrow. My hard cock slaps against my chest, encouraging me to do just that. *"Please, Varek, can you come? I'm afraid..."* She hesitates. *"I'm afraid something very wrong is happening."*

Her words bring some clarity to my mind. Through the clouds darkening my senses and telling me to do one thing and frakk the consequences. Because my mate is human. Not Kari. She has no clue what I want to do to her. What I *need* to do to her. This is why I must stay away. I must prevent myself from going to her and damaging what little foundations we've just built, because if I leave this outbuilding, she will be beneath me, impaled on my cock over and over again and there will be nothing either of us can do about it.

I can barely think, barely hold on to the last shreds of my control as I turn and head farther into the outbuilding. There are chains here, lying on the ground in one corner, and I grab them now. The beast within me roars, thrashing against its cage at the first realization of what I'm about to do. Gripping one of the pillar supports, I throw the chains around it before bringing them around myself. My muscles tense, my claws digging into the stone as that beast within me resists. I am becoming something primal, something ancient. An untamed force of nature driven by raw, animalistic desire.

I want Eleanor. I *need* her.

But there is one thing I didn't explain when I told her the story of my past. That the Tasqals didn't simply want our virility. They wanted our power. This monster that rises with the insatiable urge to rut. That when a Kari finds his mate, the urge turns him into an uncontrollable beast with a singular focus. That many female Kari have died during the rut. That I thought it would never happen to me because of the Tasqal's experiments. No displaced Kari has found his mate since. I thought we were broken. But then I never imagined a little fluttering bird to perch on my arm and awaken something inside me I long thought dead.

Her wings are finally reopening after being tied down for so long. The last thing I want to do is break them again. And so I bind myself. Each rotation of the chains around me is a struggle, a losing battle to maintain even a semblance of control. At the final turns of the chain, I secure it with the last of my logical mind. For my mind fragments, thoughts shattering under the pressure of instinct. Images of Eleanor beneath me, writhing in pleasure, fill my mind, fueling the fire raging within, eclipsing everything else. I can almost taste her, smell her, feel her, and I'm dimly aware of my body reacting. Of my knot swelling. Of spend seeping from my tip to soil my thighs and the ground beneath me. The anticipation is maddening, the desire an all-consuming inferno.

Rationality fades, replaced by the sheer, unadulterated need to claim. To hunt. To dominate. I am lost in visions of my kahl, my grasp on the present slipping away with each passing moment. Only one thing remains clear in the chaos of my mind.

I must stay away from her, even though everything within me demands that I have her now.

19

ELEANOR

$\mathcal{I}$ told Varek everything I could. At first, when he answered the ping, he was smiling, fangs slightly visible, and I realized that smiling must be a thing he and Zynar learned to do to put species like myself at ease.

On Varek's face, it's even less natural than Zynar's. So much so I noticed. His smile and every other change on his face as I told him what was going on.

That Zynar and I were 'resting' when I suddenly heard the vibration. That he was burning up but refused my help. That he locked himself in the barn. I even mentioned that his color was more vibrant. More pink.

From the moment I began explaining the symptoms, Varek's carefully cultivated smile slipped. He became expressionless. So much so that looking at him through the vid feed felt like I was looking at some kind of predator I had no idea how to read. It sent a shiver down my spine, a realization that they are so different from myself. It's no wonder Xarion had advised I hire a Raki. Just staring at Varek without his mask and I can tell that, in another time, me in my humanness would have been his prey.

So why am I hurrying back outside in the rain? Why am I

heading back toward the barn? I saw Zynar, how he was. How his eyes had changed. How he looked even bigger, stronger than usual. I saw how he reacted to my proximity. He locked himself away, probably with good reason. Why am I going back there?

I bang on the barn doors, calling his name. There's no response, but I'm sure I hear chains rattling. Picking up the wet skirt of the robe I'm wearing, I head around to the back of the barn. I find the place where there's a missing strip of wood again and I stand on tiptoes, peering in.

What I see makes my breath hitch.

Zynar's secured himself with chains against a central pillar in the barn. He's wrapped his arms, his torso, and even then, he's struggling to release himself, as if two versions of himself are warring—the one that tied him there and the one that wants to get out.

"Zynar," I whisper and he suddenly goes still. A trickle of fear goes down my spine as his head snaps in my direction. Sheets of his damp hair obscure his face and still I can see the glow of his eyes underneath. Focused on me. The air seems to still, seconds passing with the singular stare before he suddenly jerks against the chains. I jump, losing my vantage point on the tips of my toes and causing him to disappear briefly from view.

The chains begins to jangle with almost deafening intensity and when I manage to go up on my toes again, it suddenly stops. Zynar's staring at me through that sheet of his damp mane, his chest heaving, his fangs bared….and his cock…

My eyes widen as my gaze lowers to his groin.

He's hard. So very hard, it looks painful. It jumps as I look at it, pre-cum seeping from the tip as his hips jerk in a forward motion at my attention. My wide eyes fly back to his. Memory of what we just shared comes back immediately, and that fear that had trickled down my spine disappears. Because this is the same male that worried about hurting me. The same male that held me close in the aftermath and cuddled me like he never wanted to let me go.

The same male who answered my job ad and helped me with my roof. The same one that volunteered to help me get this place up to par. The same one that gave me space when I needed it. He's the male that's made me feel alive again after so many years of feeling like I was simply existing. The first male who has lit a fire in me after so long. The first one I actually think I could...love?

The thought makes me hardly breathe as I stare at him through that crack in the wall. I watch as he struggles to release himself. As he struggles to get to *me,* and it all becomes clear that this isn't about him. It's not about him at all. It's about *me.*

Zynar's locked himself up because of *me.* Chained himself because of *me.*

He wants to protect me from something. From himself?

"I'll find a way to help you," I whisper, and he jerks at the chains, his gaze heightening on me through the shadows. "I will."

Something hard rises in my throat as I move away from the barn, something I'm unable to swallow down as I walk away from the building. Because losing sight of him feels like I'm abandoning him there even though I'm not. I can hear the chains jangling as he tries to release himself to come after me. He doesn't even speak. Doesn't call out my name. Whatever's happening has him relying on his base self, one that looks like it wants to tear me apart. But I refuse to believe that's all there is to it.

My heart is heavy. A heavy beating thing that slams into my ribs with each thump. As I head back to the cottage, I still hear the chains jangling and my heart breaks. I cast my gaze to the front gate, the rain obscuring my vision, but not enough to see that Varek's not arrived yet. He won't be here for a while. My chest shudders with a heavy breath as I turn to head out of the rain. The best thing I can do is some research on my communicator. Figure out what's happening and how best to help Zynar. But as I step onto the porch out of the rain, a distressing bay reaches my ears.

I tilt my head trying to figure out where it came from when I hear it again. Oh shit, that frickin' ooga in the field. It bays, crying so loudly and so hard that I'm left conflicted.

Zynar needs my help but so does the stubborn beast.

Wrapping my robe tighter, even though it's wet and provides little cover, I step back into the rain, jogging toward the field. I see the ooga through the sheets of gray as the rain comes down even harder. It's standing in the center of the field. Why doesn't it move? If it's stuck in the rain, surely it has enough sense to try to get out of it.

I glance back at the barn and then at the gate. No Varek yet. I don't even want to go inside my house with Zynar in the barn suffering. Might as well help the ooga.

I'm on the field, the rain so hard it's blinding. With nothing to hold it back across these flat plains, the wind hits me with a full gust that has me planting my feet into the wet earth and bracing against it as raindrops try to batter every inch of my exposed skin.

I grunt, pushing forward toward the ooga. The closer I get, the more I realize it's not simply just standing there. It's stomping its feet. Beneath it is a wide ring of overturned dirt that it has trampled as if it was turning in circles but unable to go anywhere else.

"Hey! Come on out of the rain, you troublesome thing!" I shout at it over the wind, my heart still doing somersaults, my mind still on Zynar. Perhaps that's why I don't immediately hear the little snarl underneath the sound of the rain and wind. Perhaps my distraction and preoccupation with Zynar's state dulls my other senses. Because as I near the ooga it spins, making that distressing baying sound as it stomps.

I jump back, alarmed, my heart thumping in my throat now for several reasons.

The little snarl comes again and something darts in my peripheral vision, too fast to see. A little black ball?

"What the—" I spin, one hand over my brow in an effort to see better. "What the hell was that?"

There's the snarl again and the ooga stomps, spinning in a circle as the little black ball appears again. I catch sight of it. I don't even know what I'm looking at. When it stops to snarl at the ooga, I see that it's a little fur ball with small, round eyes. It looks like a pompom on legs, but with wicked little teeth showing beneath its fur.

Before I can even understand what's going on, the little tyrant charges at the ooga. I'm standing right by the large animal and as it spins to get away from the little fur demon, it collides right into me. I feel the pain before I feel myself hitting the ground. Heat erupts in my skull, a strange sensation with the cool rain falling down.

I blink, vaguely aware that the ooga is running around the field, baying and trying to get away from the fur demon. Everything feels like it moves slowly in my sight, even though I can hear that it's not.

"Zynar," I grunt. I should have never come out here to help this silly beast. I need to get back to the house. Need to find out how to help Zynar. But as I try to lift my head, as I try to rise, I realize I can't. My head feels too heavy. That warmth in my skull increasing.

THUNDER ROLLS. My eyes flutter open. It must be the thunder that woke me up, but it's not the sky that's in front of me. Purple iridescent scales are. Zynar?

"Kahlesta?" A worried face hovers over mine. But that's not Zynar's voice.

"Who—" Oh goodness, my head *hurts*. I wince as I try to rise. I don't manage it, but the face before me gets less blurry. It isn't Zynar. It's his brother. "Varek?" I croak.

My head throbs and I lift a hand to my cranium.

There's a sound as if he curses. My eyes flutter open some more, the cool rain falling into my face as I stare at the heavy clouds that look like a thick sheet above me.

What...happened?

There's movement and Varek's face appears again. He's looking at me as if I'm a patient in need of urgent care. For a moment, I wonder if this is all a dream. My thoughts are hazy and time doesn't feel like it's on the same linear path or moving at the same speed.

I blink at him, my lids moving slowly. "What...?"

"Stay still." His voice is gentle even though his tone hardens with the order. "You've had a fall."

I grunt, lifting a hand to the side of my head. When I bring it before my eyes, I can see there's only a little blood, but there's no telling how much the rain washed away.

I groan. "How long have I been lying here?"

"From the looks of it, about an hor. I came as fast as I could." There is some regret in his voice, but that's not why my eyes widen.

"An hour? Oh my god...Zynar!" When I reach for Varek's arm, it's out of habit. Just reaching for something firm I can use to pull myself up. But the moment I do, Varek suddenly jerks back, putting himself out of the reach of my grasp. I'm momentarily stunned, but he recovers quickly, giving me a slight dip of his head in apology.

"Touching me would not be wise, kahlesta. Any male scent on you will send my siblingkin feral."

That…doesn't make sense. Why would touching me have any effect on his brother? But my head is pounding and it's taking all of my focus. I grunt, pushing myself up on my elbows when I slip and almost go down. Varek reaches for me, claws coming inches away from my skin before he freezes again. He seems caught between wanting to help me and being unable to. He grimaces.

"I'm sorry, kahlesta." He's still looking at me as if I've been through something terrible. "I cannot help you like this. Please, wait here. I will return."

"Hmm?" But he's already gone, dashing across the field, his purple scales blending into the sheet of gray as he disappears.

I grunt, pressing my palm to the side of my head as my gaze shifts around the field. The troublesome ooga is now sitting on the ground, legs and head tucked in as it protects itself from the rain. From what it looks like, everything is peaceful again. There's no sign of the little fur demon thing.

When Varek suddenly appears again, running across the field toward me, I wonder if I'm hallucinating. He's covered in some sort of protective plastic-looking suit. Is he wearing a raincoat? I frown as he crouches and his gaze meets mine through the transparent visor of the suit's head covering.

Everything feels out of place. Maybe I hit my head harder than I thought and this is all in my imagination.

"We have to get to Zynar."

"Not before we get you help first, kahlesta."

"Eleanor," I groan. Each word feels like an effort. "Funny way to properly introduce myself, but my name is Eleanor."

"Eleanor," he whispers. Then he does the Kari salute, tapping two fingers to the center of his chest. "My siblingkin's *kahl*."

He says the word with such reverence that I momentarily forget the ache in my head. I'm pretty sure 'kahl' doesn't mean 'employer', because Varek suddenly falls to his knees on the wet earth before me, head bowed. I don't know how to react or respond.

"Varek?" I don't understand. "What's going on?"

He doesn't answer me. Instead, he bows lower. "Please forgive what I am about to do."

What he's about to—

Without warning—or, I suppose, he *did* warn me—Varek lifts me into his arms. The protective suit crunches as he grips me tight.

"I need to get you to shelter," he says, standing and turning toward the cottage. I wince as the shift in position makes my head pound.

"I'm fine, really. It's Zynar you should worry about."

Varek only grunts as he hurries across the wet field and toward the cottage. Hunching, he leans forward so his body blocks the brunt of the rain as he carries me. I blink at him, my gaze shifting to the farm buildings, then back. He's here, but he's not with Zynar. After what I told him over the communicator, the fact he's not rushing to his brother's aid is only raising questions in my mind.

When we reach the house and he heads straight up to the porch, I get even more confused.

"Varek...Zynar is in there." I point weakly to the barn.

Varek's gaze shifts to the barn, but that's it.

"You were right to call me, Eleanor." He uses a shoulder to push the front door of my cottage open. There's a depth to his voice that makes him sound so much like Zynar. It only makes a part of me ache deep inside at the fact that Zynar's not here. It feels like only a moment ago he was holding me in his arms and now something's happening to him and I have no clue what.

I wince as my head continues to pound. "Zynar needs you," I try to communicate the gravity of the situation with my tone. "*And* a doctor. When I last saw him—" I breathe hard, pushing through the pain. "—he—"

"Kahlesta." Varek stops me with the one word as he steps

into the house. "Zynar didn't want me here so I could help him. He wanted me here to help *you*."

His words cut off any thought in my mind. I'm so confused, I don't even immediately notice he's brought me straight into the bedroom until we're standing by the bed. Balancing me on one arm, he uses the other to strip the sheets and fold them into a padded area that he sets me on, probably because I'm soaking wet.

As soon as he puts me down, I try to rise. I end up swaying, my vision going blurry for a second.

"Wait here, kahlesta." He disappears into the other room, and I hear the front door open. A breath of relief makes my shoulders sag. He's finally gone to Zynar.

I'm wrong.

Varek returns far too quickly. When I hear him talking to someone on his comm, I try to get up again, but end up going so dizzy, I have to sit my butt down.

I am *not* okay. Just how hard did I hit my head?

Varek suddenly returns to the bedroom, still wearing that hazmat-like suit and with a small trunk in hand. He didn't go to the barn then. Did he go to his truck?

"She is conscious. Tell me what to do." His voice carries an edge of urgency beneath his calm as he still talks to the person on his communicator. The response of whoever he's talking to is distorted, but I catch fragments. Instructions, concerns— terms I don't fully grasp in my hazy state.

"Kahlesta," Varek turns to me, "the medic can't reach us quickly." Medic? "He will guide me through helping you until he can get here."

I try to protest, to tell him I'm fine, but the pounding in my head intensifies, forcing me to rest against the padded bed. My vision blurs and steadies, blurs and steadies. Okay, I'm not fine.

The comm crackles and the being on the other end of the line speaks. "Have you taken precautions?"

"Fully," Varek responds. "There will be no contamination."

Contamination? I lift my head despite the heaviness, as if looking at him will give me understanding.

"Varek, what's going on?" I hate how weak my voice sounds. I only fell. It can't be that bad. I'm tougher than this.

Whoever's on the line begins giving instructions. Varek's hands are steady as he moves over to me and follows what they say. I don't even protest as he checks my pulse and places a gloved claw lightly on my chest to monitor my breathing.

When he crouches, searching for supplies in the trunk, I look down to see that it's filled with what looks like medical items. Retrieving a device, something that looks like a barcode scanner, he continues following the instructions relayed through his communicator.

Gently, he positions the scanner over my head. A soft hum fills the room as it activates, emitting a faint blue light. He watches the readings with complete focus, adjusting the device as instructed.

"Keep your eyes open, kahlesta," he says softly, his eyes flicking from the scanner to my face. "I need to check for any serious injuries."

"I really am fine," I murmur. "It's just a little bump. I can walk it off."

His gaze flickers with doubt as he listens to the person on the comm.

"I will do my best," he says to them before ending the ping and taking out a small patch that looks like a circular Band-Aid.

"This will help with the dizziness," he explains before gently pressing it against my neck. Immediately, I feel a cool sensation spreading through me.

Next, he takes out a bandage. I don't move, allowing him to part my hair as he looks at my scalp.

"It isn't deep," he murmurs, reaching back with one hand for a bit of gauze, which he uses to clean the area. "But Zynar will have my throat for not arriving soon enough to protect you."

I shake my head, wincing again with the movement. "This isn't your fault. I went to help the silly ooga and found out it was simply spooked by some furry demon."

Varek tilts his head, the protective suit he's wearing rustling with the movement. "Fuhree demon?"

I shrug. "I don't know what it was. First time seeing an animal like that. It was small and round and filled with fur. Tiny little legs I almost couldn't see underneath the fur. It looked like a rolling cotton ball."

"Ah, an umu."

I wince as another pang goes through my head. "Are they dangerous?"

Varek chuckles and I wonder how he can laugh when it feels like everything is falling apart around us.

"No," he says. "Sounds like the ooga stepped on it and it got angry. "They can turn into terrible little beasts when annoyed."

"Just my luck," I grunt. "It was snarling at the ooga and spooked it. I don't think the ooga meant me harm. I was just in the way."

"I should have been here. If we knew there was a chance…" He trails off as he secures the bandage over the wound. A cool sensation spreads from the spot, too.

"Thanks," I whisper, gaze shifting up to him as he steps back and closes the trunk. "Did you check on Zynar?"

Varek stills before nodding so slightly I wouldn't have seen it if I wasn't looking at him.

"So, you saw that he isn't alright." I frown, closing my eyes for a moment to ward away the pain still in my skull.

"No," Varek's voice lowers. "He is not."

Whatever he's done is making me feel a bit better already. The dizziness is fading fast but the pounding in my head is still there. I open my eyes, my gaze moving over the suit he's covered head to toe in.

"What's this about…about this *contamination?*" I gulp. "What's that about?"

"A precaution," he says. His claw clenches and releases on the handle of the trunk as if he's not quite sure what to do with his hands.

"Precaution?"

Varek nods again. That slight, almost easily missed motion. "I cannot touch you."

I blink at him through my still-pounding headache. And then it dawns. The hazmat-like suit. The fact he refuses to touch me. The fact he won't go near his brother. "Oh no…" My heartbeat slows down as dread slowly fills me. The longer I think about it, the clearer it seems. Zynar's change in color. His fever. The way his whole demeanor has changed.

"Oh, no no… He's sick, isn't he? Did we… Did I…" I can't even say it. I don't know anything about pathogens. Who knows if us having sex did something. Some people are allergic to semen and Zynar had copious amounts of it. What if it's a reverse reaction to being mixed with my fluids?

Varek keeps his gaze down but shakes his head. "No, kahlesta. What is happening to Zynar is no disease or illness."

I ease up on my elbows, blinking away the pain in my head. "I don't understand."

When Varek doesn't move, urgency fills my tone. "Varek, please, I'm starting to freak out here."

Varek meets my gaze for a few moments before looking away. Whatever this is, whatever he's not telling me, it's hard on him. I can see that. But it's becoming terrifying for me.

"This is not how you should learn about this, kahlesta. It is all too soon. Too abrupt." He runs a claw over his face—a gesture so humanlike that it almost distracts from the fact that the male I'm falling in love with is stuck in my barn while his brother is here, obviously with a burden he doesn't even know how to articulate.

Love? There's that word again. Only, it doesn't make me want to run. Doesn't make me want to hide. Each second that passes with Varek's silence makes my heart beat harder. Makes something deep inside me ache. Makes a fear I didn't think I'd be feeling start to grow in my gut.

When he finally continues, his voice is low and somber, a stark contrast to the raging storm outside.

"Zynar will view any male, even his own kin, as a challenger if he senses they've had contact with you. I am no exception to the danger."

His words echo in a way I didn't expect, leaving me able only to blink at him in stunned silence. "I...don't understand. Why would that happen?"

"Zynar made you ping me for one reason. He was himself enough to realize what was happening. And so I am here." He faces me now, yellow eyes unreadable. "My sole purpose here is to protect you—from *him*. You are his kahl..." He bows. "And my *kahlesta*."

"I—." My heart is thumping so hard, it's as if it understands something I don't. "Kahlesta?" I whisper. The same word he's been calling me all along.

"Varek..." His gaze shifts to mine. My heart thumps as we stare at each other, the weight of whatever's hanging around us like an invisible cloud more present than at any other instance. "What does kahlesta mean?"

20

ELEANOR

"I'm his *what?*" I'm in dry clothes. Varek refused to continue talking until I changed, repeating fears of me getting ill by remaining in my wet tunic. He kept stating he refuses to let anything else happen to me. And since I declined his well-intentioned proposal to help me change into dry attire, I struggle to do it myself. It takes me way too long to pull on a dry tunic and underwear with my head still feeling heavier than it usually does. And the entire time, the nervous energy building inside me has not quelled, only increased.

It feels like I've suddenly stepped into territory in which I didn't expect to find myself. But whether it's dangerous territory or not, I'm not sure. Instead, there's a strange sort of anticipation mixed with unease. Solely from the fact that what Varek said to me is the last thing I expected him to say.

Mate.

He said I'm his brother's mate.

My heart does that strange ski-boop thing at the thought, but I push the feeling down. I have to be real with myself. We had sex, and maybe, somehow, Varek knows. But that doesn't make me his brother's mate. Disappointment swells within me so swiftly I can't even hide it.

Now, sitting on the bed with fresh, dry sheets, I stare at Varek from where I rest upright, a pillow braced at my back so I can rest my head against it. The headache hasn't gone and so I try to ignore the pain. It's not hard. My mind fixates on Zynar instead. My frown deepens as worry dominates my thoughts—worry about the male chained in my barn and the fact that no one has checked on him in hours.

I've gone from having the best night of my life, excited about what comes next, to now wondering what the future holds for the male I spent that night with. Frustration mingles with my concern. I'm so worried about him that I can't focus on anything else.

And Varek? Well, Varek dropped that bomb on me just before the medic arrived.

My focus on Varek is briefly interrupted by the medic as he leans forward. Using a device to press on different sections of my skull, he checks the extent of my injury. He's some type of avian. I can't quite be sure what type because he's dressed in his own version of the suit Varek's wearing. Glimpses of feathers show through the transparent section that he can see through.

"Varek," I shift my focus back to the male standing like a guard at my bedroom door. "I need you to say that again."

"You're his mate, kahlesta."

Once again, the word silences me. His *mate*? I want to tell him exactly what I'm thinking. That though the idea of being Zynar's mate thrills that part of me I've tried hard to fight, it doesn't mean anything. But that's not a conversation I can have with the medic right between us.

"Tilt your head back for me..." the medic hums. He ignores our conversation, seeming to be completely engrossed in his examination.

"I'm not the one that needs all this attention." I shift my eyes to the medic.

He emits a huffing sound I interpret as mirth. "While the blow you sustained poses no mortal danger, summoning medical aid was prudent. The force of the impact was substantial." He eases back and searches in the trunk he has resting on the bed. Taking out a vial, he instructs me to tilt my head back as he administers some fluid. It's bitter and my face scrunches.

"I have never worked with a human before, but I assure you, this will assist in your recovery." He gets a needle and lifts it up to the light. A spurt of fluid squirts from the tip and he hums appreciatively in his throat.

"What's that for?" I eye the thing.

"Neuroprotectant," the medic says. Taking my arm, I watch as he administers the medication.

The prick is minor but, within moments, the ache in my skull begins to dull.

The medic withdraws the needle and applies a small bandage. "Rest is imperative now. No exerting yourself for at least one sol."

Closing the trunk, he makes a movement like he ruffles his feathers underneath the suit. It looks like he's about to leave and I sit up too quickly. My head protests. "What about Zynar? You have to help him, too."

The avian picks up the trunk, his confused gaze shifting to Varek and then back to me. "You have not told the female?"

I blink, gaze shifting from him to Varek. "Told me what?"

"I am sorry, human. There is nothing *I* can do for the Kari. He is far past what I can remedy. He needs to complete the rut."

The rut?

I sit in stunned silence as Varek escorts the medic to the door. He doesn't try to stop him either. Doesn't get the medic to go examine Zynar. As if he knows what the medic says is true.

When the house falls silent, I wonder if Varek has left, too. Wincing against the heaviness in my skull, I start to rise before movement catches the corner of my eyes. Varek. He's there again, blocking the doorway.

"What's going on?" I say immediately. "What's the rut? Varek..." It's a struggle ignoring the pain in my skull, even though it's starting to ease. "Please, I need to know. Tell me what's truly happening to Zynar."

Varek is silent. He stares at me from where he's standing by the bedroom door. "I would explain, kahlesta...but...I do not want to scare you." Words his brother has said to me before. It seems that time is repeating on itself, only with a new circumstance. But just like the last time, I'm not afraid of what this Kari has to say. In fact, there's a part of me that *needs* to hear it.

"So many things have happened in the last few years that little can scare me, Varek. I'm a grown woman. I can take it."

He hesitates still, gaze shifting from mine to move around the room.

"Does your species rut?" he finally asks.

I shake my head. "No. But I have a good idea of what that is."

He stares at me for a moment before releasing a long breath. Enough that it fogs up the transparent rectangle in his suit that he's watching me through.

"I would spare you this distress," he finally says, "but you deserve truth. It is what I would want for my mate, if my core-rhythm ever awakened. If there was ever a chance..." He's looking at me strangely now and it isn't difficult to see the yearning in his eyes. But that's before he suddenly looks away, the emotion seeping from his yellow pits as if I imagined it there.

I give him a moment, allowing him to feel the emotions he's clearly trying to hide from me.

"Your existence..." he finally says, "is of dreams, Eleanor. A kahl. A mate. You are something every one of us displaced Kari has always hoped for."

The last sentence is said almost underneath his breath and his focus goes somewhere far away, to memories, hopes, and dreams I cannot see. I remember seeing the same look on Zynar's face before. Those times he told me about his past. Behind the suit, the intensity in Varek's eyes changes. Softens. Almost like mine would do if I was about to cry.

"You're really serious, aren't you," I whisper. I go still as his gaze suddenly heightens on mine. "You really do think I'm your brother's mate." The words choke from me, my heart beating a little harder at their utterance.

"I don't think you are. I *know* you are, kahlesta." He looks at me, his face unreadable still. "You are fated."

My heart thumps so hard in my chest, it makes the pain in my head increase. Fated. Me? To Zynar? Does such a thing actually exist?

But Varek is completely serious. There's no sly grin. No muffled laughter. His words hold weight and they're coming from deep within.

Moments pass with only the rain breaking the silence between us. No words come to my tongue. Because I'm trapped sitting still, his words repeating over and over in my mind.

Fated.

My heart does another hard thump that forces me to inhale deeply. A fated mate. Such a thing hardly seems possible or believable. Like a fairytale. So…why doesn't it feel strange? Why doesn't it feel wrong? Why doesn't my heart protest?

I swallow hard, my heart thumping heavily in my chest. Because despite that it's a thing of dreams…maybe I *want* it to be true. Maybe I want to imagine that leaving Earth was really all for a reason. That it needed to happen just so I could meet *him*. Zynar. The male that's been awakening me in every aspect.

This electricity that's been swirling around us from the first day I met him…this *need*. Maybe I want to believe it's because there's been a greater plan all along. Maybe I just want to hear that the hunk of an alien I've been falling in love with is head over heels falling in love with me, too.

There it is again. That word. Love.

The word that made my heart feel like a cavernous pit for so many years, but is now making it swell and fill in a way that I never thought would ever happen. It almost makes it hard to breathe.

"How?" I whisper. My voice is but a croak, barely audible. "I'm human."

"Yes, kahlesta. This isn't something that happens with your kind. But it is the Kari way. Our core-rhythms only awaken once in our lives and only for our perfect mate. There is no other way. No other dream. With my life, I vow this is true." Varek is about to kneel before me again, as if he fears that despite everything he's done and said, I'll still disbelieve him. I stop him with a lift of my hand.

Bowing slightly, Varek remains standing. "You are now the reason my siblingkin breathes. The reason he exists."

I stiffen, my throat tightening. What woman doesn't want to hear those words about the male that she's falling in love with? Again, my heart swells. And yet, there's the doubt. Because, th ough thrilling, this is also terrifying simply because of the odds. I'd have to be the luckiest girl on Earth. But then I remind myself, I'm not on Earth anymore. My ideas, my preconceptions, all the societal demands and expectations—none of those things matter. Here, I'm just a girl. I'm just Eleanor. All that happened in my life before this point has no weight in this.

I swallow down my fear. "And you're sure that's what's happening to Zynar… You're sure this…core-rhythm is happening. That his body is telling him *I'm* the one."

I know I'm simplifying it, but putting it into human terms is the only way I can process this. But even saying the words, they sound unbelievable. Too good to be true. And I fear I'm imagining this all. That I hit my head in that field and I still haven't recovered yet.

Varek nods, the suit making a shuffling sound as he dips his head. "It is unmistakable. His pigment has changed, his grasp on things. When I dared to venture near the outbuilding, I heard the song. His core-rhythm has...*ignited.*" His yellow gaze lights up in some kind of awe. "It will only get stronger now, interfering with his core-beat as the sols pass. His very breath."

I wait for him to continue. To explain what he just said, but he doesn't. I rise slowly off the bed. "Varek. Are you saying..."

When my feet hit the floor, I sway, my balance still a little off. Suddenly Varek is there holding me up. My wide eyes pierce his through the rectangular viewing hole in his suit. "Are you saying that the intensity of this thing will break his heart...*literally?*"

Images of how Zynar's chest was heaving as if he was having trouble breathing comes right back to me and complete horror fills me. So much so my own breath stutters in my chest under the weight of the realization. No. That's can't be what he means.

Varek grimaces again but nods. "Yes."

My belly bottoms out and I would have fallen to the floor if Varek's arms didn't shoot out to catch me again. "Varek, it's been hours!"

He doesn't seem alarmed. Doesn't release me. Doesn't run to his brother's assistance. There seems to be a condition I'm missing, even though he doesn't utter it. Something that tells me there's more to all this. More he has to say but is hesitating.

"Tell me..." I whisper.

"My siblingkin is not a weak male. He would make a fine provider. A fine protector. A fine mate." He says the words like he's trying to convince me of all those facts. But he doesn't need to convince me. I already know.

I swallow hard, gripping the bed as I lean on it. He eases away from me then, and steps back toward the door.

"He is strong," Varek says, and I don't know what I catch in his tone, but it's as if he's trying to convince himself. "He will last several sols."

My brow knits. "What do you mean *last*? You say that as if…" I shake my head because he can't be saying what I think he's saying.

"He won't be going through the rut, kahlesta. And if he won't be marking you as his, that is death in itself. A few sols is all the time he has left."

I swallow a lump, stepping back. "Are you…" I choke on the rest of the words because my brain refuses to put them into reality. "Are you saying Zynar's going to *die?*"

"Few can endure the intensity of a newly awakened core-rhythm. Few can endure the need to claim," he says. Then as if to bring the point home, his gaze locks with mine again. "Many Kari females have died during the rut." He pauses. "You are human. To accept Zynar's rut is a pressure we will not place on you."

I stop breathing. "Oh my God. That's why you're here. That's why Zynar has locked himself away. You're giving me a choice."

When he doesn't respond, only dips his head, I know I'm right.

Maybe I inhale sharply. My eyebrows rise on my forehead as I stare at him.

"Just what are we talking about here?" I whisper I'm missing something, aren't I. "His rut. It's just…sex, isn't it? The mate bond?" At least, that's what I think it is. This may all be new to me—most of it might be a shock—but, it's just…sex. Right?

I can do that.

Varek shakes his head. "No, Eleanor."

Use of my name makes me stand straighter, waiting for whatever he's about to drop on me.

"He has not just lost control; he's locked himself away because he's driven by something primal. An ancient need. Zynar will claim you over and over again, each time more fiercely than the last." Varek steps forward slowly, almost as if he's stalking me, and I'm reminded once again that although he and his brother can be so gentle, they're big strong apex predators and I'm just a little human. I stand my ground, facing him even as his words and slow approach make me swallow hard. "He will mate you again and again until his scent mingles with yours. Until your essence is interwoven with his. It's not a gentle process, kahlesta. It's relentless, consuming. He will not stop until he's satisfied that the bond is forged. Irrevocably so."

His voice drops to a near whisper as he continues. "You will be marked. Marked in a way that no other being could ever hope to erase. He will bite, scratch, and hold you with a force you've never known. The rut isn't just about pleasure or mating; it's about *possession*. Dominance. It's a ritual of survival and legacy, deeply ingrained in our species' core."

As if realizing the intensity of his words and the complete passion with which he said them, Varek suddenly turns away to face the door. "He locked himself away to protect you. And… there is nothing I can do to help him. If I enter that barn, he will tear me apart."

I gasp. "You're his brother."

"I am male. He will only see a challenge. Competition."

I release a slow breath, everything he said making me start to pace despite the faint pressure in my skull. I hold on to the bed and make my way around it. His explanation ties everything together. Even the fact he's wearing a protective suit just so his scent doesn't get mingled with mine. Protection against his own brother who might now be feral. For minutes, the room fades into silence between us.

"Did this happen because we..." I clear my throat. "Me and Zynar...we..."

"He mated with you."

I don't even want to ask how he knows, and so, I simply nod.

"It is deeper than that, kahlesta. It is fate." He glances at me over his shoulder. "It is a blessing."

But his words tell me one thing. Varek is mourning his brother because he's sure this is the end. But it isn't.

I've spent my whole life not doing what I wanted to do, and now it feels like the universe is telling me to go ahead. To finally live. I'm not throwing it away.

"If I don't accept this bond..." I can see when Varek's shoulders stiffen. He answers me smoothly anyway.

"Over the next few sols...the rut will consume my siblingkin. The need to claim you will slowly drive him insane. I can only hope his core-beat gives out before then." He turns to face me then but there is no judgment in his gaze. Instead, there is sad resignation. It hits me then that this male traveled all this way, came here knowing that his brother was in heat, going through something that would drive him to insanity, and yet still he came anyway to protect *me* from his own blood. He came with the thought that I wouldn't even consider this bond, and he stayed even when he realized his brother locked himself away and I was safe. He stayed and tended to me even while knowing his brother was slowly dying *because* of me.

I stare at him, the realization painting him anew in my eyes.

"Even with you rejecting the bond, kahlesta, I am still in honor of having met you." He bows his head again. "For Zynar to experience this gift—his core-rhythm's dawning—is a privilege he will count worth his final breath."

I absorb this silently, processing the sobering implications. Varek pauses, likely reading my turmoil through body language alone.

"How long does this...rut last?" My voice is but a whisper.

"It varies. For some, days. Others, mere hors." He meets my stare intently. "Why are you asking this, kahlesta?"

A thousand swirling thoughts tangle in my head. Why am I asking? Because I'm actually considering it.

"What if it doesn't work?" I blurt.

Varek blinks, his gaze heightening on me. For the first time since he arrived, I see a spark of hope in his eyes. He stares at me for a moment as if my words weren't ones he expected to hear. Frankly, several days ago, they weren't words I'd have expected to say either. But that was before I came to Hudo III. Before I met Zynar.

"If what doesn't work?"

"The rut." I clear my throat, all sorts of images coming into my mind with just that word alone. Images I'll have to dissect *after* we settle on this. "What if he goes through the rut and it doesn't work?"

There's definite hope in Varek's eyes now. "You are worried you might not survive."

I let out a nervous chuckle. "Ha, that too, but I'm really asking about what if he doesn't come out of this? What if Zynar is still...feral in the end?"

Varek shakes his head immediately, as if that's something that would never happen. "Your very presence will soothe him. You are all he needs."

I am all he needs.

Those words make my heart swell as if they're words I've needed to hear for a very long time.

I begin pacing again, rubbing my forehead to ward off the faint twinge of pain still in my head. Zynar didn't look so calm when he saw me through that crack in the wall. As a matter of fact, he seemed even more feral. I realize now that he was being pushed by the urge to rut.

I can feel Varek's gaze on me as I pace and when I look at

him, he is indeed tracking me with yellow-slitted eyes so much like his brother's.

"You...feel something for my siblingkin?" There it is again. That note of hope. As if it's something unbelievable. Something unprecedented.

But his words make a tingle go through me at the thought of his brother. I try to breathe through it. All that happens is that the memory of the past day shoots through my mind and everything that I felt with it.

"I do." I close my eyes, stopping my pacing as those words whisper in the room. I admitted it out loud. I like Zynar. These past few days, I've been falling in love with him.

"His scent." Varek suddenly sounds really close, and when I open my eyes, he's looming over me with that same look of hope on his face. "It calls you? His touch makes you feel something? You...*want* my siblingkin?" There's still that doubt in his voice, all mixed in with the hope.

I blink, looking away from him. I won't admit to him that I took his brother's sweaty towel to bed like some creep. That the thought of washing it almost sent me into tears. That I rubbed my clit on his shaft until I climaxed and only his fingers were inside me at the time. That when we finally had sex, it brought me to tears because everything had felt so right and I've never had that feeling before.

Instead, I nod. Varek's shoulders sag.

"Gods," he whispers, staring at me as if I'm a creature he's never seen before. "This is more than we ever imagined could happen. Your species is compatible with ours, that is clear. If we'd known of your existence, kahlesta..." He trails off, watching me.

"That's just the thing." I meet his gaze, hands fisted at my side. "We aren't supposed to be here."

His face goes completely unreadable again.

"But we *are* here. By some twist of fate, me and the other

humans that were taken survived and we're here. I'd like to think I was taken away from my planet for something other than pure bad luck. I'd like to think that this is really some act of fate. Meeting your brother has..." It's my turn to trail off and I look toward the door. "Zynar's reminded me what it feels like to fall in love again."

My heart swells and I press my hand over my mouth with the surge of emotions going through me. It all comes with a sudden surge of clarity.

"What am I doing?" I whisper. My gaze slides to Varek, and he shifts on his feet. "I have to go to him."

I move toward the door but Varek steps in my way, blocking my exit yet another time.

"Varek." My tone is hard. "We've already wasted too much time."

"You cannot go to him like this, kahlesta."

I frown. "What do you mean?"

"Zynar would have been listening to every word, every occurrence, since I brought you in from that field."

"He's in the barn. He can't possible have heard that...right?" My voice fades by the end of the sentence at the look in Varek's eyes.

"He is not the same male you had here working on your roof, kahlesta. He is...different now. His senses are primed for the ultimate act of his existence. And he will be enraged." He drops his tone so low, it's almost impossible to hear him. "Enraged that he can't have you. Enraged that I am here with you. Enraged that you're so far away from him even though he's the one to put the distance between you."

I swallow hard.

"If you are sure and we are to do this, kahlesta, we must make a plan." He watches me. Waits for me to change my mind.

I nod. "I'm sure," I whisper back, lump in my throat going down. Surer than I've ever been. I know that if I do this, I'm accepting Zynar as my mate, and offering myself to him as same. The thought is heady. "So…what's the plan?"

Varek brightens. "Simple. To ensure you're not harmed and that this…" his gaze shifts back around the bedroom, "…is a success."

ELEANOR

My heart's thudding hard in my chest as I pace in front of the bed. I'm dressed in a clean tunic. I've brushed my hair. I'm ready. And yet, each breath I take sounds loud in my ears. I close my eyes for a moment to just breathe.

A whole other sol has passed. Varek flat-out refused to enact his plan simply because the medic said I needed at least a day's rest. Nothing I said could convince him. The only thing that settled my nerves was the fact that after I begged, he at least let me venture outside to check on Zynar.

My heart broke. He was still in the same spot. Hair still hanging over his face, and his body still chained to the pillar. His gaze had snapped toward me even though I hadn't made a sound. His muscles strained against the chains, rippling with a power that seemed barely contained.

A heavy breath stutters through my nose now as I swallow hard, gaze shifting to the energy brews—as Varek called them—that are sitting in sealed cans on the floor. Apparently, I'll need them. My heart moves up into my throat as my gaze shifts to the carving knife next. It's there, tucked under the bed. 'Only precautionary,' Varek had said. The fact he insisted on me having it to use against his own kin has my breaths coming harder. I don't know if I'll be able to do that. It's Zynar. I couldn't…I *can't* hurt him.

Varek placed it there anyway.

His complete seriousness in this whole thing only makes my worry rise. Am I crazy for even attempting this? But there's still that nervous energy flooding through me. Anticipation. Need. Hope. I… I want to help him. I want Zynar to come through this. But more importantly, I want this to work. I smile for a second, remembering when he chased me in that field before handing me the bouquet.

Oh God, I hope Varek's plan works.

The loud bang that echoes through the now softly falling rain makes me jump, my eyes flying open. I know what it is, knew it was going to happen, and still it makes my heart ricochet in my chest.

Varek's driven the hover truck into the barn doors. I'd been skeptical but apparently, it's worked. The sound of the wood breaking is enough proof. I stop pacing, staring from the bedroom to the open front door, my heart still in my throat.

When Varek suddenly appears there, my heart thuds again.

His headgear is off and he gives me a small, hesitant smile, his shoulders heaving.

"Done?" I ask.

He nods. "I broke it down. Now he has to come out."

He's walking toward me, all business as he grabs ropes from where he's left them on the floor just outside the door.

"That was easy," he says. "Now for the hard part."

A lump rises in my throat even though there's an excited little quiver in the center of my chest. "Are you sure he'll be able to get out on his own? He's chained up."

"Trust," Varek says, that still slight smile on his face. "The lure will work."

My focus shifts to the front door, my gaze landing on the doorknob. I can feel my cheeks heating, that quiver in my chest spreading down to my core at the thought of what's about to come next. Because hanging on my front door is the 'lure'—one of my worn panties, swaying in the wind.

A peculiar way to go fishing, but I'm not trying to catch a trout here. I'm trying to catch my mate.

The word sends another quiver through me. One that ramps up the nervous energy in my bones.

"I can hear him," Varek suddenly says. "He's breaking free." His gaze shifts around. "I must hide."

Before I can open my mouth to go over the plan with him one more time, I hear a sound. One I can only describe as a roar that comes from somewhere outside. There is the sound of chains, and then everything goes silent.

"Varek, I'm trusting you in all this. If Zynar hurts himself I will beat you personally."

All I hear is a deep chuckle from somewhere in the room. I don't get to even check where he's hiding before there's movement on the window facing the porch. It's fast. A flash of fuchsia that sends my heart hammering against my ribs. My breath stops as I wait, standing there like some bait. But that's exactly what I am. Bait that's about to be rutted well and good.

A nervous quiver goes through my privates. After spending the majority of my life never reaching those mind-bending orgasms I used to read about, I'd prayed to God one time about it. My ma used to say all prayers are answered—

My heart stutters as I see a claw reach for my panties. He touches them so gently before his head comes into view. Crouched, Zynar grips the fabric, bringing it to his nose. The low rumble that goes through him vibrates through the air and everywhere around us before his head turns and those piercing eyes of his lock onto me.

—I guess I never, in my wildest dreams, expected my prayers to be answered like this.

I take a step back, the backs of my legs bumping into the bed as I stare at Zynar.

I'm not afraid, but there's a thrill. A thrill that makes me shiver. Something in the back of my mind says I shouldn't be getting turned on by just one primal look, but instead of that voice growing louder, there's a little throb between my legs.

Because despite the strangeness of this, the intensity, this is the most vivid experience of my life.

It's how I imagined my heart should have beaten at my wedding. Only, it didn't. How I imagined nervous energy should have gone through my veins my very first time. But, it didn't.

This is all different. As if I'm starting over. And after all the pain, I shouldn't be giving this a chance. Except I am. Because some part of me says this isn't the same as those other times.

Zynar stands, his gaze still locked with mine. He does look bigger. Bulkier. Taller. Stronger. Faster.

He's still naked and my breath hitches as he walks in, locks of his hair swinging slightly with the movement and something else swaying down below that I refuse to look at. Not yet. We have a plan and I have to stick with it.

"Zynar," I breathe. His ears flick and a lump rises in my throat. I have to keep his attention on me. That was the plan. If he realizes his brother is hiding in here, the whole thing will go upside down. He steps closer, nostrils flaring as he inhales. I just have to hope the other panties I placed on various furniture will dampen Varek's scent. I have to keep Zynar focused on me. And so I smile. It isn't hard. Relief is flooding through me just from the fact that he's here again. But my smile falters when I spot the fresh bruises on his arms and torso. Some of them bleeding from where the chains dug into his skin.

"You hurt yourself," I whisper. I blink away tears and he notices; a low growl starts in his throat. I sniffle, wiping them away. He can't think I'm hurt or in pain. He'll look for the source and destroy it. Well, that's what Varek said, and right now I'm trusting he knows what he's talking about.

Looking at Zynar now, he doesn't look like a mindless beast whose brain is taken over by an uncontrollable urge to rut. I find it hard to believe he'd kill his own brother for a female he only just met. But as he comes closer and I inhale, a deep groan releases from my lips. My lids flutter and I catch myself just as a surge goes to the center of my thighs. Zynar freezes, watching me.

I can smell him. And his scent is even thicker. Even more intoxicating.

Probably Varek is right. He's Kari after all. He should know. Because just a whiff of Zynar's pheromones and I'm already weak in the knees. The opposite effect must be true, too.

"Come to me." I beckon to him and Zynar moves, far too quickly for my eyes to keep track. My breath hitches as I tilt my head back to look at this alien who has come on my farm and on other things… With my nerves in a bunch, a surge of need I don't expect almost completely overtakes me.

Zynar lifts one claw slowly, bringing it up to my jaw. I lean into his touch, my eyes fluttering closed at the softest brush of his skin against mine.

"Liora," he whispers.

My eyes fly open and we lock gazes.

He's not completely out of it. Zynar's still there. Maybe we didn't need this plan after all. Except, only one of us seems to have realized this. I can't even stop the next event from happening as Varek shouts my name.

"Eleanor! Now!"

"Oh, crud." The curse slips past my lips at the same moment that Zynar extends his claws, his entire demeanor changing before me as he turns in the direction of Varek's shout.

Varek is a blur that appears out of nowhere. I barely get out of the way before he slams into his brother. A vicious snarl vibrates the air around us as they crash into the bed.

They struggle. Claws out. Fangs bared. I thought they were similar sizes but Zynar looks suddenly twice the size of his brother. He lands a punch into Varek's jaw that has Varek's neck twisting in the opposite direction. My eyes widen.

"Zynar, stop!"

But he doesn't. With one powerful kick, he sends his brother flying backward. Varek collides with the wall, his body going limp. He's down. The plan has failed. And as Zynar rises, his complete focus on his brother, I know I have to do something.

"Zynar…" His head snaps in my direction, his snarl lessening just a little. But then Varek shakes his head. He hasn't lost consciousness after all. He groans, shaking his head again, as he staggers upright. Zynar's focus slips from me immediately, the snarl on his lips making his fangs look deadly as his complete focus goes to what he perceives as a threat.

"Oh frakk," Varek says a moment before the air shifts. Zynar moves so fast, I only feel the breeze. The next moment he has Varek by the throat, squeezing so hard that Varek's eyes bulge.

I stand there in shock, my heart refusing to beat. I have to do something. Anything to get his attention back on me.

"Zynar!" I scream, hoping to divert his focus.

For a moment, it seems to work. His head snaps toward me, pupils still that narrow little line. But then he shifts back to Varek, grip tightening as a guttural growl rumbles from his throat.

Varek's face is changing color, desperate claws pulling at Zynar's iron grip to no avail.

I have to act, and fast. Spotting one of my panties, a part of me cringes. I grab it anyway, steeling my nerves for what I must do.

"Zynar, look at me!"

When his eyes find mine again, I rip the fabric. The sound of the linen tearing, combined with my commanding tone, succeeds in grabbing his attention.

Zynar drops Varek, the latter collapsing into a crumpled heap that pulls a huge breath into starved lungs. Zynar's focus remains fixed on me as he takes a step closer.

Heart pounding, I raise the panty and sway it in the air, using the primal cues Varek instructed to draw his focus. "Here, Zynar. This is what you want. Hmm?"

A rumbling growl escapes him, claws twitching at his sides. His expression is caught between beastly instinct and fleeting recognition of me. I pray the latter wins out.

Slowly, hesitantly, Zynar takes another step my way. Then another, eyes locked on the makeshift lure. When close enough, I stand my ground and hold it out between us.

For a breathless moment, nothing happens. Zynar hovers, breathing heavily through flared nostrils mere inches from me. Then his clawed hand rises to grasp the flimsy fabric, drawing it toward his face.

As he inhales deeply, something shifts behind his eyes.

"Eleanor," he groans.

I swallow hard, happy tears rising in my eyes. "Yes! Yes! It's me. I'm here."

It's just a simple moment, but my heart swells. But I don't get to reach for him. The moment doesn't last because Varek makes his move.

Coming in from the side, he tackles his brother from the side, throwing them both on the bed once more.

"Now, Eleanor!"

It takes me a startled second, but then I'm in motion, moving around to the side of the bed to get Zynar's attention. But Zynar is completely focused on his brother again. The moment I catch sight of his face is the moment I realize this male has never once been angry in my presence. Because right now, he looks down-right murderous. I don't know how Varek does it. He somehow secures one of Zynar's arms with one of the restraints. That doesn't stop Zynar, though. It only makes him more livid.

With one powerful kick, he sends Varek flying away again. His murderous gaze turns to his restrained arm.

"Oh no. Zynar! Zynar, I'm here! Look at me." This darned plan sounded doable when Varek came up with it, but now I'm wondering if we just made a horrible mistake. "Zynar!"

I touch his arm and he jerks. He's still snarling as his focus snaps in my direction. For a moment, I wonder if he will attack me too, but then his snarl dies a little. I take that as a green light to go on. Braving it, I get my ass up on the bed.

"Shh," I run my palm across his jaw. Zynar purrs, suddenly gripping me with his one free arm and forcing me to sit on his belly. I'm immediately brought back to our little tryst in the barn. How I'd sat on him just like this and ground myself into oblivion. "It's going to be alright. I'm here."

He seems to calm a little with my voice and my touch, something that makes me smile. Eyes locked on me, Zynar even seems to forget one of his arms is bound. It's as if he can only see me again. As if I'm the only thing that matters. It's such a heady feeling that I become lost in his eyes, no longer even aware of Varek in the room.

When he secures both of Zynar's legs in quick succession, Zynar's arm tightens on me before he bucks, trying to release himself. I notice now that he hasn't used any other words except to acknowledge my presence. As if he's unable to speak. He snarls though, fangs looking more wicked and deadlier than I've seen them before.

"I'm here, Zynar." I clasp both sides of his jaw, forcing him to focus on me. "We'll get through this. Together. I'm right here. I'm not going anywhere."

He snarls when Varek suddenly appears beside us. That murderous gaze shifts to his brother and, with one swipe,

Zynar's claw tears into him. The protective suit rips, long vertical tears where Zynar's claw digs into the material. The fabric darkens. I gasp and Varek grunts before holding down the final arm.

"You're only so frakking strong because your kahlesta has been feeding you delicious meals," Varek grumbles before choking on a laugh. My eyes are wide as I look at him. He's bleeding, and he has the time to joke? He secures Zynar's final arm and collapses against the wall, breathing hard.

"He told you about our meals?" I ask. Heck, maybe I need a distraction from the weight of what I'm about to do, too.

Varek shrugs. "He enjoyed them immensely." Then he grumbles. "Wouldn't stop boasting about it."

I sense a hint of jealousy, or perhaps sadness there, but Zynar's snarling and buckling again now that he's fully restrained. Varek rises, grinning down at his brother even though Zynar's gaze is spitting fire.

"You lucky brute." He grins. Zynar growls. "We can fight it out later. For now, enjoy your rut, brother…" His gaze shifts to mine, a soft smile on his lips. "And your new kahlesta."

Stumbling, he heads out of the room and I watch him go, my gaze shooting over my shoulder.

"There's a first-aid kit somewhere in my stuff out there."

"I'll be fine, kahlesta. Don't worry about me, I have a medkit, remember? Save your energy. You'll need it."

"Where are you going now?"

"Me?" Varek looks over his shoulder as he leans on the wall. "I'll be out here. My job is to protect you. If you need me…if you change your mind…I'll be by your side in a click."

I blink at him, wide-eyed, as he closes the door behind him. A lump forms in my throat as I turn my attention back to the unbelievably hot alien before me. Zynar is burning up. His skin. His entire body. His gaze. As soon as my eyes meet his, he bucks, hips shunting upward. My whole body moves like I'm paddling on a surfboard that's caught a massive wave...and about to catch a massive dong.

I stare down at him. What now?

I suddenly feel like a virgin faced with the first experience of her life.

"I...I never thought we'd be in bed like this again." I hedge. "Not so soon at least."

My cheeks burn as his gaze drops to my lips and a soft purr rises from his throat, cutting through a low tone that, in the confusion, I didn't notice till now. That low vibration is still there. So is the unsteady, uneven rise and fall of his chest as if he's still having trouble breathing.

He needs me.

And maybe, I need him too.

"Liora," Zynar whispers, and I close my eyes briefly.

"Zynar..." I slide against him, a tingle going through me. Am I just supposed to do this the regular way or is there something else? A method to this. I never asked Varek for the details.

Zynar needs to rut. Do I just let him?

My breaths quicken with the idea. To be at his mercy while he fills me over and over again. That sounds like the sort of heaven only present in the depths of the filthiest fiction. Can I really live it?

As I move my body against his, the sensation sends trickles of energy straight to my core.

"I've never done this before," I whisper, eyes rising to meet his. The absolute heat in his almost sets me aflame. "But I guess neither have you."

I run my hand down his jaw and grind my hips against his belly again. Zynar purrs so loudly, I feel a trickle of need go through my core.

"You knew I was yours?" I whisper. "Is that why you volunteered to work here?"

Zynar doesn't answer and judging from the rising fire in his eyes, he's being consumed too.

"Did you feel it?" I whisper, still rolling my hips. "You thought I was yours all along?"

He growls then and it isn't a growl of encouragement. He's pissed.

I smile a little. "Did I say that wrong?" I whisper. "Fine. I am yours, Zynar. Not a thought. Not a doubt. I'm yours."

Goodness, should it feel so good to say that?

Zynar growls again and bucks. Beneath my bum, his cock is like a hard pole I've been ignoring. I shudder, my eyes growing heavy-lidded with pleasure and need.

I'm so turned on, I don't think I can continue without the one thing I'm really craving for. I release him to brace up on my arms as I look down between us. I'm still clothed, in the tunic at least. There's nothing underneath. My throat goes dry as I see his cock jerk. Hard. It slaps against my ass, a string of pre-cum hanging from the tip as it rises and slaps down hard again.

Breaths coming hard, I reach for him, my entire body humming and a feeling of sweet honey gathering in my core as I align him with my entrance. I rub the sloped head there, a moan deep in my throat as I smear his spend all over my channel in preparation for him. I'm slow as I bear down, a groan rumbling from my lips at the same time that Zynar suddenly slams his hips upward. He slides in, *deep,* and I gasp, taking a moment to realign myself and breathe. But there's no slowing down. No time to catch a breath. My arms slam down, gripping his shoulders as Zynar begins to pound into me with a fervor that is unmatched. My eyes roll back, words fail to come to my lips as I stiffen, thinking this is going too quickly, too fast.

But the pleasure. My body opens to him. With each thrust, I stretch, wrapping around him and taking him all. A groan barrels up into my throat as Zynar's hips move. Even without the use of his arms and legs, I feel the power he's sending through each thrust. When he goes too deep at one point and I wince, he goes suddenly still. My eyes flutter open and I look down at him from where I'm bracing with all my might.

My chest is heaving as his cock throbs deep inside me. Right. He's still in there. He's not all gone. Zynar doesn't *want* to hurt me, but he needs me to be open to him.

I allow myself to relax. Settling against him, I wrap my arms around his shoulders and bury my face into his chest, inhaling deeply.

"Do it, Zynar. Make…make love to me like you want to."

I'm not sure he understands, but when I move my hips, he suddenly slides upward again, pushing him so deep my clit responds again. It stretches with the pressure of his thrust, making me groan once more.

I melt, releasing all the pent-up energy inside me. I don't fight the thrusts. I don't fight the call. I lean into them both. I let myself feel. I let myself feel real desire.

His pumps become fast, long, and deep, so much so that I'm happy I decided to stop resisting and just let things happen the way they should. My knees could never hold up riding him with this intensity. Not with the pressure of the pleasure shooting through me.

I cry out, an orgasm crashing through me that probably even eclipses the last one. For a moment, I remember that Varek is just in the other room, and that he can hear everything. But that thought is quickly erased when Zynar groans so loudly, the walls shake.

He comes. So much, that I feel it bursting through the seam between us.

I collapse, breaths coming hard as I shift my gaze up to Zynar's. "Feel better?" I whisper.

His cock, still hard, jerks within me. What was I thinking? They apparently don't call this a rut as a joke.

As he begins thrusting again, mingling the remnants of his

spend and mine, I ease forward as much as I can. Zynar tilts his hips and follows me as I place a soft kiss on his chin.

"I've been falling in love with you," I murmur as he begins thrusting harder. He probably won't even remember any of this and yet I speak anyway. "Where I come from, we don't have bonds like this." His pace picks up and it's an effort to speak now. "So if this doesn't work, I'd like to tell you something."

I bite back a moan as he slams his hips up hard, as if to tell me that he doesn't agree with my line of thinking. I almost choke on a laugh and a moan at the same time.

"Well, I'd like to tell you anyway. I want to try." I have to hurry before I swallow back the words. "With you. I want to try to make it work, if you're up for it."

I begin to vibrate as he sends me into oblivion. I climax again, and, as if set off by my orgasm, Zynar stiffens, his cock jerking as streams of spend shoot deep inside me.

I collapse against him again, completely wrecked. My chest is heaving as I lie there for a bit, just forcing myself to breathe. He jerks, his entire shaft adjusting inside me with the movement, and I tilt my head to look up at him again. He's still deep within me, that swollen part of his base like a seat I'm sitting on. As I adjust my hips, he pulls back and slides deep again.

I whimper.

"More?" I stretch up and kiss him under his jaw. "Do you want more?"

He purrs and slides out then in again. I encourage him, running my tongue along the line of his neck as I shift my hips once more. It's all the encouragement he needs before he starts pumping again.

I cry out, letting myself get lost. This is like a dream. I've never had anything like this. It feels like…it feels like I've never lived till this moment.

And so I let myself go. I climax. Not once. Not twice. Not three times. I lose count and still after all of that, his member remains rigid. When I can take no more, I force myself to slide off of him and I collapse on the side of the bed.

Breaths heaving from my chest, I turn my gaze to Zynar to find his chest is still heaving too and his entire body is still burning up.

I thought there'd be a change by now. Something at least, to tell me this is working. Brushing a hand between my legs, I shudder with the tingles that go through me. I'm absolutely soaked in spend.

Breaths still heaving, I look up at Zynar.

"You need more, don't you?" My gaze shifts to the restraints holding him back. "This isn't going to work, is it? Not like this."

22

ELEANOR

I pant as I stand by the side of the bed, gaze shifting to the door I just locked. The moment the lock slid into place, I heard Varek move.

"Kahlesta?"

"I'm fine. All is well."

The doorknob moves, then there's a sound like he bumps his shoulder into the door. "Kahlesta! Are you alright? The door is locked."

"I locked it myself!" My gazes slides back to Zynar. He's snarling again. His focus is on the door and the sound of the other male—his *brother*—who is on the other side.

"It's not safe. Zynar will have my head if he harms you and I let it happen."

"It's fine. He…" My chest heaves as I stare at Zynar, knowing that I'm a bit crazy, but also knowing this is a risk I'm willing to take. "He won't harm me."

The door bumps again, the doorknob rattling.

"Don't come in here. He'll attack you if you do." There's a slight pause as my gaze shifts back to the restraints.

"Kahlesta…what are you doing?" When I don't answer, he

continues. "I know this is hard. When I was a chid, I would hear females of our tribe talk about the moment they met their kahl. It is why I restrained my brother. So you can go as slowly as you need. It will take several sols, but his urge will eventually ebb. I will bring you meals. I will keep you hydrated. Whatever you desire, I will provide in my brother's stead."

"Varek…" I breathe. He doesn't even know me but I can tell he's worried. I can tell he's terrified of his brother hurting me. When I don't say anything else, he continues.

"If you grow tired…if you wish to abandon this mission." He pauses. "If you decide you do not want this anymore…"

"I'm not changing my mind," I whisper. He hears anyway. Because if there's one thing about me, it's that once I make up my mind I stick to it. I'm loyal to a fault. It's why my life turned to shit on Earth. But somehow, I don't think that's the same case here.

Zynar's gaze snaps to me the moment that I touch the restraint binding his arm. I try to loosen the knot, but it's impossible. Kneeling, I grab the carving knife Varek had insisted I place underneath my bed for security. It makes a slight *shick* sound as it scrapes across the stone floor.

"Kahlesta?" Darn it. Curse their good hearing. "Kahlesta, what are you doing? Has Zynar gotten free?" Varek bumps against the door again. Zynar snarls, teeth completely bared as he tugs against the restraints.

"No." *But he's about to be.*

The knife trembles in my hand as I bring it to Zynar's arm. He growls, his arm jerking back and tugging on the rope.

"It's okay," I whisper. "I'm not trying to hurt you. I'm just going to cut this."

"Kahlesta?!" Varek obviously heard that, too. He slams his shoulder into the door. Well, I guess the cat's out of the bag.

"If you come in here, we're both gonna kill you!" My heart's hammering as I bring the knife to the rope, sliding it just between Zynar's wrist and the rope itself. There's another thud at the door and my heart bleeds. Varek is committed to protecting me, even if it means his brother will try to disembowel him for coming even an inch near me. What did I do to go from nothing to having two people in my life who care for me so much?

The moment the rope snaps, time stills for a second. Zynar snarls, his gaze shooting to the door. I drop the knife and climb on the bed immediately, pulling off my tunic as I do. His attention refocuses on me.

"There," I whisper, my body heating from his mere attention. I feel beautiful. Absolutely alluring.

With a swipe of his claw, Zynar shreds the other rope, freeing his other arm. My eyes widen as he grips me with both and pulls me down to his face, his lips closing around my nipple in a hungry groan. A moan whimpers from my lips. He holds me there, making me straddle him as he alternates, running his tongue and teeth across the sensitive buds that harden at his insistence.

"Zynar, I—" But I'm moving again. My eyes widen slightly as Zynar spins with me in his grasp. As if my weight is negligible and he's simply moving a doll. I'm suddenly on my hands and knees. Eyes still wide in shock at how fast he flipped me, I look over my shoulder. The moment he shreds the ropes holding his legs restrained is the moment I know there's no turning back now.

So I lean into it. I relax.

When a claw finds my clit, the digit swirling and circling the little nub, fireworks go off in my veins. There's little warning before he sinks inside me, filling me with a single thrust. I cry out, almost collapsing beneath the pure power of this male as I pant his name. Zynar rubs my clit as he thrusts hard, never easing up, never relenting as he pulls another orgasm from me. I collapse then, unable to remain on my knees as he readjusts himself and grabs my hips instead.

His claws dig into my skin, not breaking it but holding me with a grip that says he won't let go. Each thrust is powerful, driving him deep inside me, touching places I didn't know could feel this good. The sound of our bodies meeting fills the room, a raw, primal rhythm that matches the urgency of his rut. I can feel the heat wafting off him, the overwhelming need to claim and mark me as his.

With each stroke, he drives me higher again, pushing me to the edge of pleasure that feels pulled from the depths of my being. I don't think I have it in me, but soon it's building again. Swelling deep in my core. Zynar leans forward, his teeth grazing my shoulder, a possessive growl vibrating through his chest. The sensation sends shivers down my spine, intensifying the pleasure already rising in my core. My breath comes in ragged gasps, my body trembling with the force of yet another climax.

He's relentless, his pace never faltering, each thrust more intense than the last. I can feel his need, his desperation, to claim me fully. It's overwhelming, and yet I crave it. This raw, primal connection. I *need* it. I realize now it's all I ever wanted. This utterly raw, pure, distinct declaration that I'm wanted. As his claws rake down my back, leaving trails of fire in their wake, I arch into him, crying out his name.

"Zynar!" I scream, my voice breaking with the intensity of my pleasure mixed in with pain. Tears fill my eyes, my whole soul ignited.

"Kahlesta?!" Varek sounds frantic, not sure if I'm experiencing pleasure or pain. Zynar growls, slamming into me harder.

"FUCK!" I've never cursed so hard in my life. "I'm fine, Varek! I'm alive! Don't break in!"

The embarrassment of having what, in essence, would be my

brother-in-law listening to me get railed has long gone. I don't care about anything outside this room anymore. All I care about is the male at my back.

Zynar responds with a deep, guttural growl, his thrusts becoming even more forceful. Each deep thrust presses his thickened base at my entrance, filling me to the brim as his sack swings forward, slapping against my swollen lips. I can feel the tension building in him, the imminent release that he's holding back. Those teeth that just grazed my shoulder sink in and I cry out again. The pain is immediate and I choke on the sharp intensity of it. But then there's warmth. Warmth as Zynar licks the wound at the same time that warmth spreads within. Like liquid fire running into my veins and spreading through me. Zynar growls, his pelvis still slamming into me as he licks the mark he just left and I know it's a claim that I am his.

The sensation, that pleasure-pain pushes me over the edge once more, my body convulsing with the force of my orgasm. My vision blurs, and all I can feel is him, his heat, his strength, his unyielding need. He roars, a sound of pure primal satisfaction, as he finally lets go, his release flooding me with warmth.

But it's not over. He's still hard, still moving, his need not yet sated. I can feel his cock throbbing inside me, the relentless rhythm of his thrusts driving me to the brink again. I'm helpless in his grasp, lost in the overwhelming pleasure he's giving me.

His claws tighten on my hips, and he pulls me back against him. Somehow we've shifted and I'm only partially on the bed now, half my body draped over it as he starts thrusting once more, each more powerful than the last. The raw strength of him, the uncontainable desire that drives him is like an energy cloud filled with spores that intoxicate. Because my body sings. Where I should be sore and pained, I tingle, desperate for more. Each stroke sends an electric bolt of pleasure crashing through me, my body responding without prompt or input from me.

"Zynar," I gasp, my voice a breathless whisper.

He growls in response, his lips brushing against my ear. "You are mine, Liora. Only mine."

The possessiveness in his voice sends another shiver down my spine, and I moan, arching into him. His teeth graze my neck where he just marked me, his breath hot against my skin. The sensation is intoxicating, driving me to the edge of sanity all while reminding me that this isn't a dream. It's real. It's real and it's happening to *me*.

I can feel the climax building again, the heat pooling in my core, ready to explode.

"Oh God," I whimper. "I don't think I can…"

His thrusts become frenzied, each one pushing me closer to the edge. I'm lost in the sensation.

"Zynar, please," I beg, not even sure what I'm asking for.

He answers with a deep, possessive growl, his hips driving into me with unrelenting force. The world fades away, and all that exists is him, his touch, his need, his love. My body shatters under the force of my orgasm, waves of pleasure crashing through me, leaving me trembling and breathless.

And still, he doesn't stop. His need is insatiable, his desire unending. He thrusts into me again and again, each stroke sending me higher, until I'm lost in a sea of pleasure, my mind and body completely consumed by him.

I'm not sure how much time passes, how many times I come, how many times I scream his name. All I know is the pleasure, the overwhelming, all-consuming pleasure that he gives me.

I was a fool. Why was I fighting this? Out of everything that has ever happened in my life, this is the only thing that feels undeniably right. From the moment I saw him, I should have known. This pull, I've never felt it with anyone else. And now, it feels like that all makes sense. I've never believed in soulmates. Not after my experiences. But…maybe I was wrong. Maybe I was just on the wrong planet all along.

Tears fill my eyes as I bury my face into our soaked sheets.

He…he's mine, and I am his.

Days pass. Time feels warped and strange. Every section of my skin buzzes, my core swollen and yet still seeping. The energy brews Varek supplied are drained, and yet, my energy is non-existent. Zynar's thrusts slow, the intensity ebbing away as the time passes. They become languid as he cradles me and still manages to bring me to climax, even though my body feels completely shattered. When he thrusts deep and gives one final groan, I know we've made it through.

Zynar barely manages to lift me onto the bed before collapsing. He pulls me into his grasp, tucking his body around mine as he trembles with the aftershocks of his release. I can feel his heartbeat, strong and steady, a comforting rhythm that grounds me more than I could have ever imagined it would. And beneath that, an almost silent hum, a rhythm I only hear because my ear is pressed against his chest.

I think we did it.

He's still inside me and when his cock jerks, the last of his spend releasing, I wince. I'm sore. So very sore and still there's a stupid smile on my face. I look up, my tired eyes meeting his. There's a tenderness there, a vulnerability that takes my breath away.

"Eleanor," he whispers, his eyes almost closed. "You are my… kahl…my mate."

Tears fill my eyes as I reach up to cup his face. "And you are mine, Zynar."

At this moment, it feels like I've actually found a new home.

23

ZYNAR

I wake from what feels like a haze that lasted several moons.

There's a buzz all over my frame, a sense of great accomplishment, and…something new.

My eyes flutter open, and I sense her presence immediately.

I freeze. Here in my arms, tucked against me, is my Liora. Eleanor. She's here and… The fog of the last few sols lifts slowly and my core-beat quickens. That's when I feel it. The new rhythm, settled and comforting underneath every single beat that keeps me alive. My core-rhythm is there. It is strong. I can breathe without effort. I feel better than I have ever felt in orbits and that can only be because…

My gaze shifts down to the Liora tucked in my arms. The scent of sweat, spend, and mating is thick in the room. My core-beat quickens even more.

I completed…I completed the rut?

Horror grips me at the same time that I catch the scent of something else. Lifeblood. My breath stills as I lift my claw to see the red fluid crusted at my claw tips. It's with effort that I cast my eyes lower, too afraid of what I might see.

But Eleanor is alive. She's breathing. I didn't... I swallow hard. I can't even think that thought. If I had taken her life in my state I would never forgive myself.

But there is still the scent of lifeblood. When my gaze shifts down further, I go still again. For I see it. The source. There are lines across her back where my claws no doubt trailed down her. Red lines where her lifeblood must have seeped from.

"Gods forgive me."

I'm not sure if I should pull her toward me or force her away because of what I have done. I completed the rut. That is clear. My core-rhythm is settled. My awareness is back. It's all cloudy but I'm remembering slowly. How I took her over and over till her soft body could take no more. How she relaxed in my grasp, even though I hurt her. How she let me sink into her over and over again.

I have a mate. A kahl that I always dreamed of.

Eleanor let me rut? Willingly? Or was she too afraid of doing otherwise?

Even though I wish to remain entangled in her arms for far longer, I shift, sliding my arms from around her. I only see more damage as our bodies part. Where I bit her on her shoulder has a deep red bruise. And her skin. Splotches of brown adorn her hips where I must have gripped her too hard. When I see the bandage on her head, it's the last snowflake that sets off a massive avalanche.

My core-beat goes unsteady again. I cannot breathe as I rise from the bed.

Eleanor's perfect sleeping space is destroyed. The room is in tatters; so is the bed. Some parts of the mattress are torn, ripped by my very claws and the bed itself is resting on a single leg.

The sight of her injuries, the evidence of my loss of control, fills me with a crushing guilt. I promised to protect her, yet here she lies, marked by my own claws and her nest destroyed. I stumble back, my chest tightening as I struggle to breathe. This isn't how it was supposed to be. I should have been able to control myself.

"Brother?" Varek's voice sounds behind the door and a surge of anger rises. He was supposed to protect her. From *me*. Why did he allow me to get to her? He should have taken her away! Far from this place. He should have let me dissolve into madness if it didn't mean Eleanor would be forced into a mate-hood she probably knows nothing about.

I was supposed to bide my time. Prove to her I can be an asset here on her farm. Win her over. Except the gods had other plans.

The greatest thing that could happen to any Kari occurred. I found my mate. I found my kahl, but I have hurt her. There is no telling if we even have a chance now.

The anger that rises is quickly tamped down. This isn't Varek's fault. It is mine.

I stare at Eleanor. Her golden strands with those fine specks of silver are damp and limp, hanging over her face and obscuring her beauty from me. I dare to move closer, to shift the strands away so I can look at her. She's a sight to behold. I could stare at her for eons and feel like my soul is being satisfied by the sight of her beauty itself.

I should have known. Known that she was something special to me from that very first sol we crossed paths. Which Kari can come face to face with his one true mate and not know? I am a fool.

Claw trembling, I brush a digit across her jaw, taking a liberty I might not be allowed again. Because, despite the odds, Eleanor survived this. She survived my rut and I have no clue how she will respond to it, to *me*, when she wakes. Because she has no core-rhythm. Her life organ doesn't sing like mine does by simply a brush of my claw on her skin. The mere thought of her rejecting me, even after the rut, makes my core-beat stutter.

The mere thought of having to leave, of being separated from her is already making me hyperventilate.

But even as I brush a digit over her skin, Eleanor doesn't stir.

"Brother?" Varek's call is more insistent this time, but my focus is on my mate. Her skin is hot—hotter than I've ever felt it. Concerningly so. Her breathing is so light, it's almost not there. Alarm makes the scales along my arms lift and shift.

"Kahlesta? Are you alright?" Varek bumps the door this time. "It's been several sols. I have no choice but to break this door down."

Several sols? Just how long have we been in here?

When I hear him about to break the door down like he said, I rise and unlock it. His stills when he sees me.

My brother isn't one to show his emotions much. Prefers hiding behind a facade ever since we found our mor lifeless, unmoving. But in times like this, I see that he still cares.

His shoulders sag and he releases a breath. Running a claw through his hair, he says, "I was worried sick."

"You let me in the room with her."

He stiffens. "She wanted to."

His words catch me off guard. "Eleanor is human. She didn't understand what a rut is. Her species doesn't go through such a thing. Nothing I read about her kind suggests she would be prepared for what I did to her."

Varek tilts his head, crossing his arms now. "She's as stubborn as you are, you know. I explained it all to her and she still wanted to help you."

Emotion chokes me, swelling in my throat. "She what?"

"She didn't want you to *die*." He frowns, fangs showing. "I'm beginning to think that was the wrong decision." Despite what he says, I can tell he didn't want me to die, either. Just from the fact that that relief reflects in his eyes before he hides behind his mask again.

Releasing a breath, I reach back into the room for a piece of the torn bed sheet and wrap it around my lower half. At another time, I would have argued with my brother. I would have been angry at him like logic says. But there are more important things.

"Where's your comm?" I brush past him into the room, staggering in a way that makes me frown. I'm weak. Weaker than I thought I would be. My core-beat's a little frantic as my gaze skips around the room. I have to shake my head to clear it, grogginess still making what's before my eyes go blurry.

It's clear Varek spent the last few sols in this room. There's a makeshift bed on the floor beside the table. The scent of burned meals from where he must have been trying to make something to eat. He was keeping watch, making sure my mate was safe while I was completely out of it. A rabid beast. It's not how I wanted Eleanor to ever see me. And my brother, he's done his best. It's not like we had a plan if this were to ever happen. Neither of us thought it was ever possible.

"Why?"

"Something's wrong with my mate." I stagger again, having to shake my head to dispel the blurriness.

He stiffens before going to the doorway, his gaze falling on Eleanor. "What's wrong with her? Did...did you...Gods Zynar..."

I growl, but he's right. I lost so much control that my mate's lifeblood is embedded in my claws. "Yes," I admit. Because whatever's wrong with Eleanor is directly because of me. I can't even face my brother with this fact. If I were him, I'd probably punch my lights out. "She's burning up. And she isn't moving. I need a medic." There's a tremor in my voice even though I try to hide it. Nothing has ever made my voice tremble before.

It's probably the only reason Varek's anger doesn't rise. When I turn, still trying to spot his communicator because I'm pretty sure mine is lost somewhere in the outbuilding, I catch the fact his demeanor shifts from caution to urgency. "A medic?"

"Can't take her to the clinic. I am in no state to pilot the hover truck, but if I must..." I try to stand taller, but my frakking strength wanes. I probably didn't ingest anything but my mate's juices for the last several sols and though that makes my entire being swell with an unknown warmth, I'm aware it isn't the best of things right now. Because Eleanor needs me and I am incapable in my current state.

"Like frakk you will. I will drive her—"

I growl, eyes flaming. My gaze shifts to lock with his. "She's my *mate*, Varek."

He hesitates. "Your core-rhythm it's..."

"Wrapped around my core-beat. I cannot be away from her. It would kill me." But then I hesitate again. "But if it means she will survive..."

Varek makes a sound in his throat. For the first time in a long while, I see his brows dive to his nose. He snarls. "No."

I step closer, my own brows furrowing as we glare at each other. "I can't lose her, Varek," I snap. The desperation that creeps into my voice is so evident I think it alarms us both. I growl again. "Where's the comm. I need help now!"

Because the thought of losing her when I've only just found her is unbearable. I stagger, leaning against the wall as Varek rushes around me. I hear him hurrying back outside, probably to the truck, as I make my way back in to Eleanor. I hover over her, my mind racing with dread. Every click feels like an eternity as I wait, my core-beat pounding in my chest.

When Varek returns, comm in hand, he's already speaking rapidly into it. "This is Varek of the Korruk line. We need immediate medical assistance. It's the human female. She's unresponsive, high fever."

I don't move from Eleanor's side, my hand brushing her

damp hair back from her forehead. Her breathing is shallow, each rise and fall of her chest a fragile promise of life.

"Help is on the way," Varek says, his voice steady but his eyes reflecting the same fear I feel. "We'll get her through this, brother. We have to."

Can he sense it? My desperation?

I might as well die if Eleanor doesn't survive this. I don't deserve to live if I have hurt her so badly she doesn't even have the chance to recover.

As we wait, every second stretching unbearably, I silently vow to do whatever it takes to save her. This is not how our story begins or how it ends.

ELEANOR

J grunt. My head feels like someone dropped a boulder on it. Trying to sit up, I become confused as my fingers fold into soft, fresh sheets beneath me.

"Hmm?"

I could laugh at myself to notice something as mundane as the sheets, but they're a stark contrast to the chaos I remember. I shift, wincing at the dull ache in my muscles. My eyes flutter open. I'm in my room and the sun is shining. My gaze shifts to the window and the bright pink sky out there. The roof held through the rain. He did a great job.

It's another random thought that feels almost like my brain trying to scramble for things to distract me with. There's heat all along the center of my chest and I breathe a little harder as I rub at the spot.

Trying to rise, I grunt. My entire body aches. My neck. My back. My...everything. And now that song is stuck in my head. I groan and that's when I realize there's been voices in the background all along. Arguing male voices. Several of them. As soon as I groan, there's silence. And then there's the sound of scrambling feet.

It's Zynar that I see first. Just the sight of him sends an electric shock straight through me that culminates in my core. I blush. Shouldn't I be sated? If memory serves me right, we shared this same bed for days without stopping.

"Little Bird," he grunts. He's looking at me strangely, his eyes slightly wide. Gone is that predatorial look he had when I'd peeked through the crack at him in the barn. That same look that had followed him inside before he took me to oblivion. Instead, the strange look in his eyes makes me more alert.

"Zynar, is everything…" That's when I see the other male that suddenly appears at his back. Varek has the same strange look on his face, right before it slips behind an unreadable mask. When two white fluffy ears separate them and Xarion steps into the room, my eyes widen even more.

"Xarion?"

Xarion adjusts his collared jacket and stands tall. "Eleanor."

Behind him, the two Kari stand tall too. For all appearances, Xarion looks like something those two would have hunted in times past. Now, he stands before them like he has no fear at all.

"What's…what's this about?" I rub my head, wincing slightly at the bump that's still on my skull. At the sound, Zynar's ears flick, that strange look in his eyes increasing. My gaze shifts back to Xarion. "Is something wrong?"

"I was alerted of your critical state by the Kari who you seem to have…mated?" His ears straighten as if it's something he can hardly believe, and I feel my cheeks warm.

"My critical state?"

"You've had a fever," Xarion states, folding his arms behind his back. "One that held you unconscious. Coupled with the wounds you sustained during the rut, it was severe enough to cause great concern."

"Wounds?" My gaze shifts down but I'm covered by a sheet. "I don't remember any wounds." But then I recall Zynar's bite. My fingers move to my shoulder now, a slight wince going through me at the warmth that emanates there. "Oh, you're talking about Zynar's bite? It's nothing. Doesn't even hurt."

None of the males before me look convinced. Varek is a mask of unreadability. Zynar still has that strange look in his eyes. And Xarion is frowning. He's angry. At me? At them? Certainly at them, because his glare shoots to Zynar a second later. Zynar's throat moves, his gaze never leaving me. The absolutely broken look in his eyes has me sitting up a little straighter.

"There were also wounds across your back where the Kari used his claws to rip into you."

My mouth falls open. "What? No. No that's not what happened at all."

"You *bled*." Xarion doesn't budge, and I realize that I under-estimated him as a male. This no-nonsense attitude isn't one I'd have expected from him. He's taken charge. "In addition, there are bruises all over your frame. I will file a report and the Kari will be removed once you sign the documents."

His words make some part of me choke in what can only be fear. "What? No. Why would you..."

And that's when I realize that the look in Zynar's eyes isn't a strange one I can't read. Because I completely understand it now. It's fear. Zynar thinks he hurt me. They all do.

I take all three men in before I slump in the bed and groan. All three basically tumble through the doorway to get in. I resist the urge to chuckle despite the seriousness of the situation.

"I'm fine." I hold up a hand to stop them. "I feel better than I've felt in...years."

Xarion stands straight again, adjusting his clothes as if what just happened wasn't a lapse in his facade. Even the Saffion cares about me. I smile.

"Your wounds..." Xarion begins, frowning again and keeping the two Kari at his back as if he's protecting me from them.

"Are nothing. Inconsequential. I bruise easily. At least, on this world I do. Even on Earth, we get cuts and scrapes from things that should be harmless like, I don't know, paper." I can tell none of them understand what I mean. "What I'm trying to say is that Zynar was incredibly gentle with me." My gaze shifts to him. To Zynar. To my mate. At just that thought, there's an undeniable heat that spreads through my chest so fast that I feel like I'm burning up.

Zynar stares at me as if I'm still his world. As if I'll *always* be his world.

"You didn't hurt me, Zynar. The scratches, the bruises, each one holds a memory I don't want to ever forget." His ears flick at the sides of his head. "I enjoyed every second of it."

It's not how I imagined speaking to him after everything that happened over the past few days but it's clear he needs my reassurance. And that they need it too, Xarion and Varek.

"Are you…" Xarion frowns. "Are you saying you accept the mate bond of this Kari? You still have a choice, Eleanor. He will have to obey your wishes whether or not he completed the rut."

I nod. "Why would I not accept?"

Xarion stares at me. Behind him, Varek's brows rise as he stares at me too. Are they surprised?

"We are prey species." Xarion's ears fold slightly as he says that. He gives the other two males a side-eye that tells me that this bravado is actually taking a lot out of him. And he's doing it all for me. A female he simply had to show her farm and leave alone after that. "Fangs and claws are…"

"Scary?" I smile.

Xarion brightens. "Precisely. They're terrifying. And not just to us, Eleanor. To many species, claws and fangs represent danger."

I glance at Zynar, seeing the concern in his eyes. "I suppose. But not for me. Not with Zynar. He's shown me nothing but care and respect."

Xarion shifts uncomfortably, clearly still struggling to

reconcile my words with his own instincts. Varek, however, seems more accepting, his tense posture relaxing slightly.

"If you are certain," Xarion begins, his tone still skeptical, "then I will respect your decision. But understand that this bond is not something to be taken lightly. It will change you, bind you to him in ways you cannot fully comprehend yet."

That heat in my chest burns so much I can't ignore it anymore.

"I'm sorry." The words are all I can say as I push the sheets down. It feels like something is searing into my skin and the pain is so much that it's bringing tears to my eyes. "But something's wrong."

"Gods of Karicek..." Varek mutters.

Zynar's suddenly before me, having pushed his brother and Xarion out of the way. His claws hover over my chest, his eyes wide as he looks down at me.

There, between my breasts in a path that goes down the center of my chest and disappears beneath the sheets, is a swirling pattern that looks like a raised tattoo on my skin. Except it's not dark. It's red and it *burns*.

"Are those..." I hear Varek's voice as I cover my breasts and stare down at the thing on my chest, my eyes wide with confusion and a bit of fear. "Are those kahl sigils?"

"That is...unheard of," I hear Xarion say. But when I lift my head, I can only look at Zynar. He's staring at me, his chest heaving as he looks into my eyes.

"Eleanor..." he murmurs.

"Zynar, what is this? What's happening to me? It hurts." I wince, biting down on my lower lip as a wave of heat and pain emanates from my chest.

"Get out," Zynar breathes, looking over his shoulder at the other males. "*Get out!*"

The urgency in his tone sends Xarion and Varek scrambling

to obey, their concern evident but overridden by the clear command.

The door closes behind them, leaving just the two of us. The silence is thick, broken only by my labored breathing and the low hum of energy that seems to emanate from the markings burning on my chest.

"Zynar," I whisper, the pain making my voice tremble. "What is happening to me?"

He's staring at my chest and even with the pain, his proximity is making something within me sing. The marks burn harder as his scent wafts into my nose. I hum and whimper at the same time.

"The sigils…I've never seen them before," he whispers.

"Then…" I wince, clenching my teeth. "Then how do you know what they are?"

"This is…this is something we heard about back on Karicek when we were chids. Old stories that those with no corerhythm who mated with our kind, would be marked in some other way. This too, we believed to be a myth."

I nod, understanding yet not really understanding this whole mating thing. Apparently on Earth, we're so primitive that it isn't this complicated. Just wham, bam, thank-you ma'am.

"Will it always hurt?" I grip on to his claw that's still hovering over me and Zynar purrs before he cuts off the sound.

"It shouldn't." His gaze shifts to mine, a trembling claw coming to cup my jaw. "I am sorry, Liora. I have only brought you pain."

I shake my head. "No. You've brought me life." I grit my teeth. "But yes, there is pain. I need you to soothe it for me."

His head pops up like a dog that's just heard the word "walk" or "park". If he had a tail, I'm sure it would wag.

"Anything for you, Liora." Zynar straddles me and my entire body flutters. When he dips his head and runs his tongue over the marks, my head falls back in a moan. How do I still have the energy to even get aroused? As Zynar licks and sucks on my skin, I run my hands through his hair, looking down at the male that's made me feel more than I've ever felt in such a short time.

His tongue is like a salve against a wound. Every swipe soothes my skin, sending tingles right through me and straight to my core as he follows the path between my breasts and lower. He goes over my belly until he gets to where the sheet bunches at my hips. With a low purr, he pulls it down and continues going down.

The tension in my shoulders ebbs as I look down. The pain in the marks is ebbing and they're being revealed even more. It's like a purple tattoo that's marked me as his. A flutter goes through me when Zynar continues to go lower.

"Oh, I'm not hurting there. As a matter of fact, the marks are —" When his tongue swipes over my center, I jerk at the over-sensitivity left behind from the days of rutting.

"I must soothe you here too," he purrs. "It is my fault that you had to endure so much."

"Endure?" I whimper. I wouldn't call it enduring but—my thoughts turn to mush as Zynar licks and sucks me. He doesn't just stay between my legs. His lips and tongue move over every inch of my skin till my entire body is tingling from his kiss. When he finally makes it back up to my face, I giggle. He pauses as if surprised by the sound. When I open my eyes, he's staring at me.

"What is it?" I sober a little.

"You do not wish for me to leave? To reject this bond that I have forced upon you?"

I sober completely, brow furrowing slightly. "Won't you die if I push you away?"

When he doesn't answer, I wrap my arms around his neck and pull him in. Zynar braces his arms up, trying not to crush me as I hug him.

"Doesn't this mean you're mine now?" I grin at the words even as he dips his head and inhales my hair.

"For as long as you want me to be."

I hug him tighter. "Why wouldn't I want you?"

He grunts and I realize it's a scoff. "You're a desirable female many males would fight for if they had the chance. You have your pick of males from many worlds and species. You have no core-rhythm. The bond…"

"I can feel it too."

He stiffens, almost as if it's been something he's been hoping for.

"I can feel it. It's not like the core-rhythm, I suppose, but I feel it. Call it human instinct. A gut feeling. When we know something's right. It's an inexplicable sense that guides us. I trust it."

Zynar lifts his head and looks down at me. "You choose me?"

"Zynar," I whisper. "I think fate put us together for a reason."

He stares down at me before his head tilts, his lips brushing against mine almost hesitantly.

I open up to him, accepting his slow soft kiss and realizing it's the first real one we've shared as a mated couple. *Mated.* I can't even really believe it, but I'm smiling against his mouth by the time the kiss ends.

"It is nice to see your joy, Little Bird. I worried…"

"That I would run away?" I smile, shaking my head. "Never. I've got a mate now, and a farm to run, remember?"

Zynar grimaces. "About that…"

ELEANOR

J step out of the room, a fresh robe wrapped around me and Zynar following like a guard at my back. I'm very aware of the fresh flush on my face and the fact that everyone in this room knows that I've been freshly, well, mated.

"Oh, Xarion. I didn't expect that you'd still be here."

Xarion turns from where he'd been standing by the window, both arms clasped behind his back. His gaze skips over me and then moves to Zynar then back.

"I would have already left if the human didn't insist on meeting you before we headed to her farm."

At first, I think he's referring to me. But then that doesn't make sense and I frown. "The human? There's another human here?"

"Affirmative. With your budding relationship with the Kari, the New Horizons Initiative is well underway." He blinks, long lashes floating over his red eyes. "Accepting the Kari's mate bond," his gaze slides to Zynar again, "will do well to improve the success of the initiative."

I clear my throat. "Yes." As if that's the reason this all happened. I'd all but forgotten I was supposed to be getting along with Zynar for some other reason. "Well, where is she now? The human."

Xarion's gaze shifts back to the window. I step up beside him. "And...where's Varek?" My eyes widen when I see that there, at my gate, are two oogas lazily eating grass. Sitting on top of one is a human woman who seems to be telling Varek a story. Meanwhile, Varek himself is standing by the ooga, looking up at the female. His back is turned so I have no idea what his reaction is.

"What the frakk..." Zynar murmurs. "Is he...being *sociable?*"

"Indeed," Xarion sounds bored and just about fed up with all of us.

"Xarion! You should have told me! We made her wait so long!"

Xarion grunts. "You were indisposed. I didn't think you would want her to come in and hear you getting...well...whatever it is that you and your mate were doing behind that closed door." He inhales deeply. "Whatever newly mated pairs do."

Is that a sense of longing in his voice? I'm not sure. It's so fleeting that I don't get a chance to decide.

I hurry back in and change into a tunic, not before taking an extra minute to marvel at the design etched into my chest. A sense of pride and longing sweeps over me as I step out of the bedroom again. Zynar's waiting right there.

"Liora, are you sure you're well enough to go outside?" He steps up to me, worry on his brow. "If you wait here, I can bring the human to you."

I shake my head. "She's probably as nervous as I was about this move. It would be best if I'm the next person she sees." I'm saying this as I head to the door, though, when I step outside under the warmth of the sun, it's clear the other human still has company.

Varek shifts on his feet, head dipping slightly as he notices my approach. I nod to him too before turning my attention to the other woman.

Her eyes are a brilliant green not faded by time or hardship, and they widen with curiosity and excitement as she notices me approaching. She looks about my age, perhaps a bit older, I can't tell. I've never been good at guessing people's ages. But what I do see with absolute surety is the air of determination and resilience that reminds me of myself when I first arrived here.

"Hi there," I greet her warmly, trying not to wince at the still-lingering aches as I try to put her at ease. "I'm Eleanor."

The woman smiles, a bit nervously, but there's a spark of friendliness in her eyes as she leans forward on the ooga to shake my outstretched hand. "Catherine. It's nice to make your acquaintance, Eleanor."

Both Varek and Zynar stare at our exchange. Zynar stands protectively close to me, his presence a comforting weight at my back. Varek, meanwhile, seems almost awkward, his usual confidence replaced by something more tentative as he listens to Catherine speak.

"Varek here has been telling me all about the farm," Catherine continues, her gaze flitting between him and me. "It sounds like you're building something really incredible out here."

I chuckle softly. "Well, I can't take all the credit. Zynar has been a huge help."

Zynar purrs softly, the sound sending delightful shivers across my spine. The mark on my chest warms up and I try not to react as I shift my gaze upward to look at him. There's a small smile playing on his lips. The first smile I've seen since I woke up to his worry.

"It is a joint effort," he rumbles.

Catherine looks genuinely impressed. "You already have a field ready for tilling. You'll have crops in no time, I'm sure."

I smile and shrug. "Zynar here will have to teach me how to use the tools, but we'll try our best."

Catherine smiles. "It's inspiring, really. Makes me feel like there's hope for us humans out here after all."

I take in her words, quite sure she has no idea of the weight of that utterance. With Zynar at my back, those words feel almost filled with certain promise.

"There definitely is," I whisper.

There's the sound of someone clearing their throat and I turn to see Xarion waiting patiently behind us.

"Right," Catherine sits up straighter, inhaling deeply as she does, her gaze cast in the distance. "I've held Mr. Xarion here for far too long. I just didn't want to pass by without meeting you." She turns her gaze to me. "He tells me my farm is that way." She points east. "A bit of a ways away from yours."

She smiles a little but she's human. I can see the uncertainty underneath her bravado. Reaching up, I squeeze her hand and she jerks slightly at my touch before she presses a soft smile to her face.

"I'll visit whenever I can," I assure her.

Catherine's polite smile falters just a little, the uncertainty in her eyes more pronounced. Her expression softens with an almost apologetic look.

"That's very kind of you, Eleanor, but I wouldn't want to be a bother. You've got enough on your plate here. I'll manage, somehow." Her voice carries a quiet resolve. "I've lived on my own for a long time, so don't you worry about me."

I squeeze her hand one more time before letting go. "You'd never be a bother. Don't hesitate to reach out if you need anything, even if it's just for a chat." Then my face lights up. "We have these handy smartphones that can do anything. Just give me a ping!"

Catherine nods, her smile becoming more genuine, but the

hesitance is still there. "Thank you, Eleanor. I'll keep that in mind."

Xarion steps forward, his presence commanding attention. "Catherine, it's time to go. We have a long journey ahead."

With a final nod to me and a glance at Varek, Catherine turns to follow Xarion as he hops on his ooga with such grace, I'm only reminded of how clumsy I was the first time he took me out here on mine.

"Goodbye, Eleanor." Catherine waves. "Good luck with your farm."

"Goodbye, Catherine. Stay safe," I call after her, watching as she and Xarion head off into the distance.

My gaze skips to Varek, who is watching them leave, and then to Zynar, whose attention is solely on me. Warmth pulses from the sigils as I turn to face him.

"Well, this has already been a long day. Want to go inside?"

I don't get an answer but a yelp escapes my lips as Zynar suddenly swoops in and lifts me into his arms. I hear Varek groan and it makes me chuckle.

"Let's go back inside." It's not the words but the way Zynar says them. That growl that sets my insides alight.

Varek groans again and my gaze shifts to him when he walks in the opposite direction—towards his hover truck.

"Um, Varek, what are you doing?"

He pauses, gaze shifting to me before moving to his brother. "Leaving before he remembers I let him rut when I shouldn't have. The last few sols have been very…eventful."

I frown at Zynar. "Have you been arguing with your brother?"

He frowns immediately, too, eyes piercing in Varek's direction. "He was supposed to keep you away from me."

"And let you die?"

"If I'd hurt you more—"

"You *didn't*," I stress. "You wouldn't have."

Zynar stills and I know he's still wrestling with himself over what happened.

"Either way," I turn back to Varek, "you can't leave. Not without getting some rest and proper nourishment."

Zynar frowns again. "You will not be on your feet preparing any meals."

I grin. "Good. Because you're the one who is going to cook for him." He looks surprised enough that I laugh. "And me."

That makes him purr.

I face Varek again who is still hesitating by the truck.

"Come on." I jerk my chin toward the cottage. "You're family now."

"Family?" Zynar parrots.

"Kin." I'm not smiling now, I'm serious and when Varek freezes before his gaze shoots to Zynar, I know I've said the right thing.

Varek's shoulders loosen and he releases his hold on the hover truck door.

As you wish, kahlesta," he gives me a slight bow.

"As you wish, my kahl." Zynar grins.

As we make our way back to the cottage, I see the extent of the damage to the barn. My eyes widen.

"Are you sure this is what you really want?" Zynar whispers, noting where my focus had gone.

I look up at him, nodding without hesitation. "I have no doubt."

Somehow, I think we've both found something we've wanted. Something we've both needed.

EPILOGUE

ZYNAR

I have a kahl. And she is beautiful.

My core-rhythm sings each sol at just waking to see her face sleeping peacefully against my chest.

This is the life I've always dreamed of. The one I thought would never find me. But Eleanor made it possible.

The farm is growing. I've redoubled my efforts in repairing all the outbuildings to bring them up to par. I've mended every tool that's still in working order and gotten Varek to dispose of the rest. He's been acting strange lately. Whenever he thinks I'm not looking, I catch him gazing at me when I have my Liora in my arms. It's not hard to tell what his thoughts might be.

I've found my kahl, and that means that there's a possibility he might find his, too. If I were my siblingkin, it would be the singular thought on my mind. Just like Eleanor is on mine at every moment.

I gaze down at her now; at how her hair dances in the soft breeze that rushes past where we rest on the porch. Eleanor had me set up what she called a 'hah-mok', a strange swinging seat made of textiles strung up from the roof. It sways slowly as we rest within it. It is my favorite spot to rest after a sol tending the field. Here, Eleanor has no choice but to allow me to wrap myself around her. It's the only place I feel completely at ease.

I purr now as she adjusts herself, one of her legs sliding across my crotch and the ever-present hardness there.

It has been this way since the rut. Every second in her presence feels like an opportunity to slide within her heat. Even her smile makes my cock jerk in anticipation of sinking deep within her again. But I must withhold myself. I will never forget the sight of her lifeblood on my claws. Of the marks I left on her perfect skin. And though she's healed completely now, it's still like a haunting memory.

My kahl is far too precious. I will treasure her till the end of time.

She snuggles against me now, whispering something about making me meatlohf. It's now my favorite meal. But I don't want her to move. I want to lie with her in the quietness of this home. *Our* home.

Eleanor has decorated the walls with blooms that grow from hanging pots. She's added color to the walls. A soft pink a few shades lighter than the sky itself. She giggles when she does these things, as if they make some part deep inside her unequivocally happy. It was the same with the garden I dug at the side of the lodge. She squealed the moment she saw it, pulling me into an embrace and smashing of lips that made me purr so hard I immediately started thinking of what else I can do to make her react with such fervor. She'd tucked a bloom into my mane and giggled at the effect. Each day, her happiness grows, and that is all I need.

Dipping my head, I inhale deeply, her scent filling my nostrils. I can't help it, my claw slides down the center of her chest, skipping across the sigils there until I reach the center of her thighs. Eleanor gasps and clamps her legs shut with my claw trapped between them.

"Zynar," she whimpers. "I've already come twice today."

I huff a laugh through my nose. "Is that supposed to make me want you less?" I dip my head to her ear. "You're so beautiful when you come, Little Bird. It only makes me want you more."

Her breath catches and she shifts her hips so her core rubs against my palm.

All else falls from my mind. Nothing else matters.

For I have found my kahl. I have found my home.

ELEANOR

I stand with a mug in my hand, drinking some iced-tea—or at least the equivalent of it out here.

Zynar's in the field, planting crops. He's been doing so much work here, work that would've taken me months or maybe years, that I wonder how I would have even managed to do it all alone. He's planting a wheat-like plant and by the next season, we will have a harvest. Our first one. I even have a garden with more flowers than I can bear to keep for myself. With Zynar's help, I'll be setting up a stall in the town soon.

Xarion, of course, is completely delighted with the progress. His short little comments on our progress make me laugh. And that's all to say that the New Horizons Initiative is fully under-way. Apart from Catherine, he's told me they've settled two other females out here on the plains. We humans are settling in. My gaze slides from Zynar to the new hover truck parked in the yard. Zynar's addition to the farm. I have no idea how to pilot the thing, but know I just have to say the word and he'll take me to introduce myself to the others.

He's so selfless. Even more than I first realized.

Turns out, that job the comm had told me Zynar cancelled was the job he completed. He refuses to take payment for doing my roof, even though it was before we became official mates. Thinking about Catherine, I have an idea of what I can use the funds for. I pinged her recently, and just like my farm, hers has a lot of work that needs to be done. Sponsoring her on Zynar's behalf seems like the right thing to do and he even agreed.

I smile now. The changes in my life are staggering. I feel younger, more vibrant. My mornings start with a sense of purpose, a far cry from the lonely, aimless days I had back on Earth. I've found a rhythm here, a balance between the farm work and my relationship with Zynar. We're building something real, something lasting, and every step forward fills me with pride.

Zynar catches my attention again and when I look his way, he waves to me from the field, a broad smile on his face. His presence is a constant source of strength and reassurance. I wave back, my heart swelling with affection. This bond between us is something I never expected, but it's become the cornerstone of my new life.

I take another sip of my drink, savoring the moment. Catherine's words echo in my mind. *"It's inspiring, really. Makes me feel like there's hope for us humans out here after all."*

Hope. It's a powerful thing. And out here, amidst the fields and under the vast, open sky, I've found it in abundance.

AFTERWORD

❋☆❋☆❋

Whoo! You reached the end of Eleanor and Zynar's story. What a ride!

When I first started writing this book, I knew I wanted my heroine to be someone who finds love later in life. I've always wanted to do a series like this and hesitated because it's not the genre norm. But, I'm going to publish them nonetheless, hoping that some of you will read and find joy in them.

All books planned for this series will have heroines who find love later in life after divorce, widowhood, or whatever life threw at them.

If you've ever wondered if love could bloom again after heartbreak, loss, or life's unexpected twists, this series is for you. The Kari are waiting to welcome you with open arms (and maybe a few growls)—and trust me, their ruts are *legendary*.

Happy reading—and get ready to fall in love with the Kari all over again in the next book!

♥ A.G.

NEXT IN THE SERIES

An Alien for Her Heart

Catherine

On the alien plains of Hudo III, I seek refuge from a past haunted by loss. My solitude is my sanctuary, or so I believe—until Varek appears. The alien warrior stirs something within me I thought was long dead: *desire*. He promises a bond forged in fire and intensity, one that leaves me lost—torn between the fear of opening myself again and the yearning to embrace a love that could heal my broken heart..

Varek

She's captivating. From the moment my eyes land on the human female, she becomes not just a puzzle to be solved, but the mate I desperately want by my side. I must convince her that together we can forge a future, if only she'll give me a chance. But I'm a broken male. I do not deserve her. My persistence should be tamed.

Only, I cannot stop. *I want her*. Broken or not, deep down, I know, this female is *mine*.

Heck, she's not even in the same galaxy, and the face hovering so close she can make out every detail? That face is definitely...not...human.

But before she can really figure out what's going on, Kerena realizes she's caught in the middle of a war—one she was thrust into as soon as she was ripped from Earth.

She's surrounded by aliens in a rebellion, but there's one—the one with the strange golden eyes, minty-teal skin, and rippling muscles—that holds her attention.

His presence is magnetic and his heated gaze makes something stir deep within her.

He's battling something that has nothing to do with the war and his warning that she should stay away does not go unheeded.

He's a dangerous rebel fighter. She gets that. So...why is he still hovering so close? And why is he growling at everyone that so much as looks in her direction?

Most of all, why does he keep looking at her like she belongs to ... HIM?

Other books in the series: V'Alen

Riv's Sanctuary
Series Title: Riv's Sanctuary

Abducted from Earth over a year ago, Lauren spent most of that time getting accustomed to her new life as one of the "animals" in an alien zoo.

When she's sold by the zookeeper, her life takes a turn she wasn't expecting. She has no idea where she'll end up till she's brought to a sanctuary owned by a tall blue hunk of an alien called Riv.

Riv's life is quiet and peaceful in a place as far away from civilization as he can manage. So when an annoying chatterbox of a human ends up on his doorstep, he's less than pleased. The human disrupts his life and his solitude and he can't wait to get rid of her.

He's not interested in helping her, and he's definitely not interested in love.

Except…she's managed to wheedle her way in and suddenly those barriers around his heart don't seem so strong anymore.

He has two options: Let her go.

Or let her in.

Other books in the series: Sohut's Protection, Ka'Cit's Haven

Arrival

Series Title: Captured Earth

Adira

The machines came, and they trampled us all.

I have nothing left. No family. No friends. No home.

They harvest us. They breed us. They feed from us…

There is no hope…Not until one fateful moment when my eyes open and I see something streaking across the skies.

What appears is like a demon before my eyes…

But can they be worse than the evil already upon us?

I will just have to wait and see.

Fer'ro

Sailing across the stars for what feels like eons…we have followed our enemy to a little blue planet.

We had wanted to arrive before them…now I think we may be too late.

But when we kill the first Scrit and I see the being drowning within its depths, I know I have to save it.

And *it*…turns out to be a *her*. **A female.**

This planet has hope yet. I will save her and her kind.

…Little do I know…she's the one who ends up saving me instead.

Dark. Steamy. Gritty. A thrilling romance intertwined in a plot that will give you chills.

Other books in the series: Base Zero, Cataclysm, War

Claiming His Mate

Series Title: Fated Mates of the Atari

When I get a once-in-a-lifetime chance to go on a luxury space cruise, I jump at it.

This cruise is the beginning of something amazing, and nothing is going to stop me from going.

But when things go wrong shortly after departure, it's clear I have made a mistake.

Suddenly thrown into a world where I have no way of defending myself, the last thing I expect is an Atari warrior coming to my rescue.

This cruise has been full of surprises…but the Atari is the biggest one of all.

He's tall, growly, possessive, and he sends my pulse into overdrive with just the slightest look.

Why the heck is my body reacting this way to this stranger?

And did he just declare that I am his mate?

Other books in the series: Craving His Mate, Fighting for His Mate, Guarding His Mate

Outlaw
Series Title: The Midnight Seven

Our colony is dying.
We're out of time. Out of hope. Out of options—*unless I risk everything on him.*
The outlaw.
One not bound by rules or mercy.
With lives at stake, I offer him a deal he can't refuse. And one I can't go back on.
Bargaining with a demon to save my people, only time will tell if I've sealed their fate, or found their salvation.
And mine.
Find on Amazon

Scan the QR code to view all books

ABOUT THE AUTHOR

A. G. Wilde is an avid reader, a gamer, a lover of all things space, alien, and sci-fi.

She is addicted to intense romance, irresistible heroes, and deliciously naughty things.

❀☆❋☆❀

facebook.com/agwilde

instagram.com/authoragwilde

tiktok.com/@authoragwilde

x.com/authoragwilde

bookbub.com/profile/a-g-wilde

amazon.com/author/agwilde